The
DIRECTOR'S
CUT

D0950414

Books by Janice Thompson

WEDDINGS BY BELLA

Fools Rush In
Swinging on a Star
It Had to Be You

BACKSTAGE PASS

Stars Collide
Hello, Hollywood!
The Director's Cut

BACKSTAGE PASS ★ BOOK 3

The
DIRECTOR'S
CUT

A NOVEL

Janice Thompson

Revell

a division of Baker Publishing Group
Grand Rapids, Michigan

© 2012 by Janice Thompson

Published by Revell
a division of Baker Publishing Group
P.O. Box 6287, Grand Rapids, MI 49516-6287
www.revellbooks.com

Printed in the United States of America

Library of Congress Cataloging-in-Publication Data
Thompson, Janice A.
    The director's cut : a novel / Janice Thompson.
        p.   cm. — (Backstage pass ; bk. 3)
    ISBN 978-0-8007-3347-6 (pbk.)
    1. Women television producers and directors—Fiction. 2. Hispanic American television producers and directors—Fiction. 3. Camera operators—Fiction. 4. Situation comedies (Television programs)—Fiction. 5. Hollywood (Los Angeles, Calif.)—Fiction. I. Title.
PS3620.H6824D57 2012
813'.6—dc22   2011052500

Scripture quotations are from the Amplified® Bible, copyright © 1954, 1958, 1962, 1964, 1965, 1987 by The Lockman Foundation. Used by permission.

Published in association with MacGregor Literary Agency.

The internet addresses, email addresses, and phone numbers in this book are accurate at the time of publication. They are provided as a resource. Baker Publishing Group does not endorse them or vouch for their content or permanence.

12   13   14   15   16   17   18   7   6   5   4   3   2   1

To Erin Brinkle, my trusty assistant. Girl, your backstage help on *Johnny Be Good* was much appreciated, but I'm still convinced you belong in the spotlight.

And to the only Director in my life, the one who puts up with me when I try to rewrite the script—praise you for sticking with me, even when my "I'll take it from here, Lord" attitude kicks in.

Casting the whole of your care [all your anxieties, all your worries, all your concerns, once and for all] on Him, for He cares for you affectionately and cares about you watchfully.

1 Peter 5:7

My So-Called Life

Like most Hollywood directors, I like to keep my drama on the set. It doesn't always work out that way, of course, but I give it my best shot. If only my chaotic life outside the walls of the studio matched the calm, calculated goings-on inside, then I'd have it made.

In my director's chair, I'm the epitome of poise and composure. And why not? My cast and crew jump to attention when I give them instructions. When I step outside the doors of Studio B after a long day of filming, however, I must admit the truth—I have absolutely no control over anything in the real world. And when you're a director by nature, losing control is pretty much equivalent to appearing on *Dancing with the Stars* in your underwear.

I do my best to cope. Most people wouldn't even know I'm struggling. But I am. I have serious need-to-know issues. What Hollywood director doesn't? If I can't control it—i.e., "fix" it—then what good am I? I've been trained to whip everything into shape. That's why I spend my days on the *Stars Collide* set tweaking scripts, fine-tuning actors' lines, and fretting over camera angles—so that everything is as close to perfect as it can be before I commit an episode to film.

It would be nice to have those same capabilities once I step out into the real world. Problem is, the good, bad, and ugly scenes of my life never seem to get tweaked before they're committed to the history books.

Okay, so I'm a control freak. I admit it. But hey, a director works off the script she's been given. If I'd been handed the script of my real life in advance—the one outside the studio walls—I would've asked for a rewrite. First thing to go? My upbringing in South Central L.A. I would've asked the writers for a home in the valley, at the very least. Next? The many, many times my dad attempted to trade my mama in for a newer, younger, thinner partner. Those scenes would definitely have to go, replaced by family-friendly episodes of *Father Knows Best* or *Make Room for Daddy*. Finally, I would have penciled in the perfect *Brady Bunch* siblings who all got along, even under the worst of circumstances. Oh, and just for fun, I might've thrown in a love interest for myself. Maybe. If things at work slowed down a little.

On days like today, with my cell phone buzzing nonstop, I might have also asked for a little more patience. Unfortunately, those who pray for patience usually end up needing even more of it. I found that to be the case as I raced through a conversation with my mother while I made my way up the 405 headed to the studio.

"We're so proud of you, Tia-mia," Mama's lyrical voice rang out, her Spanish accent still as strong as ever. "You've done really well for yourself in this job."

I'd just started to respond with, "Aw, thanks!" when she completed her thought.

"Yes, you've done really well. But I do hope, now that you've made it big, that you won't turn your back on your family. We've always been here to support you, and I hope you'll return the favor."

Huh?

This seemed to be another in a long line of strange comments from my mother of late. Ever since our show's Golden Globes win a few months back, she'd offered more than a few backhanded compliments. What could possibly make her think I'd turn my back on my family just because I'd achieved some degree of success in my field?

Then again, Mama was prone to beating around the bush. Likely she had something else on her mind.

Sure enough, she piped up with the real reason for her call moments later, now speaking in fluent Spanish. "I want you to get your little sister a job at the studio doing hair and makeup."

I drew in a deep breath and counted to three before responding. "Mama, just because I'm the director of a TV sitcom doesn't mean I have the ability to hire my siblings at will. Those decisions come from above."

"From God, you mean?" She took a deep breath. "Yes, I know. But I've already asked him about it, and he's keen on the idea, so I figured you would be too. I know how close you two are."

I sighed. If, as Mama so aptly put it, the Lord had placed his stamp of approval on this "*hair*-brained" idea, who was I to nix it?

My stomach churned as I responded. "I'll do what I can. Maybe I can talk to our producer. But Benita will have to fill out an application just like everyone else, and there are no guarantees, even if Rex goes along with this. As I said, these decisions come from above. The studio executives, I mean."

"But she really needs a new job as soon as possible, honey. And I heard you say that your hair and makeup girl was taking another position on a movie set in mid-April. Isn't that right?"

"Well, yes. Nora's leaving in a few days, in fact. But why does Benita need a job, anyway? I thought she had a new one at that great salon in Beverly Hills." I put on my turn signal, checked my rearview mirror, and eased my way into the right lane. "When I talked to her last week, she told me she had special connections that were going to keep her at the salon for years to come. She even said she was earning more money now than ever. And she mentioned something about perks. Sounded promising."

I managed to make it to the exit ramp just as a Mercedes flew up behind me. The driver honked and rode my tail all the way down the ramp.

Mama released an exaggerated sigh. "Well, see now, she ran into a little problem there, Tia-mia."

I did my best not to groan aloud as my mother called me by the familiar nickname again. Instead, I focused on the road, finally shaking the Mercedes at the light.

"It wasn't a hair- or makeup-related problem, thank goodness." The lilt returned to my mother's voice. "That would have been more difficult to overcome. This was something else. Completely unfair, I might add."

"Hmm." My sister's degree in cosmetology was relatively new, but no one could fault her makeup skills. They were flawless. She put my mascara and lipstick skills to shame every time. There had to be more to the story than what I'd heard thus far.

Mama's next words were rushed, as if she had to force them out. "Okay, from what I understand, she had a little fling with the owner. How was she to know he had a fiancée? The man led her on, and you know how vulnerable she is."

"Mama! And you want me to bring her onto the set of *Stars Collide*, which is filled with handsome men?" My thoughts drifted not just to our show's stars but to our cameramen as well. One in particular. Jason Harris might be hard as nails when the cameras got to rolling, but I still caught my eyes drifting his way on occasion. Not that he appeared to notice. No, his gaze was directed through the camera, not at me.

Mama continued to carry on about Benita's cosmetology skills, but she lost me about halfway into a speech about the importance of lip liner. Listening to her lyrical Spanish conversation with its lifts and curls took me back several years to my childhood. Back then, Mama's voice brought comfort. These days I was so distracted that I rarely took the time to revel in those familiar feelings when they did come. No, I had far too much work on my plate for that.

In the background, I could hear Angel, my mother's Chihuahua, barking nonstop. That dog was enough to drive even the sanest person crazy.

"Angel, calm down. Stop all that yapping!" Mama hollered so loudly I had to pull the phone away from my ear. "It's just a car driving by, baby. Come and sit in Mama's lap."

The next couple minutes were spent listening to my mother comfort her dog. Go figure. She had the time and energy to be compassionate to a canine.

I pulled up to another stoplight and glanced in the rearview mirror to check my appearance. "Mama, I have to go. I'm almost to the studio. And it's Monday. You know what that means."

"Yes, I know." She reverted to English. "You tell me every Monday. It's the weekly roundtable reading. One of the most important days of the week."

"Yes. We go over every inch of the script and iron out the wrinkles. So I really have to go." I continued to peer in the mirror. A few tight lines around my eyes let me know that the wrinkles in the script weren't the only ones I needed to deal with. All of this stress was aging my face prematurely. Someone who'd just turned thirty shouldn't have lines around her eyes . . . right?

"Okay, okay. Just one more thing before you go," Mama said. "I wanted to double-check that you're coming over for dinner on Friday night. We'll all be here, as usual—the whole family. I'm making tamales."

"All? So, Daddy's coming?"

She paused, and I could almost envision the look on her face. "No, I don't think I'm quite ready for that. Not yet." Her voice sounded strained. Then again, who could blame her? My father's issues were enough to drain even the strongest of women.

"He called again last night," I said.

"O-oh?" Now she really sounded nervous.

"Yes." I wondered why I'd mentioned it at all. Should I tell her that he'd admitted to his latest indiscretion and had even managed to work up a few tears afterward? Nah, better not. Still, those tears—real or fake—had caught me off guard. Maybe he really planned to do right by Mama this time. You could never tell with him.

Thankfully, Mama got another call, and I turned my full attention to the road. Well, mostly. My thoughts kept drifting to her comment about how I'd made it big. If only she realized how insecure I felt, even after working on a major sitcom like *Stars Collide* . . . then she would know just how far I had left to go.

Oh, sure. A Golden Globes win should have been enough to squelch any lingering doubts I might've had about my directing abilities, but it had accomplished just the opposite. Now I felt the pressure to perform as never before.

I pulled my car onto the lot, determined to face the day with a more positive outlook. Before long, I'd be safely inside the studio, where everything was scripted and safe. There I could breathe normally again. Be myself. Take the reins and whip everyone—and everything—into shape. Praise the Lord and pass the scene board! I could hardly wait.

2

The Office

I arrived at the studio ten minutes later. Whipping my Beamer into the parking lot, I saw a familiar pink car. Climbing out of the passenger side of the late-fifties convertible was one of our show's most beloved stars, Lenora Worth. The seventy-something waved as I pulled into the spot next to her.

I exited my car, and she grabbed me by the arm, the soft wrinkles around her blue eyes more pronounced as she offered up a warm smile. "Tia! Rex and I were just talking about you." She gestured to her husband, who now stood behind her. I couldn't help but notice how dapper Rex looked in his suit and tie. In fact, they both looked like they'd been dropped onto the set from an episode of *The Donna Reed Show*, especially with Lenora wearing that white chiffon dress with its flowing sleeves and pinched waistline.

"Who are we today, Lenora?" I asked.

She primped and gave a little turn. "Vivien Leigh. *A Streetcar Named Desire*. 1951."

"Lovely. You look angelic."

"Thank you. The costume director for that movie won an Academy Award for this dress." Her girlish giggle made her seem almost childlike. "What do you think of that?"

"It's fantastic," I managed. "I've always been a fan of chiffon."

On other people.

"I'd like to see you dolled up for a change, Tia." Lenora gave me a scrutinizing look. "You've got such lovely outfits, but they're so structured."

"Structured?"

"You know, prim and proper. And you do seem partial to the color gray, don't you?" She pointed to my slacks.

"I—I do?" Strange. I'd never thought about it before. Then again, most of my skirts and jackets were in varying shades of black or gray.

"You need to kick back every now and again. Add some color to your life. Wear a red dress or something. Put on your dancing shoes. Something in a great shade of hot pink with high heels. Let some fella waltz you around the set." She extended her hand in Rex's direction, and the two of them did a couple of turns around the parking lot. She giggled. "Whoops! Feeling a little woozy, like you were flying me across the parking lot and all the way to the moon."

Rex kept a tight hold on her until she stood upright. "You want the moon, sweet girl?" he asked. "Just say the word, and I'll throw a lasso around it and pull it down."

"Oh, I know that line!" Lenora giggled. "*It's a Wonderful Life*. Jimmy Stewart." She paused for a minute, then snapped her fingers. "1946. Is that right?"

"Right as rain." Rex kissed her on the cheek. "And so are you. Not feeling woozy anymore, are you?"

"Only woozy for you." She flung her arms around his neck

and planted a tender kiss on his lips, causing him—and me—to blush.

Afterward Rex reached over and wrapped me in a fatherly embrace. In that moment, I almost forgot he was our show's producer. Felt more like the grandfather I'd never known. Someone kind and dependable. Someone who would stick around no matter how tough things got. In other words, the polar opposite of my father.

I gazed up into his sparkling eyes, fairly sure he was up to some mischief. "What's up?" I asked. "Please don't tell me you want to refilm that scene from last Friday, because—" I never had a chance to finish. Rex shook his head.

"No, it's something completely different. Or, rather, some-one completely different."

"There's a new member to our *Stars Collide* family, Tia!" Lenora clasped her hands at her chest and grinned. "We've been dying to tell you."

"Oh!" My heart quickened. "Kat had her baby?" Our show's female lead was due to deliver in a few weeks. We'd managed to work the pregnancy into the storyline quite nicely, but we hadn't filmed the delivery scene yet.

"No, silly. KK's right there." She pointed to where Kat and her husband Scott sat in their car, drinking coffee and laughing. "It's someone else. She should be here any minute. I'm pretty sure she said she'd be in a red Beetle."

Sure enough, a red VW bug pulled into the spot next to mine, and a tall, slender young woman emerged. She dropped a half-eaten donut and nearly tripped as she reached down to pick it up. "Oops." Shoving the messy donut into a napkin, she looked our way with a smile. "Guess the five-second rule doesn't apply in parking lots." With a giggle she tossed the donut into a trash bag in her car.

"Tia, this is Erin Brady." Rex smiled as he made the introduction. "She's in her first year at LAFS. Erin's going to be your new production assistant."

"Production assistant?" Interesting. I'd gone without one for months. Why the sudden rush to fill the position?

I took in the unfamiliar young woman with her short blonde hair and whimsical smile. She seemed a bit overeager, ready to jump in with all arms and legs, gangly as they might be. Her endearing Southern drawl captured my attention right away and held me captive as I led the way into the studio.

Erin chattered all the way, barely pausing for breath. Only when we reached the inside of the studio did she fall silent. She stood, eyes wide, looking around the room. After a couple minutes, she blinked away tears.

"You okay?" I asked, sensing some sort of problem.

"Oh, yes." She nodded, her face now awash with joy. "I'm just so happy. See, I've dreamed of working on a sitcom my whole life, but I never thought I'd get the chance. Texas is a long way from L.A., ya know? I probably still wouldn't be here if my mom hadn't met Lenora Worth and Kat Murphy at that fund-raiser several months ago. I can hardly believe it, but I'm standing in Studio B, working for Tia Morales, my favorite sitcom director in television history." Tears now covered her lashes. "Can we say, 'Died and gone to heaven'?"

Well, if that didn't boost my morale, nothing would. So much for worrying that Miss Sunshine had come to steal my job. And if her words hadn't won me over, the Southern drawl would have. The girl had clearly been in L.A. only a short while. Not long enough to be tainted by the industry.

I stuck out my hand and smiled. "Erin, I'm glad to have you on board. You've worked as a PA before?"

She shook my hand, the sugary residue from the donut almost causing our palms to stick together. "Not on a sitcom, but I did a short stint on a feature film. I know there's a lot of grunt work involved, but I don't mind. I can grunt with the best of 'em. Besides, I enjoy being behind the scenes. Never really aspired to much more than that, to be honest."

Funny. When I took in her overly dramatic style and her words and mannerisms, I had the strongest feeling the camera would love her. She had that natural way about her that we directors loved to see on film. Hmm. I'd have to think about that. In the meantime, I really needed to get this sugar off my hand. I fished around in my purse, coming up with a tissue. Rolling it around in my palm, I managed to make things worse instead of better. Before long, my hand was coated with sticky tissue.

"Anyway, your wish is my command." Erin's face glowed with excitement, and her Southern drawl grew more pronounced. "What can I do for you? Help the kids run their lines? Act as your go-to gal? Make a run to Starbucks for coffee? I'm ready to roll, Miss Tia. Just let me know where to start."

Ugh. Had she really just called me Miss Tia? Why not announce to the whole world that I was single?

Still, I could hardly fault someone with a smile this genuine. Clearly her words were meant to be endearing. So I came up with a job for her to do.

"I need someone to pick up this week's copy of the script from the writers so we can start our roundtable reading. Down that long hall to the right." I pointed. "Our head writer's name is Athena. Please tell her to give you the copy with the changes I made over the weekend."

"I can't wait to meet her, and all of the writers, for that matter." Erin's cheeks flushed as she smiled. "I fancy myself a scriptwriter. Who knows? Maybe one day I really will be."

"Sounds like you've got a lot of interests."

"All film related." She shrugged. "I guess I need a twelve-step program. I'm hooked on the industry."

Me too. But beware, you poor, naive thing. It can eat you for lunch if you're not careful.

I patted her on the shoulder and forced a smile. "There are worse fates." Lowering my voice, I added, "And by the way, I'd appreciate it if you just called me Tia. None of this 'Miss' stuff, okay?"

"Of course." She giggled. "Sorry about that. Back in south Texas, everyone was 'Miss.' Well, except the women who were married." She laughed. "Anyway, I meant it in a nice way. We just call folks 'Miss' to be polite. Ya know?"

"Right. I'm sure that makes sense." *Deep in the heart of Texas.* "Now, go ahead and get that script for me, okay?"

"Sure!"

In her haste to cross the studio, she tripped over a row of cables attached to Jason's camera. For a minute I thought he would scold her, but he managed to get things under control. In fact, he appeared to be smiling, and his gaze lingered on her. Was he interested in our young prodigy? Surely not. She definitely didn't seem his type.

Not that I knew his type, come to think of it.

"New girl?" he asked as he came over.

I did my best not to let his nearness distract me, but that early-morning stubble on his face was strangely endearing. He usually showed up to work clean-shaven. I liked the new look—so much so that I apparently lost the ability to construct an intelligible sentence with Jason in my sight line.

"Y-yeah," I finally said. "Erin Brady, my new PA."

"Ah."

As he smiled, two perfectly placed dimples arose. I'd seen them before, but today they seemed to hold me spellbound. *Pay attention, Tia. To something other than Jason, anyway.*

"She seems energetic," he said.

"Weren't we all energetic when we first started out?" Immediately I wanted to bite my tongue. How dare I sound so jaded after only a few years in the industry myself? Forcing a smile, I tried to smooth things over. "She's in her first year at LAFS."

"Best film school in the country." He nodded.

"Agreed." I did my best not to sigh as I reminisced about my days at the Los Angeles Film School. I was a different girl back then . . . ready to take on the world, to prove my worth—to my family, my peers, and myself. "She reminds me of myself a few years back." I coughed. "Well, maybe more than a few years back. She's got that 'I can conquer the world' look about her but is plenty green around the edges. I recognize that for sure."

"Me too." His laugh caught me off guard. "But I hope her enthusiasm and innocence catches on. We could use a dose of that around here."

Hmm. Was that all he hoped was contagious? Surely he wouldn't be interested in her. Not that it was any of my business. No, I had no claim on Jason. Sure, we made a sport out of bickering, but beyond that, we had no relationship. Not really.

Before I could help it, a sigh escaped.

"Just seems like . . . " He lowered his voice. "I don't know, maybe it's just me. But ever since those Golden Globe awards a few months back, everyone around here's gone a little crazy. You know what I mean?"

"Oh? How so?"

He shrugged. "Paparazzi everywhere. People doing interviews around the clock. Writers in a frenzy, trying to come up with newer, better scripts just to keep the audience hooked. It's a lot of work to keep things going."

I lowered my voice. "Maintaining momentum is critical, especially at this stage of the game. *Stars Collide* has been on the air for several seasons now, so it's more important than ever to keep things fresh so the viewers won't abandon us."

"Right, but . . ." He raked his fingers through his sandy hair. "I dunno. Things have been just a little too perfect. You know? Kind of feels like we're all in a pressure cooker, and sooner or later someone—or something—is going to explode."

Interesting image. I'd never really thought about it from that angle. Still, I did recognize the fact that we needed to keep our audience interested, now that our show and its lead players had received so much acclaim.

From the other side of the studio, the children entered with their tutor. Candy, our resident diva-child actress, made a mad dash for the stage and began to belt out a song at the top of her lungs. Behind her, one of the boys gave her a little shove and took her spot center stage, where he began to sing a different song, one I didn't recognize. Before long, their teacher got them under control and moved them off the stage and toward the classroom.

As always, my frustrations kicked in as I watched my younger cast members in action. They tended to get under my skin more than I cared to admit. The idea of dealing with small children left me feeling unsettled. Perhaps it was my upbringing with so many siblings. I'd had enough of the chaos and just longed for peace and quiet.

Then again, how would I ever marry and have kids of my own if I couldn't even handle the ones I had to direct?

As little Joey made his way across the stage, he turned to holler something to Ethan, the cast's youngest. The cup of chocolate milk in his hand shot up in the air and landed on the sofa. Candy let out a squeal. So did their teacher.

Jason ran toward them. I half expected him to throttle Joey, but instead, he gave him a hug and helped clean up the mess. Before long, Scott, our show's male star, joined him. Between the three of them, they got the sofa and floor cleaned just as the janitor arrived. Crisis averted.

"Kids up to tricks again?"

I turned as I heard Kat's voice, taking in her wider-than-ever midsection. Wow. I couldn't even imagine being that pregnant and still smiling. Yet she managed to do both, and her contented expression looked genuine. Crazy.

"Mm-hmm." I looked at Jason, watching as he wrestled with one of the little boys. "All the kids."

Kat chuckled and rubbed her belly. "Heaven help me when this baby girl arrives. I know very little about children."

"After working here for so long?" I turned back to face her. "You of all people should be ready to raise a child." I pointed to the children of the *Stars Collide* cast, who had now gathered around Jason and Scott like chicks around a mother hen. "Look what a great job you and Scott have done raising all of them."

Kat laughed. "They're our cast members, not our children."

"Still, they've looked up to you as parental figures for several seasons now." I gave her a smile. "Don't worry, Kat," I said. "You're going to be a great mom."

Out of the corner of my eye, I caught a glimpse of Erin in the hallway, loaded down with scripts. She glanced Jason's way. He rose and gave her a nod.

The feelings that swept over me were swift and sudden. Jealousy snaked its way around my heart. Still, it made no sense—especially in light of the fact that Jason and I had started out as mortal enemies. He'd made my first few months in this position a nightmare, in fact. Until a month or so ago, we rarely spoke to each other beyond what was necessary on the set. Now we seemed drawn together by some crazy, invisible force. Well, at least in my imagination.

Still, the idea that feelings could be stirring inside of me terrified me.

And excited me.

Now, to see where those feelings would take me . . .

One Life to Live

Minutes after the fiasco with the spilled chocolate milk, I headed into the conference room to wait on the others. Erin arrived in the room, her arms loaded with scripts and her eyes filled with tears.

"Sorry." She sniffled. "I just came from the writers' room. It took me longer than expected."

"Everyone okay?" I asked. Surely she hadn't gotten her feelings wounded this early in the game. If so, then we needed to have a "stiffen that backbone" talk right away. I couldn't abide a weak, teary-eyed assistant.

"Oh, yes, sorry." The cutest grin turned up the edges of her lips as she put the scripts on the table. "I just met our fabulous scriptwriters. Paul and Bob are a hoot. And Athena and Stephen are so . . ."

"Talented?"

She sighed. "Romantic."

"Ah, well, they're newlyweds, just back from their honeymoon." With a wave of my hand, I dismissed her silliness.

"I know." Her eyes took on a dreamy, far-off look. "To Greece. They went to the Acropolis and saw the Parthenon. They even went to Santorini. Can you imagine?"

"Not really, no." Frankly, I couldn't imagine traveling anywhere right now, not with such a critical season in full throttle. Maybe one day I'd get to see the world like other people, but for now I'd have to be content viewing it from my director's chair.

"They also saw Mount Olympus and the ruins at Delphi." Erin's eyes fluttered closed, and she clasped her hands at her chest. "I heard all about it." Her eyes popped open, and she leaned over and whispered, "Did you know Athena brought baklava today? They have a whole tray of it in the writers' room. And gyros. And some kind of yummy lamb dish that I've never even heard of before."

"Yes, it's Monday. Athena always brings leftovers from her parents' restaurant on Mondays."

Erin kissed her fingertips, looked skyward, and whispered, "I'm going to love Mondays!" She grabbed my hand and gave it a squeeze. "And I'm going to love working with you. Could life get any better?"

"That all depends on your point of view." Jason entered the room and took a seat at the table. "If you're an optimist, then the best is always yet to come."

"Ooo, I am an optimist." Erin giggled. "So I guess life really will get better and better from here." Off she went, talking about how great life was going to be. I paused to think about her words. They were free-flowing, sure, but laced with passion. Not the Hollywood version of passion either. The real deal.

"I like that attitude." Jason's smile let me know that he

really meant his words. "We need more people like you around here. Things have been way too serious, and pessimism seems to rule the day. A cheerful disposition will go a long way to change all that."

"Yes, well . . ." I cleared my throat and brushed a loose hair behind my ear. "Erin, the others will be joining us in a few minutes for the roundtable reading. Let me go ahead and fill you in on how the week runs so you'll be prepared. Things are very structured around here, especially so late in the season, so you might as well get used to it."

"Oh, I know your production schedule already," Erin said. "Rex told me. Roundtable reading on Monday. For the cast and crew, anyway. The writers are already working on next week's script. Is that right?"

"Yes."

She tapped her finger over her lips as if in thought. Then she snapped to attention. "Oh, I remember now. Tuesdays you do a run-through with the actors and crew. The writers fine-tune their script for the following week."

"You've got it!" Jason flashed a smile.

She grinned. "Then on Wednesday, you have a dress rehearsal. Only, you don't call it a dress rehearsal. You call it the final run-through, which I love. The words *dress rehearsal* always strike such fear in the hearts of the actors, right?"

"Never really thought about it. I—"

"That same day wardrobe and makeup folks work their magic. You've switched your filming day to Thursday. Used to be Friday. Thursday night after filming you watch the dailies. Friday you leave open to clean up anything that didn't work on Thursday. Have I missed anything?"

"You left out two turtledoves and a partridge in a pear tree." Jason leaned back in his chair and grinned.

"Oh." Erin giggled and then did the strangest thing I'd seen in ages. She clasped her hands together and belted out, "Five actors acting, four writers writing, three cameras rolling, two producers smiling . . . and a partridge in a pear tree!" The whole thing came out in overdramatic flair but with perfect pitch. One more thing to keep in mind: the girl could sing. But her enthusiasm was starting to wear on me.

Good grief, Tia. Are you really that jaded? Don't you re-member being new to the industry?

Jason applauded and she took a little bow, her cheeks now rosy. "Sorry. Sometimes I get carried away."

"Don't ever apologize for being cheerful," Jason said. "You're just what the doctor ordered."

Hmm. Better keep moving. I offered Erin a smile. "Sounds like you've pretty much got everything memorized," I told her. "But just be aware that things don't always go as planned. Sometimes people get sick. Sometimes our guest stars don't show. Sometimes the kids are temperamental. All sorts of things go wrong."

"But mostly all sorts of things go right . . . right?" Her blue eyes sparkled with a youthful merriment that I almost found contagious. Almost.

"Yep. She's an optimist." Jason chuckled.

I took my seat and pulled one of the scripts close. Thumb-ing through it, I added, "This week we need everything to go right. This episode is more important than any we've ever filmed because it's Kat Murphy's last show before she goes on break to have the baby. I'd like to see her go out in style. Perfect timing, since we're nearing the end of this season anyway."

"It's just so sad that she's going to step away for a while. She's my all-time favorite actress."

"She'll be back at the beginning of next season, hopefully. But for now, we're going to have to do without her. I want her last show to be memorable, for her sake and the sake of the viewers."

Erin's eyes sparkled. "I hear ya. Athena said this week's episode has a Greek flair. Sounds like lots of fun."

"Yes, just what the doctor ordered. We're sending Kat out on a high note."

"Someone talking about me?" Our leading lady waddled into the room and eased herself down into a chair, a look of bliss settling over her. "Ah, that feels good."

"Just telling Erin here that you'll be out on maternity leave for the next few months."

Erin's eyes brimmed with tears as she reached out to touch Kat's hand. "Oh, sorry. I just had to touch you to make sure you're real. I've seen you on television, but in person . . . wow."

Kat chuckled. "I like you already. But don't make too big a fuss over me. Tia here is the real brains behind this operation. And Athena and the rest of the writing team, of course."

"We were just talking about them." Erin's eyes widened. "Athena and Stephen went to Greece on their honeymoon."

"I know."

"I want to go to Greece on my honeymoon someday. Or maybe Italy. Or maybe France. I can't make up my mind." Erin giggled and her cheeks turned red. "I'm barely twenty-two, but I've been planning my wedding since I was seven."

Just a baby.

On the other hand, I was thirty and had hardly given a moment's thought to my wedding.

Kat's words interrupted my thoughts. "Scott and I went to Mexico for our honeymoon. I hear the beach is lovely there." She giggled. "We didn't actually see it."

Awkward.

"Oh, I know all about your trip to Mexico." Erin waved a hand. "Trust me, I did my research on all of you before coming to work here. I could tell you pretty much anything you want to know about anyone in the cast or crew of *Stars Collide*. I've committed it all to memory."

"O-oh?" Just how much did this girl know about me?

"I don't know if you remember," Erin said to Kat, "but you met my mama at a fund-raiser you did awhile back with Brock Benson." Her eyes glazed over. "Have I mentioned he's my favorite actor in all of television and movie history?"

"Then it's your lucky day." Kat glanced at the clock on the wall. "He should be here by now."

"W-what?" For a moment, Erin looked as if she might faint. "Are you serious? You're just teasing me, right?"

"He's our guest star this week," I said.

At this news, Erin promptly pulled out a compact and went to work adding lipstick and a touch of blush. "Sorry." She giggled. "But if what you've just said is true, I have to be ready. A girl only gets to meet Brock Benson once in a lifetime . . . if she's lucky." Tears covered her lashes again. "I must be the luckiest girl in all of America today." She drew in a breath, wiped away her tears, and grinned. "Sorry. Couldn't help myself."

"Understandable."

"Brock filmed a movie in Texas a few years back, and I tried to get a bit part just so I could breathe the same air as him. But I wasn't able to, and it almost killed me. Seriously. I couldn't get out of bed for three days. I've always been such a fan."

As if on cue, the room flooded with people. Scott entered first, followed by Rex and the cast of kids. Brock was close behind them, carrying little Ethan on his shoulders. I thought Erin might take a tumble out of her chair when she saw him. We'd been fortunate to get the megastar for this episode, and even more fortunate that he'd been willing to take on the role of a Greek talent scout—a role far removed from anything he'd ever played in the movies. Most of his fans knew him as Jean Luc Dumont, the pirate you loved to hate. Or would that be hated to love? Anyway, he'd never played a talent scout before—that I knew of, anyway. And certainly not one named Basil.

Erin hurried over to Brock, her face aglow with excitement. Not that I blamed the girl. The guy was pretty much the hottest thing in Hollywood—literally and figuratively. Even I was a little weak in the knees when he came around, and I'd met more than my share of stars over the years.

"C-can I get you anything?" she stammered.

He looked her way, eyes lighting up as he took in her enthusiasm. "Sure. I'll have a latte if you've got it."

"If we don't, I'll drive to Starbucks and have one made for you. Or I'll go to culinary school and learn to make one from scratch." She turned to me, a frantic look on her face.

"Down the hall on the right. We have one of those coffeemakers that uses individual premixed cups. You'll find a variety of them in the desk underneath. The latte's on the right."

"There is a God and he loves me." She whispered the words then giggled. After turning to leave the room, she looked back at me, nearly tripping over herself in the process. "You want anything?"

I nodded and said, "Coffee. Black." Not that I really liked my coffee black, but drinking it that way in front of others made me feel tougher somehow . . . like I didn't need anything sweet to survive. At home I drank the real stuff—half coffee, half Italian sweet cream, two artificial sweeteners. Just the way I liked it.

Jason raised his hand, likely hoping to get Erin's attention. "I'll have a—"

Unfortunately, she didn't see him, her gaze never leaving Brock as she backed out of the room. She returned moments later with my coffee in hand, sloshing a bit of it on the script. "Oh, pooh." She put the coffee down on the table, then reached for a napkin to dry my script. Her hands trembled so violently I reached out and touched them to calm her down.

"It's okay. Really." I gave her an encouraging wink, and she moved on to give Brock his latte, then settled into the chair next to him. Convenient.

Out of the corner of my eye I caught a glimpse of Jason, who rose and left the room, whispering something about needing coffee.

Minutes later, everyone else joined us. Lenora sashayed in, wearing her white chiffon dress, and did a semi-arthritic spin to show it off.

"You look like a million bucks, kid," Brock said with a wink.

"Seeing her in this dress makes *me* feel like a kid again," Rex said as he pulled out Lenora's chair. "I was barely a teenager when *A Streetcar Named Desire* came out."

"One of my favorite movies." Brock nodded and flashed a broad, white-toothed smile.

"Oh, Vivien Leigh was beautiful, wasn't she?" Lenora released a contented sigh.

Rex ran the back of his hand across his wife's cheek. "Not half as beautiful as you are right at this very moment."

The whole room seemed to come to a standstill at his proclamation. His words—and Lenora's teary reaction—held us spellbound. In fact, the scene they'd just inadvertently acted out in front of us was probably more emotional than any we'd filmed in weeks.

Still, we had work to do. And how could I call myself a director if I couldn't manage to get a simple roundtable reading started?

I finally got control of the room, and Scott dove in, reading the first line. The story took several twists and turns, each one more humorous than the last. Before long, we were all laughing aloud, even the children. By the time we ended, there wasn't a dry eye in the room.

"This is brilliant," Brock said as he lifted his script in a triumphant manner. "The funniest thing I've ever read. No wonder you guys took home the Golden Globe back in January."

High praise coming from a man whose last movie had garnered five Academy Award nominations.

"We've got some great writers." As I looked Brock's way, my gaze lingered on his gorgeous face—perhaps a moment too long. Still, who could blame me? No harm in looking, right?

Jason cleared his throat as he reentered the room. "Should be a lot of fun to film."

I startled back to attention. "No doubt. Let's get together and talk it through, okay?"

As he nodded, a hint of a smile creased his lips. I found myself torn between the prettier-than-a-picture actor seated across from me and the intriguing-sometimes-sarcastic-always-has-something-to-say-about-everything-even-the-things-I-don't-care-to-talk-about cameraman taking a seat to my right.

Thank goodness I didn't have to ponder this dilemma for long. Kat's words interrupted my thoughts. "Tia, I love this whole episode, top to bottom, and I'm sure the viewers will too. I just think it's hilarious that Angie goes into labor in an elevator and Scott—er, Jack—has to deliver the baby with Brock's help. Pure genius."

"My favorite part is that we don't even know that Brock's character is a rival talent scout." Scott grinned. "Thinking he's a gyro delivery guy is what makes it so brilliant."

"And dressing Jack and Angie up like Mr. and Mrs. Easter

Bunny is the icing on the cake," Kat said. "I can't even imagine how funny it's going to be to add that element." She giggled. "I also can't imagine what it would be like to have that happen in real life. Can you?"

Frankly, no.

Still, I'd better respond. "Well, we figured since the show will air so late in the spring, it just makes sense. Jack and Angie are on their way to see the kids they represent at an Easter egg hunt. Brock's character wants in on the action, so he sets himself up as a sandwich delivery guy to get into the party."

"Hey, I love all of it." Brock's smooth voice caught my attention once again. I turned to look at him, again captivated by his gorgeous eyes. "It will stretch me to use a Greek accent, but I think I can handle the role. I'll work on it until I've got it right."

"Oh, I feel sure you can handle anything you put your mind to." Erin flashed a smile so bright you would've thought she was auditioning for a toothpaste commercial.

He returned the smile, his gaze lingering on her for a bit longer than one might expect.

"It's going to be an award-winning episode," Rex added. "I can feel it in my gut."

Kat shifted in her chair. "I'm just curious, how are you going to keep things going when I'm on maternity leave?"

I'd been waiting for this conversation for weeks, so I dove right in. "I talked to the writers about that at length. We've got a plan of action for the last couple episodes of the season. Scott will play a larger role, and so will the children and several of last season's elderly guests. And we're hoping that Lenora will have more of a presence."

Lenora's cheeks turned the loveliest shade of pink. "Oh, I love having a presence."

Kat flashed me a warning look. I knew she'd been worried about her grandmother's fragile state ever since the Alzheimer's diagnosis. Still, what could we do? Lenora wanted to continue on with the show, and who was I to turn away an aging Hollywood star—especially when we needed her as never before?

"I was a big star once, you know." Lenora gave me a wink.

"You're still a big star, my dear," Rex said as he slipped an arm over her shoulder. "It's the pictures that got small."

She giggled and her cheeks flushed pink. "Oh, I love that line. Gloria Swanson said that in *Sunset Boulevard*."

"In 1950." Rex winked.

Lenora sighed. "Oh, movies and television were wonderful back in the old days. These days everything is so rushed, so much about ratings."

"Well, keeping our audience happy is key. We've got to give them what they've come to expect from us—quality acting and great stories." I turned to Kat. "But to answer your question, we've got it covered. Our audience has been following Angie's pregnancy over the last several months. They know she's about to deliver. So having her away from the show for a few weeks will be fine. But Rex and I decided that while Angie's away, the mice will play."

"The mice will play?" Kat and Scott looked confused.

"We're thinking that it would be nice to keep Brock on the show through the end of the season. We're talking only a few weeks, after all."

A little gasp went up from Erin, who apparently liked this idea—a lot.

"If he's really a rival talent scout and not a sandwich delivery guy, then imagine the possibilities. Maybe he tries to steal some of the kids away from the agency."

"Ooo, can I be stolen away too?" Lenora clasped her hands

together and giggled as she batted her eyelashes at Brock. "What fun!"

"Well, we were thinking of Candy's character first," I said. "She might be a little diva, but we've set her up as the agency's biggest moneymaker. It would be fun to have Brock's character try to snatch her away from the Stars Collide agency and make money off her."

"What's the name of this talent agency I'm running, anyway?" Brock asked. "Just curious."

"I think the writers came up with A&B Talent, which is short for Above & Beyond. Your character will pull actors away from Stars Collide by claiming that you can take them above and beyond where they've been in their careers. You'll be sort of a Pied Piper character, playing a mesmerizing tune."

"Very devious of me." Brock scrunched his eyebrows in a devilish fashion and Erin stared at him, clearly ready to follow this handsome Pied Piper anywhere he might lead.

"Your sole purpose will be to woo people away," I added. "And like your pirate character, you'll be the bad guy we love to hate. The one everyone ends up falling in love with."

He rubbed his hands together. "Now that's a role I can get into."

"It's perfect," I agreed. "Just the thing we need to keep the momentum going."

"And keeping the momentum going is what we're all about, right?"

I turned Jason's way, wondering at the hint of sarcasm in his voice. Why would he say such a thing, at least publicly? Of course we had to keep the momentum going. What else could we do?

Just about the time I gave myself over to the feelings of frustration rising inside of me, I noticed someone humming a familiar melody. I glanced across the table at Erin, who clamped a hand over her mouth. "Oops, sorry." She giggled. "I hum all the time. Can't help it. Mama says I was born with a song in my heart, and it's hard to stop it."

"Don't ever try to stop it." Brock patted her shoulder. "And if I do say so myself, we could all stand a little song now and again."

As I dismissed the crew, Jason lingered. I rose, albeit reluctantly, and reached for my copy of the script, still puzzled by his words. Maybe he would stick around long enough to explain.

Erin drew near, her face glowing with excitement. "That was great, Tia. I just know that the show is going to take off like a rocket, especially if you keep Brock Benson on. He's so . . . yummy."

Jason rolled his eyes.

I offered a little shrug. "I see great things ahead, and I think it all went well today. It's a rare day when everyone catches the vision."

"Oh, I don't know." Jason stood and stretched. "I think half the battle is sharing the vision in a way that makes people want to latch on."

"I'm just saying that whenever Athena and Stephen and the other writers come up with their ideas, they can see it all on paper. They tell those characters what to do and they do it. But then they pass the script off to actors who don't always see the vision as clearly." I paused, ready to admit the truth. "I'm not saying I always catch their vision either. But this is a team effort. I spend a lot of time every week talking things through with the writing team. And with Rex."

"Well, anyway, I think it went great too." Erin's face lit into the cutest grin, and then she began to hum again. She made her way out of the room, which left me alone with Jason.

"I owe you an apology." He sighed. "What I said was rude."

Yeah, it was.

"Well, I guess we just have different ways of looking at things," I said. "But we're on the same team . . . right?"

"Right." He nodded, his gaze lingering on me. Out in the hallway, someone called his name and he turned to leave. As he reached the door, he looked back and shrugged. "Forgive me?"

"Of course."

"I think I'm just used to bantering with you. It's a hard habit to break."

Interesting.

The smile that followed his words pulled me in, like the Pied Piper playing his merry tune. Still, I couldn't figure out why Jason had embarrassed me in front of the group. The apology was a nice touch—and so was that line about liking to banter with me. Still, his initial words hit me the wrong way.

I found myself drawn back to that melody Erin had been humming. Seemed eerily familiar. As I slipped into the ladies' room, I heard it again, this time coming from one of the stalls. Listening closely, I realized she was singing a song I hadn't heard in years.

"Oh, you can't get to heaven on roller skates. You'll roll right by those pearly gates."

In a flash, I was eight years old again, singing with the other kids who attended the inner-city street church. Strange that I'd been trying to skate my way into all sorts of worlds that weren't mine—then and now.

I pushed back the memory and focused on the day ahead.

How I Met Your Mother

Monday evening, I made the drive back to my house in Bel Air West with that goofy roller skating song on my mind. At least it helped to prepare me for the inevitable situation at home. Though I'd owned my sixties-era house off of Mulholland for a couple of years, I'd barely made a dent in the renovations. Putting my out-of-work brother, Carlos, in charge of the demo and rebuild had been a misguided act of faith. Still, what could I do? My heart went out to his wife, Maria, and to their little ones. He needed the work, and I needed my home renovated. Surely he would pull this off—with a little prayer and a lot of begging. Besides, he'd called on Humberto, my middle brother, to help. Humberto was always good for a laugh, if nothing else.

I arrived at the house, pausing at the front step to draw in a deep breath and usher up a "Lord, please help me" before unlocking the door. Knowing what awaited me on the other side made me wish I could turn around and head back to the studio. Instead, I bravely slid the key into the lock and turned the handle.

I tried not to groan aloud as I laid eyes on the mess in my large entryway. Ladders. Paint cans. Half-hung Sheetrock, semi-floated. And dust as far as the eye could see. The sweeping stairway was littered with Coke cans and even a couple of beer bottles. Lovely. Apparently my brothers hadn't made much progress today. Then again, they'd been moving too slowly all along. Many times I'd wished I could snap my fingers—or wiggle my nose like Samantha on *Bewitched*—and watch the rooms in my home take shape.

Unfortunately, wriggling my nose had only given me an itch. Or maybe it was the dust. Sure enough, I felt a sneeze coming on. "Ah-ah-ah-choo!"

After regaining my composure, I decided to slip out of my work attire and into what I'd taken to calling my real work outfit—a pair of gray sweats and a faded T-shirt with the LAFS logo on the front. Might as well support the alma mater in style.

Before starting, I flipped on the television and grabbed a yogurt container from the fridge. Nothing like dinner and a movie before floating Sheetrock. Not that I knew how to float Sheetrock exactly, but I'd watched Carlos and Humberto do it, and it didn't look that difficult. And I had to figure that if Carlos could do it with a beer in one hand, certainly I could attempt it sober and two-handed. I hoped.

Suddenly I heard Benita's words in my head: "Never do a job that can be pawned off on a man." God bless my sister. She'd become skilled in the art of pawning. Still, I had to wonder if she would ever learn to do anything on her own, without assistance from the male species. Short of applying makeup, anyway.

Hmm. Makeup. I needed to remember to call Benita later about the potential job at the studio. She would be tickled to learn that Rex had jumped on the idea. Of course, he didn't realize what a risk he was taking. And I wouldn't be telling him, at least not yet. It might come back to bite me later, but for now I would keep my mouth shut.

For whatever reason, thinking about my sister got me to thinking about guys. Thinking about guys got me to thinking about Jason. I still couldn't shake the comment he'd made after the roundtable reading. Settling onto the dust-covered sofa with my yogurt in hand, I did my best to put him out of my mind. Instead, I found myself thinking of the way Brock Benson's smile had turned Erin to mush. Some girls just couldn't see straight with a handsome guy in the room. Me? I could see straighter than an arrow.

Still, what did Jason mean with that snarky comment? I thought about it a while longer. He'd apologized after, sure, but what had prompted the statement in the first place? Did he feel we were charging ahead too fast? Taking the show down the wrong track, maybe? Surely he realized we had to keep the ball rolling. Advertisers were expecting great things from us, and we wouldn't let them down. This week's episode would prove that as never before. Why, I wouldn't be a bit surprised if Rex's prediction turned out to be true. Perhaps several of us would garner Emmy nominations. One could hope, anyway.

A knock sounded at the door, and I answered it, expecting to see Carlos and Humberto on the other side. My jaw dropped when I discovered my father standing there.

"Tia-mia." He flashed a smile almost as crooked as his conscience. "Can I come in?"

"It's a mess in here, Dad," I said. "The guys have left it in shambles." *Again.*

"I heard your brothers were working on the house for you. They need something to do." He took a step inside, and I moved aside to allow him entrance. "How's that working out?"

"Well, you know Carlos. He works four hours and thinks he's put in a full day. Claims Maria or one of the kids needs him. But Humberto's doing all right. He keeps me entertained, anyway. Both of those guys are a piece of work." I rubbed at my itching nose, willing myself not to sneeze.

"Chips off the old block." He gave me a wink that I assumed was supposed to make me laugh. It did not. While I appreciated my father's attempt at humor, I had never appreciated the fact that he bounced from one job to another . . . and one woman to another.

Ugh. Was it getting hot in here? I tugged at the neck of my T-shirt as I led the way across the entryway and into the living room. I had a feeling he hadn't come all this way just to talk to me about my house, or the weather.

I pushed aside a newspaper from the sofa and gestured for him to sit, and then I faced him, but not before ushering up a silent prayer for God's help with this conversation. He'd written a lot of father-daughter scripts over the years, so this one should be a piece of cake for him. Still, being this close to my dad had me a little unnerved, considering how angry I was with him.

"So, what's the latest with you and Mom?" No point in beating around the bush.

"Well, a man can hardly avoid a question like that, now can he?" Dad chuckled and propped his feet up on my twelve-hundred-dollar coffee table. Great.

He gestured for me to sit in the empty spot next to him, but I declined. How could I be mad at my daddy while sitting curled up at his side? No way. I'd lean against the wall and let it hold me up for a while. Unfortunately, all of the dust threw me into a sneezing fit once again. Made my eyes itch too. When I finally got things under control, I reached for a tissue and gestured for my father to begin.

"You want to know where things stand with your mama?" The sigh that followed was a little exaggerated. "I showed up at the house this afternoon to talk to her."

"No way. She would've called me." I wiped my nose then wadded up the tissue.

"You can call and ask her yourself. I've told her how sorry I am and that it won't happen again." He hung his head for several seconds, then finally looked my way. "Tia, I don't expect you to understand. You don't have a lot of experience with the opposite sex."

Perfect. Condescension and a guilt trip. Just what I needed on a near-empty stomach in a dust-filled room, after a hard day at work with people whose lives off the set were as perfect as they were when the cameras were rolling.

Focus, Tia.

"So, you're done with what's-her-name, is that right? Or is this like last time?"

"Baby girl, don't be so hard on your old dad. I'm human. I make mistakes." He offered a childish pout, then stroked his fingers across his heavy black mustache. Strange how I'd never noticed the gray mixed in with all that black before. Suddenly I felt very, very old. Right now, though, I focused on his eyes, still brimming with tears.

Look away, Tia. Don't buy into his story.

I stiffened my backbone and faced him head-on. "You've surpassed your legal limit on mistakes, Dad."

"Legal limit?" He chuckled and his features softened. "Well, if there's a legal limit on mistakes, I probably passed it in my teens, like everyone else in the world. But hey, you're

44

missing the point. We've got to forgive and move on. That's what life is all about. We fall down then get back up again. Right?"

I wanted to throw my arms up in the air and give him a little speech about falling versus deliberately walking into sin's path. My speech would include a section on God's idea of marriage and how he felt about men who cheated on their wives. I'd probably throw in something about building trust in a relationship and at least a brief mention—for the thousandth time—of how much pain his wandering eye had caused Mama all these years.

My father must've picked up on my inner angst because he rose and took a few steps in my direction. When he reached me, he extended his hand, his eyes growing misty.

Oh please, not again. You do this every time.

His voice trembled as he spoke. "Tia, my family means everything to me. Don't you see that?"

"I know you say that, but—"

"I'm a flawed man. But the Bible says we have to forgive."

"It's not a matter of forgiving, Dad. It's a matter of being smart." *One of us has to be.* "You keep falling into the same pit, and you expect Mama to pull you out. It's not fair to her or the rest of us. How do you think she feels after what you've put her through?"

"I know, I know." He paused and raked his fingers through his hair. "But what can I do, Tia? I've got eyes in my head. Can't very well close them every time a pretty woman comes along. You might as well gouge my eyes out than ask me to look away."

I bit back the "Don't tempt me" that threatened to come out. Still, a shiver ran down my spine at his blunt statement. Sure didn't sound like he planned on mending his ways. I started to open my mouth to speak, but he didn't seem to notice. No, he kept right on talking, clearly oblivious to my inner turmoil and my desire to put him in his place.

When he paused from his lengthy conversation about beautiful women, my father's expression brightened. "Speaking of pretty women, I hear Benita is coming to work for you at the studio."

"We're in the talking stages, but nothing is really settled. I'm going to call her later tonight to let her know what my boss said."

"That's one of the reasons I stopped by—to thank you. Benita's a good girl."

"Humph."

No comment.

"You're a good girl too." He squinted and then laughed. "Maybe a little too good. Like your mama. Such a saint, that woman."

I'm no saint. If you had any idea what I'm thinking about you right now, you would know that.

"Anyway, don't fret about Benita, honey. It will all work out."

"I'm not fretting."

He gave me a pensive look. "Sure you are. That's what you do. You analyze things." He crossed the room and paused in front of the family photo on the mantel. "Benita's just the opposite. She goes where the wind blows her. Carlos too."

Gee, I wonder where they get that.

"I'm afraid it's going to blow them out to sea if they're not careful," I said after thinking it through. "That's no way to live. Everyone needs a firm foundation. You know?"

My father turned away from the photo and shrugged. "Oh, I don't know, Tia. At least your brothers and sister are getting to have some adventures. I can't fault them for that. I've had a few of those myself."

46

Yeah, and look where they've landed you—living in a cheap hotel room away from your family.

Hmm. Maybe I should keep my thoughts to myself.

Or not.

"Which is better?" I asked him after pausing to think it through. "To live an adventure or to be sure of where you're going?"

He laughed. "I know where I'm going, Tia-mia. Same place I always go—back to your mama's arms. Don't ever doubt it. That woman thinks I hung the moon." He took a couple of steps toward the door, then turned back with a wink. "She can't make it without me."

I fought the temptation to slug him. Did it really seem that easy to him? Mess up—deliberately—then come crawling back, knowing my mother's big heart would accommodate him? Suddenly I wished I had the courage to tell my mother to send him packing once and for all. She had every logical reason to do so. Even the Bible would back me up on this one.

And yet . . . as my father stood here, a smile as broad as the Pacific on his face, I could see how he managed to charm people.

He walked to the door. Resting his hand on the doorknob, he turned back to face me. "Honey, about your sister . . ."

"What about her?"

"I know you said things aren't settled yet, but she really needs a job. It would ease your mother's mind if you—"

"I know, I know."

"You're well connected, Tia-mia. You know people. Big people. Important people. So, it's only right . . ."

I waved my hand, unable to take anymore. "Our producer has already agreed to meet with her tomorrow. Don't worry. It's as good as done." A sinking feeling took hold as I spoke those words. Having Benita at the studio every day would make me a nervous wreck, but I would do it—for my family. Besides, we had less than two months left in the season. Surely I could endure that much time with Benita.

He gave me an approving nod. "I never worry where you're concerned. Of all my children, you're the only one I never fret over." He gave me a look that could almost be described as endearing. "You're the one to make us all proud. The real winner in the bunch."

His flattery caught me off guard. Still, I could sense manipulation when I saw it. His words were meant to provoke me to action, as always. Tia, the worker bee. Tia, the rescuer. Tia, the only one in the family capable of carrying the load—financially and emotionally—for everyone else.

Nope. Nothing had changed. Except now the words were covered with more dust. I felt like sneezing just thinking about it.

Dad's hand gripped the door, and he turned on the charm once more. Flashing a convincing smile, he offered up a few parting words. "Think like a winner, honey. Stick with your family. Don't abandon us now, not after all we've been through together."

Funny. As I closed the door behind him, I realized I could have said the very same thing to him.

5

Family Ties

On Tuesday morning I arose feeling completely wiped out after a late night of taping and retaping Sheetrock in my entryway. Turned out it was harder than it looked. So much for those hunky carpenters on the DIY network, telling me I could do it myself. They'd clearly never seen a neurotic, overworked Hollywood director try her hand at home improvement.

My watery eyes and itchy nose made me a great candidate for an antihistamine commercial, but I didn't dare take any meds. Not on such an important day. It was Tuesday, after all. Some of my toughest work happened on Tuesdays. Blocking and reblocking scenes. Giving instruction to the actors, the camera guys, and so on. Nope. No time to think about a head cold—or whatever this was—today.

As I hit the 405, I shifted gears—internally, anyway—and gave some thought to today's plan of action. After such a great read-through yesterday, I felt sure my cast and crew would be in good spirits. That would help. Hopefully our run-through would be smooth.

My phone rang just as I reached my exit. I pushed a button on my steering wheel and Mama's voice rang out, just as it did every morning about this time.

"Tia-mia, you sweet girl! I just called to thank you for getting Benita the job. It means the world to me. And her too, of course. To all of us. Oh, you always come through for us, Tia."

"It's not really solid yet, Mama," I said. "Rex has agreed to meet with her today. I called her last night and made it very clear what is expected of her, if he does decide to hire her." A chill came over me as I thought about the potential for disaster with my sister in the studio. Thankfully, the SUV behind me provided the perfect distraction as he attempted to rush me down the ramp.

"Oh, I know it's going to be solid before the day's over," Mama said. "I've been praying about it and feel sure the job's in the bag. But I really called to talk to you about your father. I, um . . . I hear he stopped by your place last night."

"Benita shouldn't have told you."

My mother's voice kept me from saying more. "Did he . . . I mean, is he planning to . . ."

Come back home? Again?

"I guess that's your decision, Mama." I pulled my car up to a stoplight and drew in a deep breath. "It's between you and Daddy. It's not really my business. Besides, he said he talked to you already."

"Still, you're my oldest, Tia-mia. I lean on you for advice."

And a thousand other things.

She continued, oblivious to my thoughts. "And yes, I talked to him, but I still can't decide if he's telling the truth this time. Did his apology seem real to you? Hmm, baby girl?"

50

"Mama, I'd really like to talk, but I'm almost to the studio. It's Tuesday. You know what that means."

"Yes. Tuesday is one of the most important days of the week." Sounded like she was reading the words from a book or something. "It's the day the cast and crew do a full run-through of the episode for the first time. You've told me a dozen times."

"Exactly. And it's the day when I have to stay focused and give direction."

Especially today, since we're delivering a baby.

"You've never had a problem with focus, honey. Now, your little brother, he's another story. Gabe's teacher tried to tell me that she thinks he has ADHD and needs to be on medication. What do you think of that?"

I think it's about five years overdue, but I would never say that out loud.

"Just one more thing to pray about, Mama," I said. "Better hit your knees."

"With as many children as I've got, I spend half my time on my knees and the other half wringing my hands. And when you factor your father into the equation . . ." She sighed. "Anyway, I spend a lot of time praying. And my knees are calloused."

No doubt.

"I've spent a lot of time doing the same," I said as the light changed. "That's the only thing that gets me through—on Tuesdays and every other day of the week."

"I know you have to work, honey, but when things slow down, call me and give me all the news about Benita's new job, okay? I can hardly wait to hear, especially now that Brock Benson is part of your cast."

I shoved the feelings of panic aside as I realized Benita would be spending one-on-one time with Brock Benson. The very idea terrified me. Still, he seemed like he had a good head on his shoulders. Surely he could deal with a beautiful flirt like my younger sister. I hoped.

I ended the call with Mama, my mind now reeling. Thank goodness Benita was waiting on me when I arrived at the studio. I ushered her into Rex's office, and after just ten minutes of chitchat, she'd landed herself the job. So much for thinking the network execs would have to weigh in on the idea. Rex made the decision as if he'd known all along he would.

As we left his office, he leaned over and patted me on the shoulder. "I like her a lot, Tia. Never would've guessed you two are sisters, though. You're very . . . different." The creases between his brows deepened.

"Um, yes."

And not just physically.

Just as quickly, the tension seemed to lift from his face. "Still, I see something in her. And her portfolio is wonderful. She's got quite an eye for color."

And other things. I paused and drew in a breath. *Stop it, Tia. Give your sister a chance.*

"Have someone take her over to meet with Nora. They'll have a few days together before Nora has to leave. Benita can learn the ropes."

"Great idea."

By the time I'd absorbed his words, Benita was ten paces ahead of me in the hallway. She reached the set, then turned back to face me, her eyes shimmering with tears.

"Oh, Tia, it's wonderful. To think I'll be putting the finishing touches on some of Hollywood's hottest—" Her words hung in midair as Brock Benson entered the room. "Oh, mama mia," she said at last. "It's that all-American boy next door. In the flesh." She pulled out a compact and checked her appearance. Turning my way, she whispered, "How do I look?"

"Great. As always."

"Thanks." She snapped the compact closed and smacked her lips together. "Let's get this show on the road, sis." She giggled at her own words. "Show on the road. Ha!"

"Yeah, we get that a lot around here."

"Introduce me to the cast and crew, okay? And play it up like I'm used to working with stars. I've spent time with a few at the salon, you know." She lit into a lengthy list of well-known people she'd crossed paths with, but I barely heard any of it. Instead, I found myself focused on Jason, who approached Brock and shook his hand.

"Well, not everyone's here yet," I said. "I see Jason and Brock, but none of the others—"

Just as I spoke the words, the room filled with adults and children alike. Once everyone was in place, I led the way onto the set, Benita on my heels, and clapped my hands to get their attention. My little sister stood at my side nearly humming with excitement. Any minute now I expected her to take off flying around the room.

The guys—Jason and Brock, in particular—seemed spellbound by Benita. Out of the corner of my eye, I took note of the fact that she was watching them. She used her fingertips to brush loose strands of hair around her face. Whether she realized it or not, Benita always did that when flirting. Looked like she had a few girlish tricks up her sleeve. Hopefully the guys would see through her little game.

"Everyone, this is my sister, Benita Morales." I held my breath and waited for the menfolk to stop gawking.

"Hi, everyone." She giggled and gave a little wave, her perfectly lined lips curling up in a sumptuous smile. "You can call me Beni."

"I'd like to call her, all right," Bob, the youngest on our writing team, leaned in to whisper to Jason.

I chose to ignore him. "With Nora leaving in a few days, we need someone to take over the hair and makeup department," I explained. "Beni's a natural. And she's graduated from a very prestigious beauty school here in L.A."

"Cosmetology school," she whispered. She cleared her throat and spoke to the group. "I went to WBI."

"WBI?" Jason shrugged. "Don't know that one."

"Western Beauty Institute. I graduated with a cosmetology license. It's officially recognized by the National Accrediting Commission of Cosmetology Arts and Sciences. My primary focus of study was eyes and lips." She went off on a tangent talking about eye makeup techniques, but I could tell the guys weren't really interested in that. They were, however, interested in *her* eye makeup. Or maybe the lashes, which she fluttered at will as she spoke. And those outlined lips were apparently a draw too.

The males in the room appeared to be hanging on her every word. She finished up her speech and gave a little giggle. "So I guess you could say I'm a beauty expert."

"Holy cow, is she ever," Bob whispered. He elbowed a couple of the other guys. One let out a little snort.

Ugh. How could I turn this ship around? Only one way. Take command.

I upped my volume to be heard above the murmuring of voices. "We've made our introductions. Now it's time to get to work. Erin, would you take Benita to the makeup department and introduce her to Nora?" I gave my sister what I hoped would be an encouraging smile. "Have fun."

"Oh, I will." She paused at Brock's side, stammering something about his gorgeous hair, then kept moving.

Thank goodness. We could finally get to work.

Maybe. Jason drew near and touched me on the arm. I looked his way and he smiled. "She's your sister? No joke?"

"Really, Tia?" Bob asked. "You're kidding, right? One of you must be adopted."

"Of course not. We have the same parents." *To the best of my knowledge.*

"Wow." Jason shook his head, glancing after Benita. "That girl is . . . well, you have to admit, you two are nothing alike."

"She's my kid sister," I said. "Would you like to see her birth certificate?"

"Only if it proves she's old enough to go out with me." Bob wiggled his brows and everyone laughed.

"Very funny. But I don't think that's a very good idea. Dating your co-workers rarely works out." *Cardinal rule, right?*

"Oh, really?" Kat said, taking a couple of steps in my direction. She rubbed her belly. "I think I can prove otherwise."

Embarrassment flooded over me. "Well, you're an exception. You and Scott were made for each other."

"We were indeed." She laughed. "And apparently so were Athena and Stephen." She pointed at our two love-struck head writers and shrugged. "I'm of the opinion that God brought them together too." She gave me a pensive look. "Kind of makes me wonder who's next on this set."

"Ooo, pick me!" Bob raised his hand and let out a childish squeal. "Beni and Bob! I like the sound of that." He gazed after my sister and sighed. "And I like the *looks* of that."

The guys lit into an excited conversation about Benita's assets. I groaned and turned away from them, wondering— for the first time in my life—if perhaps one of us really was adopted. Knowing my father's history suddenly made that possibility seem all too real.

Calm down, Tia.

Athena approached just as I shared my heart with Kat. "I guess I'm a little jealous of my sister. Always have been, in fact."

"Why?" Kat looked perplexed by this idea.

"She's gorgeous, and she's never had trouble finding a guy. Or two. Or twelve."

"Well, yeah," Athena said, looking in the direction Benita had gone. "It's the vibe she puts off. Trust me, if you started putting off that vibe, I'd be plenty worried."

"It's not that I'm even looking. My work keeps me busy. And I'm perfectly happy single."

Liar. You are not.

"I used to think that." Kat offered a delirious sigh. "But then God interrupted my plans with Scott."

"Funny. I was always the sort of girl who found satisfaction in her work too," Athena said. "Figured if I wanted a romance I could pencil it in whenever I liked. But God had other plans. He sent Stephen when I least expected it."

"You guys—girls—are different. You're both so . . ." I wanted to say *pretty*, but I knew they would turn it around and claim that I was pretty too. Instead I just sighed.

"We're not different from you, trust me," Athena said. "Just at a different stage of the journey."

Kat patted me on the arm. "The excitement over your sister will wear off soon enough, I suppose. The guys will get over her in time."

"I'm not sure about Bob. He looks smitten."

"He's always smitten. Remember the Amish girlfriend? And the girlfriend before that? And the one before that? He falls hard and then licks his wounds."

"Guess you're right. I'm sure it will be business as usual around here as soon as the fascination wears off." The heaviness in my heart eased up a bit. Then just as quickly, it returned. I faced Kat. "Only, you're leaving. So it really won't be business as usual, will it?"

"Aw." She shrugged and reached over to hug me—not an easy

56

task with a basketball-sized belly in the way. "I'm going to miss being with all of you so much. And in case I didn't make it clear yesterday, I really love this week's script. It's the perfect swan song for me, and I'm grateful. You have no idea how grateful."

"You deserve the best, Kat. You really do. I . . ." Tears filled my eyes. "Well, I'm really going to miss you."

"Ack! Now look what you've done." Athena dabbed at her eyes. "You've made me cry."

"I'll miss you both so much," Kat said. "But I can't wait to see what the future holds." She giggled. "For that matter, I can't wait to see what today holds. I know you'll do a great job leading us." She lowered her voice. "And just so you know, I think it's a very kind thing you're doing for your sister."

"Thanks."

"Brave, even." She gestured to the guys, and one of her brows elevated slightly. "If you know what I mean."

I knew, all right. But I didn't feel brave. I felt like I'd just made a big mistake bringing Benita here. The potential for damage was huge. Still, we had to plow ahead. No rest for the weary, and all that.

Minutes later, we were off and running. I pulled the team together again, reminded them of the basic outline of the episode, and began to give some stage directions, starting with the elevator scene—the most critical component.

"The elevator set piece is being constructed as we speak and should be ready for tomorrow's run-through. But for now envision a space about eight by eight. Brock, you'll enter first, followed by Scott and Kat. Brock is holding the bag of sandwiches from the gyro shop. He's just picked them up to take to a meeting." I snapped my fingers. "Ah, that reminds me, we'll have to get Athena to bring in several sandwiches from her parents' shop for this scene. They actually get eaten, so they have to be real." I turned to Erin. "Make a note, okay?"

"Got it." She grinned. "Athena needs to bring sandwiches for Thursday's shoot."

This led several of my cast and crew members into a conversation about how great Athena's parents' sandwiches were, which took away valuable time. I finally managed to get them corralled once again.

"Anyway, Brock is in the elevator with the sandwiches when Kat and Scott—er, Angie and Jack—get in, dressed as Mr. and Mrs. Easter Bunny."

Scott interrupted me. "No, they're heading out to meet the kids. Brock gets on after the fact. Isn't that right?"

"Hmm." I thumbed through my script. Sure enough, I'd gotten it backwards. Nothing like appearing discombobulated in front of my cast and crew. I released a slow breath and dove in again, this time giving instructions about the location of the next scene. "Okay, so Angie and Jack are in the elevator . . ." I paused and turned to Erin, distracted by a niggling thought. "Would you mind checking with the wardrobe department to see if they've got the Easter Bunny costumes ready? Last I heard they were having trouble finding the fabric they needed for Mrs. Bunny's skirt."

"Will do." She took off running.

I turned back to my cast. "So, they're in the elevator dressed up for the party, where they plan to surprise the kids they represent. Then Brock gets in carrying the sandwiches, and the elevator gets stuck, which jars them all and sends Angie sprawling to the floor. At that point, she goes into labor." I looked at Kat. "Think you can manage that part?"

She wrinkled her nose. "Well, do you mean 'go into labor' as in 'have labor pains'? Or does my water break or something? The script isn't clear. Do you have a preference?"

Ack! What a question to ask a never-been-pregnant woman. I closed my eyes and tried to envision the scene. Which would be the better choice? Labor usually took awhile, right? Maybe it would be best to have her water break first. I'd just about decided on that when Kat piped up.

"I read in my pregnancy book that most women just start with a few twinges. They don't even realize they're in labor right away. And very few women have their water break at the beginning. How long is this scene going to be, anyway? I can't just have a pain and then deliver a baby, you know?"

"Oh, we'll go back and forth from the elevator to the scene with the kids to show a progression in time," I explained.

"Okay." She nodded. "So, how do you want me positioned? I mean, this is a family show. We have to be really careful how we handle this scene."

"Right. We want it to be funny but not crude."

Hmm. Looked like I needed a compass, because right now I didn't have a clue where I was headed. And how would I steer this ship if I couldn't even tell a pregnant woman how to deliver a baby in an elevator?

I closed my eyes once again, picturing the whole thing. "Okay, this is how it's going to happen. You'll be in the elevator when Brock joins you. A moment later the elevator gets stuck, and after you fall to the floor, you feel your first labor pain. That's not too unrealistic, is it?"

Kat shrugged. "Sounds okay to me."

"By the time we cut to the kids' scene at the agency and come back again, maybe you can be lying down with Jack on one side of you and Brock's character on the other. At that point you can be . . ."

"Panting?" she offered.

"Sure. Panting. Whatever. Just make sure it looks real."

Kat rubbed her belly. "Trust me, I'll make it look real."

Everyone got a laugh out of that one.

"And this would be a good time to have the guys eating the sandwiches. They're just biding their time."

"Typical guys." Kat rolled her eyes and eased her way into a chair.

"Then we'll cut back to the kids, who are trying to break into the elevator. By the time we cut back to the inside of the elevator, Jack has figured out that Brock's character is the rival talent scout, but it's too late to worry about that because the baby's coming. We'll cut back out to the kids, who hear an infant crying. When the elevator doors open, Jack faints."

"Can't wait," Scott said. "I've always wanted an excuse to faint."

"Well, now you've got it." I plastered on a smile and tried to look calm and confident as I called everyone into position for the first run-through. Unfortunately, the whole thing turned out to be a chaotic mess. And my instructions—confusing and vague—didn't help matters.

What's wrong with you today, Tia? You'd think you had never directed the birth of a child before.

Then again, I hadn't. Maybe that was the problem. I had no clue what I was doing. But I couldn't very well let them see that, could I?

Erin ran back in the room, gave me a thumbs-up, and hollered that the costumes were complete and ready to be fitted. At least we didn't have to worry about that.

We forged ahead, making a royal mess of things. The kids began to act up, creating more chaos than my nerves could handle. Poor Kat sat on the floor panting for so long I thought she might pass out. She pushed and puffed till I believed a baby might actually emerge. And the look on Brock's face was priceless as he watched. Clearly he'd never witnessed a scene like this one before. Not with a neurotic director in charge, anyway.

"Okay, everyone, let's do this. I think we should . . ." I stared at my cast, my thoughts tumbling madly. For whatever reason, every sensible idea slipped right out of my head. I'd left everyone hanging on my last word, and they were counting on me to give direction.

At long last, I said the only thing that made sense.

"I think we should take a break for lunch."

Married with Children

There are those moments in life when you feel as if you're drowning. In my case, pride kept me from calling out for a life preserver. How could I call myself a director when I felt like fleeing every time the seas got rocky? Spielberg didn't run when trouble set in, did he? Of course not. And what about the great Cecil B. DeMille? He dug in his heels and stayed put, even during the toughest of times. Even Stanley Kubrick didn't run, though some felt he should, after that scuttlebutt with *Lolita*.

No, the greats didn't run. They stayed put and directed the delivery scene in the elevator, even when everything inside of them screamed for the mother-to-be to hold that baby inside until next season.

Deep breath, Tia. This baby's got to come out.

A few deep breaths later and I realized I was panting, just like I'd seen Kat doing earlier.

"You okay, Tia?" Rex walked toward me, the wrinkles in his brow deepening. "You're looking a little pale. And you sound a little winded."

"Am I? Hmm." Mustering up my courage, I gave him what I hoped would be a convincing smile. "I'm fine."

Or at least I will be, once I get this breathing steadied.

"Okay. Well, I'm taking Lenora over to the commissary for some lunch. She didn't eat much this morning. Her appetite these days is . . . " He shook his head. "Anyway, she likes the commissary. Reminds her of when she was young. Back in those days, you never knew who you might see at the next table—Rock Hudson, Clark Gable, Doris Day . . ."

Rex disappeared, along with half of the cast and crew. Finding myself on a near-empty set, I turned to my new production assistant. "Erin, would you do me a favor and run lines with the kids as soon as lunch ends? I could tell at the roundtable reading yesterday that Joey's going to have a little trouble with pacing in that first scene, and Ethan is struggling with a lisp. I really need someone to help Candy run over her solo too. Think you can do all that when we get back from lunch?"

"Sure. Sounds like fun. Do you mind if I do some warm-ups with them first? I think that's half the problem. Their enthusiasm is waning because they're stuck in a rut. Seems like no one's excited about all of this, and that's a shame. If we make this fun for them, they'll come alive again. I just know it."

I nodded, mesmerized by her ability both to work with small children and to take charge. In so many ways, I felt like the Lord had plopped Erin down in the middle of the *Stars Collide* studio just to lift my spirits. Well, that, and to help. She seemed more than ready to assist me in whatever way I needed.

To my left, a familiar voice rang out. "Are you hungry? Do you want to go to the commissary?"

I looked over at Jason. "Oh, I . . ." Was he really asking me to join him for lunch? My grumbling stomach finally won out. "I would love that. I'm starved."

"I had some ideas about shooting this scene and wanted to talk them through."

"Sure." Naturally. He just wanted to talk shop. Figured. Then again, who could blame him? I'd always focused on business first.

"Ooo, I want to go too," Benita said from behind me.

Jason turned and gave her a curious look, followed by a shrug. "Sure. Sounds good. The more, the merrier."

Ugh.

Benita rolled her eyes. "I asked Brock if he wanted to come, but he's going to eat with Erin and the kids. Go figure."

Go figure, indeed. I watched as Brock made his way to Erin's side, a broad smile on his face.

When we reached the commissary, the smell of roast beef nearly knocked me off my feet. How long had it been since I'd eaten a real meal? Still, I could hardly shovel in the beef with people looking on, now could I? Instead, I opted for a salad with light Italian dressing. Benita, on the other hand, went for the roast and potatoes.

We took our places at a table just far enough away from Rex and Lenora to give them some privacy. I watched as Kat and Scott ate their lunch together off in the distance. What would it be like, I wondered, to eat lunch with someone who loved you as deeply as Scott loved Kat?

"Mmm, Tia?"

"Yes?" I looked into Jason's eyes.

"Would you pass the salt?"

"Oh, um, sure." Not exactly "Let's spend the rest of our

lives together," but at least he was talking to me. For months, the only communication we'd had was arguing over filming techniques. At least we were sitting at the same table. That was a start.

"This place is crazy." Benita looked around, her eyes widening as she saw a familiar male star. "Oh, Tia! That's Trace Goodnight from *Another Side of Love*. I've always thought he was so handsome."

"Yeah." I shrugged. I'd seen him around dozens of times, so he'd lost his luster.

"Working at a studio has to be the best job I've ever had." Benita looked my way, her eyes sparkling. "And seeing all of these famous people is just the icing on the cake. Now I can see why you love your job so much, Tia."

"Why wouldn't she love it? She's very good at what she does." Jason took a bite of his sandwich and gave me a wink.

My heart fluttered. *Did he really just wink at me, or does he have something in his eye? And did he actually say I'm good at what I do?*

Benita took a bite and leaned back in her chair. "I know she's good at what she does. She talks about work nonstop, even when she's at home with the family. It's 'camera angles' this and 'lighting' that. She never quits."

"I like my job. What can I say?" Nibbling on a piece of lettuce, I tried to put her words out of my mind. Besides, what did she know about my work? She'd never shown much interest in it.

Benita shrugged. "Might not hurt to give it a rest every now and again."

I bit back the words on my tongue and continued chewing the lettuce.

She turned to Jason. "Don't you agree?"

"Oh, well, I guess it's not my place to say. Besides, I'm pretty much a workaholic myself." His encouraging smile lifted my spirits. "So, what do you do for fun, Tia?" Jason took a swig of his Coke. "When you're not talking about your work, I mean."

"For fun?" I paused and shrugged, opting not to mention taping and floating Sheetrock. I finally landed on the only answer that made sense. "Watch a lot of TV and movies."

"Me too." He nodded.

Benita rolled her eyes. "You two are so boring."

His gaze narrowed as he looked my way. "Now, this isn't a trick question—or maybe it is—but are you watching TV shows and movies to rest and relax, or are you working?"

I sighed, knowing I'd been caught. "I watch the various camera angles and setups. Wide shots. Narrow shots. Close-ups versus pulled-out shots. Actors' tones and inflections. Hairstyles. Set design." I groaned. "Trust me, I'm not resting and relaxing. I'm usually looking for new and innovative ways to do things. Or I'm catching errors. Do you know how many costume errors alone I've caught? It keeps me on my toes so we don't make the same mistakes."

Benita's eye rolling kicked in again. "See? I told you. She never takes a minute off. It's ridiculous. Even God took one day off."

"I rest."

Sometimes.

"If anyone understands Tia's work ethic, I do." Jason sighed. "Especially when it comes to watching movies or TV. I'm ruined for life. Can't enjoy them at all."

Finally! Someone who understood me.

Jason leaned forward and spoke in hushed tones. "Just last week I watched an episode of *Another Side of Love* and noticed that Trace Goodnight's shirt was yellow at the beginning of the scene and brown at the end. Someone wasn't paying attention."

"I actually took notes at the last movie I went to. Beni got mad at me because I hid my iPad in my purse." I glared at her. "Don't know what her problem was. I only pulled it out a few times, and I reduced the light on the screen so it wouldn't bother anyone."

"I wanted her to have a good time," Benita said. "But she doesn't know how to do that. Trust me, we've been working on it for years and she can't get the hang of it."

"Can I help it if I'm a workaholic?" I asked. "I'm trying to make a name for myself in this industry, and that's not easy."

Even as I spoke, shame washed over me. Where had the words come from, anyway? Since when did I care about making a name for myself?

Jason gave me a sympathetic look. "I've never said this before, Tia, but I don't envy you being the director. Having that much control would be tough. And having to come up with decisions on the spot—with so many people looking on—would be even tougher."

"The worst is when we're in the middle of a scene that's not working. I'm standing there in front of the whole cast and crew, having to come up with a solution. I usually work much better alone. I block out every scene in my head—and on paper—ahead of time. So when things fall apart, I might look composed on the outside, but I'm mush on the inside."

"I never would have known." He gave me an admiring look. Seemed like I was seeing more of this side of him lately. Interesting.

"I'd take your place any day," my sister said between bites.

I sighed. "Beni, there's more to the job than most people know. I don't just have to direct the actors and actresses. I have to make sure the set design is perfect." The intensity of my voice rose, and my words were more rushed. "I have to work closely with the costume department to make sure everyone is looking the way they should be looking. Same with hair and makeup. I have to communicate with all of the department heads on a regular basis to make sure we're on the same page. Not to mention the producer and the advertisers. And then there are the kids. I have to make sure they're on the set only a certain number of hours per day, and having their lessons with their teacher the rest. That means everything has to be scheduled down to the minute."

Jason looked sympathetic. "I don't know what you're so worried about. You're the director, and a great one at that. You're accustomed to telling people what to do, and they do it—not just because they respect you as a person but because they respect your position." He shrugged. "That's got to feel good."

"Sometimes. But I guess I'd just rather have their respect as a person, not a director. When I'm not hollering out directions, people just pass me by like I'm not even there."

"Impossible." His gaze lingered, and a hint of a smile creased the edges of his mouth. "I defy anyone to pass you by."

Suddenly all the noise in the commissary seemed to come to a grinding halt. For a moment, I could hear only his words: "I defy anyone to pass you by." They rang out loud and clear, flooding my heart with joy. And surprise. And intrigue. And hope.

His face lit in a boyish smile, and all of a sudden it was just the two of us sitting in the studio commissary, eating lunch and talking about the things we had in common. Everything around us faded to sepia tone. No, scratch that. Sepia tone was highly overrated and rough on the eyes. I'd never understood that whole faded-edges thing, either. Better make it mood lighting—soft whites shimmering through transient gels positioned overhead. Or maybe a lovely beach scene in the background. Digital, of course.

One thing was for sure. If Jason had been filming this scene—if the camera had zoomed in close enough—he would surely have noticed the shimmer of tears in my eyes. And though they surprised me, I could no longer deny the fact that they reflected feelings simmering just below the surface.

Oh, mama mia! Now what?

Grace under Fire

I spent Tuesday night arguing on the phone with my brother, who claimed he'd been too sick to finish floating the Sheetrock in my entryway that day. Too drunk was more like it. From the sound of things, he'd passed "sick" about four beers back. So, once again, I tackled the chore by myself. For hours I worked alone, until my body just couldn't take it anymore. By the time I tumbled into bed at midnight, the dust had clogged my airways, causing me to cough and sneeze nonstop. Lovely. Nothing like a director with a head cold.

Wednesday dawned bright and sunny. I awoke, rolled over in my bed, and whispered up my usual "Dear Lord, please let this be a good day" prayer. Okay, so maybe it wasn't deep and spiritual, but it was all I could muster after such a long night.

When I tried to sit up on the bed, my arms and legs didn't want to cooperate. Well, not without pain, anyway. And what was up with my shoulders? Strange. They were almost as stiff and sore as my neck, which refused to turn. And then there was the issue of my stuffy sinuses. They were worse than ever. Maybe I really was coming down with something.

No, after a hot shower, I could only conclude I had DIY syndrome. Too much home improvement had nearly done me in. But no time to think about that right now, not with our final run-through happening today. Somehow I had to get through this delivery scene, even if it killed me. And I had a feeling it might, especially with my body in such a weakened state.

After showering, I did a few stretches, hoping to ease my joints into working order. Though they cried out in pain, they cooperated for the most part. Still, nothing about this particular Wednesday morning felt right to me. For one thing, Mama didn't call me like she always did as I made the drive to the studio. For another, I couldn't seem to get my creative thought processes to come into alignment where this week's filming was concerned. Instead, I had this nagging feeling that I was on the *Titanic*, slowly guiding it toward an iceberg. Heaven help me.

Arriving at the studio, I parked and did my best to emerge from the car without wincing in pain. After all, with Lenora and Rex pulling into the spot next to me, I had to keep up appearances. And speaking of keeping up appearances, Lenora emerged from her pink Cadillac convertible wearing a cream-colored blouse with a high collar, a long skirt, white gloves, and a wide-brimmed hat. I'd gotten pretty good at guessing her movie getups, but I had to admit this one boggled me.

"Who are we today, Lenora?" Jason said from behind me, and I turned to see him walking my way from the most gorgeous red BMW Z4 I'd ever seen. I'd never noticed that he drove such a wowzer car. Maybe it was new. Still, it seemed a little odd considering his cameraman's salary.

Lenora's voice startled me back to attention. "I'll give you a clue. I traveled with Humphrey Bogart up the river, facing crocodiles and renegades who tried to kill me."

"Ah, piece of cake." Jason nodded. "Katherine Hepburn. *The African Queen*."

"One of the greatest movies ever filmed." Lenora sighed. "Wasn't Bogart the dreamiest boat captain you'd ever want to see?"

Rex cleared his throat.

"Oh, don't worry, you sweet man." Lenora reached up to stroke his cheek, her eyes filled with wonder. "There will never be a hero greater than you."

He gave her a sweeping bow. "Why, thank you. Thank you very much."

A girlish giggle erupted from his wife. "It's Elvis in the flesh!"

"Then you are my Priscilla." Arm in arm, they walked into the studio, Rex's voice bellowing out "Love Me Tender."

I pulled out a Kleenex and blew my nose. "They're really something, aren't they?"

"Yeah." Jason looked their way then glanced at me. "They give me hope that some relationships really do stand the test of time."

"Me too." Just one more thing we had in common.

"Are you sick?" He pointed at the Kleenex.

"I've been stricken with a rare malady—DIY syndrome— but I'd rather not talk about it right now if you don't mind."

"DIY syndrome?" He looked puzzled but didn't comment.

"Yeah." I blew my nose again. "But don't worry. It's not contagious. If it was, the whole country would be under red alert."

As we entered the studio, I took note of Erin, who was playing with a couple of the kids. They really seemed smitten with her, and vice versa. Her laughter, lilting and carefree, brought a certain sense of joy to the place. What would it be like to live like that all the time? To have such a relaxed attitude? Likely I'd never know.

I got right to work, checking in with the writers to see how next week's script was coming, then committing to a plan of action for the day.

By eight o'clock, my cast had arrived in full. Kat looked a little pale but claimed she was perfectly fine, just a little tired. Scott looked anxious, and Brock—well, he just looked distracted. Strange. I'd never seen him this way before.

Seconds later, I noticed the object of his distraction. Benita's familiar giggle rang out from the far side of the set. She'd somehow collected a group of guys around her—no big surprise there. Jason stood in the center of the group, just a few feet away from her. She'd said something funny, obviously. Jason, Brock, Bob, and Paul were all laughing. Why this bothered me so much, I couldn't say. Probably had something to do with not feeling great. Well, that, and the comments the guys had made yesterday about Benita and me having different parents. That still bugged me.

Kat approached, one hand on her belly, the other hand clutching a churro she nibbled on. "Looks like your sister's quite a hit with the guys," she said between bites.

After a couple seconds of silence, I finally said, "There's always so much drama going on around here."

"Well, of course." Kat giggled. "That's the point, isn't it? We're a television sitcom, after all."

"I just like to keep my drama on the stage, if you know what I mean. In bringing Benita in, I feel like I've had to direct more drama offstage than on. I should have known."

Athena joined us, offering a sympathetic look. "You're worried about your sister?"

I nodded. "You have no idea. She's . . ." I wanted to say, "following in our father's footsteps," but held back.

"She's flirtatious with the guys. I've noticed that much," Kat said. She took another bite of her churro and a contented look came over her. "Yum."

"And she's a raving beauty," Athena threw in. "You can't blame them for being interested."

"Yeah, she's pretty, all right."

On the outside.

The words had no sooner flitted through my brain than I felt like slapping myself. Really, who did I think I was, cutting my sister down because of her physical beauty? Only God could see the heart, right? Besides, how would I ever know my sister's potential for inner beauty if I didn't slow down long enough to get to know her—really know her?

"Looks like she's got Brock right where she wants him." Athena's eyes narrowed to slits. "Yep. She's caught him on her hook and is reelin' him in." She chuckled. "He'd be quite a catch. Can you even imagine, Tia? If she snags him for life, that would make him your brother-in-law."

Ugh. Why did that idea suddenly make me feel nauseous?

Okay, time to get to work. I blew my nose one last time, then clapped my hands together and called the room to order. Seconds later, a roomful of cast and crew members faced me. The words of Kieren Willingham, my director at LAFS, ran through my head. *Look confident. Confident, Tia. Make them think you know what you're doing. They're going to follow your lead.* I squared my shoulders, ready to take control.

"I know we had a rough day yesterday, but today is going to be different. We'll get through this episode top to bottom and clean up the rough spots."

Everyone on that set is going to be taking their cues from you. Kieren's words again. *If you fall apart, they fall apart.*

If you look lost, they will feel lost. It's your responsibility to keep the ship from sinking. Or at least to keep it from looking like it's sinking.

But how did one go about that with a true sinking feeling in her gut?

Everyone stared at me in complete silence. After a minute, someone coughed.

Oh, right. Better get this ball rolling. I smiled and dove right in. Somehow we managed to make it through the episode, scene by scene. Kat did a superb job with the delivery, and we all cheered when Scott lifted up a plastic doll and proclaimed, "It's a boy!"

Tomorrow we'd have a real baby. I'd already arranged for an infant boy to arrive on the set early in the morning. Filming his scene would be tricky. He could only be under the lights for minutes at a time—what with child actors' activities being governed by the labor union and all—but we would manage. I hoped. And keeping the news that the baby was a boy out of the papers would be even trickier. My cast and crew had been sworn to secrecy, and studio audience members were as well. In fact, the network had gone out of its way to prepare privacy documents for audience members to sign before they were allowed on the set. Hopefully no one would leak our little secret.

By the time the lunch hour arrived, I felt completely confident once again. And as if on cue, the stuffy nose ended. Ironic. Maybe I wouldn't need to see a doctor after all.

Rex pointed at his watch—my cue that I needed to cut everyone loose for lunch. I did just that, thankful the caterers had arrived with our food for the day. Wednesday runthroughs always required a quick lunch.

Instead of joining the others, I slipped down the hallway to my office, pulled open the script, and began to scribble and scratch. My stomach grumbled, but I ignored it and kept working. There would be time to grab a few bites later. Maybe.

A rap on the door caught my attention. I turned to discover Jason standing in the open doorway. His boyish grin captured my heart. "Still working?"

"Yeah." I sighed and pointed to the script.

He gave me a fatherly look as he took a couple of steps in my direction. "So, I guess Benita was right. You do overwork yourself."

"Oh, I don't know about that. I just—"

"I'm worried about you, Tia."

Well, that certainly got my attention. "You are?"

He nodded, and I could read the concern in his eyes. "You need a break. And you've got to eat."

"Yeah, I know, but I'm worried about that one bit where Scott and Brock fight over the sandwiches. Something about the way they handled it didn't ring true. At times like this, I wish we had a choreographer on staff, someone who could actually block the scene to its best potential. It could be really funny if we get it right."

"You need a choreographer? I used to do a mean hip-hop."

"No way."

He chuckled and tried a couple of awkward dance moves. "Totally kidding. Just thought it would make you smile. And it did."

I pursed my lips, not wanting to appear so fickle. Still, what could a girl do with such a handsome guy teasing her like this?

A playful smile lit his face. "Well, why don't we go to the lunch table and wrestle over a couple of sandwiches to figure out the scene? What do you say?"

"I can think of no one I'd rather wrestle with."

Good gravy. Had I really said those words aloud? Judging

from the look on his face, yes. I rose slowly and shrugged, then mumbled a few words under my breath in Spanish in an attempt to calm my nerves.

"What was that?" He gave me a curious look.

"Oh." I paused, then repeated the words the same way they had come to me: "*Es posible que no hay nada que de más vergüenza?*"

"Ah, I see." He nodded. "And the answer is yes. I'm sure there are a thousand things you could've said—or done—that would've been more embarrassing, so don't worry about it. I'll wrestle sandwiches with you any day." The edges of his lips curled up in a delicious smile. So delicious, in fact, that I almost forgot to be embarrassed.

Then reality hit. "Wait. You speak Spanish?"

"Junior high Spanish class. But I do a lot of work with my church down in the inner city, so I've been brushing up on it."

"W-where did you say?"

"South Central. There's a street church that I've just started working with on Wednesday evenings. I'll tell you all about it at lunch." He gave me an imploring look. "If you'll come with me. I hope you will."

"I would, but I really need to get this done. This episode is so important to me."

"Me too. But there are more important things." He gave me a pensive look.

My heart did that nutty flip-flop thing again, and I tried to steady my breathing. If this guy didn't stop making insinuations, my heart might not be able to take it.

He drew so close I could almost feel his breath on my shoulder. It sent little tingles coursing through me.

"You know how people say the show's the thing?" he whispered, his voice soft but firm. "Well, it's not. I mean, we come in here and pour our hearts out to make the show the best it can be, but in the end, the show isn't the thing. It's what happens outside the walls of this studio that teaches us who we really are. Inside . . . well, this isn't reality. Reality is out there. And in here." He pointed to his heart.

Be still my heart.

"I know you're right." I rested against the edge of the table and reached for the script, which I tucked under my arm. "Reality is out there." *And I've experienced plenty of it.* Suddenly I realized my nose was stuffy again. I reached for a tissue.

His words grew more intense. "I'm just saying that the show—important as it may be—isn't really what this is all about. It's about the real world. Real relationships. Real stuff."

All the stuff I have no control over, in other words.

"I'm trying to tell you something, Tia, but it's not coming out right." He took my hand, which caught me completely off guard.

"O-oh?"

"Sometimes the lines between fiction and reality get blurred, whether we're in the studio or out. Is this making any sense?"

Out in the hallway, several of the children ran by. Candy stopped and looked into my office, her eyes widening as she saw my hand in Jason's. I quickly pulled it away.

"So, what do you say?" Jason gazed at me with greater intensity. "Want to come and wrestle a sandwich away from me? We can eat and work at the same time. Or I can entertain you with stories about the street church."

"I . . . I . . ." My cell phone rang and I glanced at it. *Great. My brother. He chooses now to call? When I'm in the middle of a potential love scene?*

I put up my finger to signal Jason to give me a minute, then I took the call. Carlos dove into a lengthy dissertation about his financial needs, honing in on the fact that he needed to buy more supplies for my house but had no money to do so. I tried ever so politely to respond, but after a couple minutes of listening to his nonsensical conversation, I found my temper growing, especially once I picked up on the fact that he'd been drinking again.

I finally shrugged and signaled for Jason to go on to lunch without me. As he lingered at the door, the most unusual feeling came over me. I wanted to toss the phone into my purse, scratch this nonsense with my brother, and run hand in hand with Jason to the lunchroom to wrestle sandwiches.

Instead, I watched as he disappeared around the corner, then I reached for a tissue while my brother manipulated me into handing over my credit card number for a lumber purchase.

8

Life as We Know It

Thursday morning, Mama neglected to call me once again. By now I was on to her. I'd seen this avoidance game before. It usually took place about the same time she reopened the door for my father to come home. No doubt I would show up at her house tomorrow night for tamales and find my father watching *Wheel of Fortune*. In the meantime, I could count on not hearing from her.

Oh well. There were other things a thirty-year-old woman could do on her way to work besides talk to her mama, especially when the topic of conversation usually rolled around to everyone else's problems. I released a slow breath as I entered the traffic on the 405 and decided to talk to someone else entirely.

I ushered up a rushed prayer, part of it geared toward the traffic and the rest covering my concerns about family matters. Then I turned my attention to today's episode, offering up a "Dear Lord, you know how important this one is to me, right?" prayer.

Superficial at best. Likely the Almighty was getting a little weary of my drive-by prayers. No doubt he was hoping for the "stop in and stay awhile" version. Still, everything in my life moved fast these days. Who had time to slow down? Slow people didn't make progress. They didn't have others depending on them. And they certainly didn't survive in the industry. Or in L.A. traffic, for that matter.

I laid on my horn as a car cut in front of me. The nerve of some people. The guy in the car gave me a not-so-friendly gesture and kept going. Perfect. Just what I needed to start my day.

Hmm, what was I doing again? Oh yeah. Praying.

I tried to dive back into prayer but was consumed with thoughts about today's filming. I still hadn't quite figured out that sandwich bit, though I'd considered it from a dozen different angles. Maybe something would come to me. Or maybe the guys would just figure it out in the moment. Sure, that was it. I'd leave it to Brock and Scott. They'd come up with something.

See there, Tia? It feels good to let go and trust, doesn't it? You don't need to fix everything.

Jason's words from yesterday suddenly flitted through my mind once again. Whether he'd meant to do it or not, the guy had convicted me. Did people really see me as a workaholic who didn't take care of herself? Couldn't take a break for lunch? Didn't get enough sleep? Tried to fix everything?

I sighed. What did it matter, really, what others thought? I knew all of those things were true. Painfully, horribly true. And all because of one goal in mind—to make *Stars Collide* the best show in television history. If I worked harder, pored over the scripts longer, spent time strategically blocking each scene, and expected more in the way of characterization from my cast, we might just make it to the number one slot this year.

I prayed.

Or rather, I didn't pray. I was too distracted by a sudden case of the sniffles once again. After working my way through the worst of it, I put in a quick call to my primary care doctor, who promised to send me the name of a great allergist.

By the time I arrived at the studio, I was in better spirits. I parked next to Jason's BMW, giving it a solid look as I exited my car. Squinting, I gave it a second look. Looked like he was sleeping inside. Odd. I rapped on the window and he startled awake. Seconds later he rolled the window down and I gazed inside, trying not to laugh when I saw the hair sticking up on top of his head.

"Everything okay?" I asked.

"Oh, yeah. Just had a late night last night, so I decided to rest my eyes for a few minutes." He yawned and stretched.

"You weren't partying, were you?" I teased.

"Hardly." He opened the door and stepped outside. "Remember I told you about that street church thing? I was there last night, working. I try to go at least one Wednesday night a month to serve food." He smoothed his hair with his hands. "A lot of those street kids don't get much to eat for the rest of the week, so those Wednesday night meals are pretty important. I like to be there. And I've made a few friends—not just the workers, but some of the kids. They're really great. Just going through a hard time, most of them. Or estranged from their parents."

"Ah."

"It was quite a night. They had to call an ambulance for a guy who OD'd in the parking lot right in the middle of the service. Never seen anything like it, but that's South Central for you. Anyway, I didn't get much sleep, so I'm a little out of sorts. Hope I can pull it together on the set."

Suddenly my insides felt shaky. "Where exactly in South Central?"

"Pretty rough neighborhood near a public park. Very different from life here in the studio, and extremely different from where I grew up. Let's just say we don't get a lot of that kind of action in Newport Beach."

"Newport Beach?" Well, that explained the BMW, for Pete's sake.

He paused and shrugged, a somber look overtaking him. "Sorry. That's my former life. My parents are still there, but I live in an apartment in Hollywood Hills just a few minutes from here. Newport Beach is part of my past, not my present."

I resisted the urge to say, "Must be nice," and just nodded.

Thank goodness Jason seemed focused on work today too. "Listen, I forgot to ask you about setting up that first shot. We need to talk about lighting for the elevator scene."

"Oh, right." I gave him final instructions as we made our way inside the studio. Funny. Once I slipped back into director gear, I relaxed immediately.

Half an hour later, most of my cast and crew had arrived. Erin came bounding in, more excited than I'd seen her yet. "We're filming in front of a live audience today!"

"I know."

"I'm going to offer to run lines with Brock before he gets his hair and makeup done. That okay?" She gave me a pleading look and I nodded. Minutes later, she and Brock were seated next to each other on the set, going over every line.

I noticed Brock's gaze lingering on Erin as they worked together. Interesting. Obviously Benita noticed too. She fussed with her hair, squared her shoulders, and headed their way, a determined look on her face. I'd seen that look before.

"Brock?" She put her hands on her hips when he didn't answer right away. "Brock."

He turned her way, eyes widening as he took in her short skirt and tight blouse. "Yes?"

"Time for hair and makeup."

"Oh." He grimaced. "We were just running my lines. Can you give me a few more minutes?"

Benita eased the script out of Erin's hand. "Oh, don't worry about that. I'll run lines with you while we get you ready. That way we can kill two birds with one stone."

Was it my imagination, or had she glared at Erin while saying "kill two birds with one stone"?

Undeterred, Benita continued. "Sound good?"

I half expected Erin to whop Benita upside the head. Instead, in her usual gracious and good-humored way, my easygoing production assistant shrugged and headed across the room to help with the children. Brock watched her until Benita started talking again.

"Well, c'mon." Benita giggled. "We've got to turn you into a Greek talent scout. Can't wait to show you what I've got in mind. Hope you don't mind if I thicken your brows a bit. And you're going to love the mustache. No one will even know it's fake."

"Hey, as long as your plan doesn't involve eyeliner, I'm okay with it." Brock laughed. "You wouldn't believe what I've been through. I had to do this one gig down in Texas that required wearing tights. Never again!"

"I remember when you were filming in Texas. I read all about it in *The Scoop*. Weren't you dating some wedding planner or something?"

"No, we never dated. She ended up marrying a guy named D.J. But you know how the tabloids are. They never get a story right."

"Yeah. But I read them anyway. They're so much fun." Benita's giggles echoed across the set as they disappeared down the hallway.

I went back to work, setting up for the day. By ten o'clock, the doors opened for our studio audience, and the seats began to fill pretty quickly. No matter how many times I went through this, having a live audience behind me still made me a little nervous. Added extra pressure I didn't need. On the other hand, pressure always caused me to up my game.

Filming for a thirty-minute show took a lot more than thirty minutes, even on the best of days. We averaged three hours at best, and that was just for the actual filming, not the prep work or the dailies.

The studio audience added an entirely new dimension to the process. Though we instructed them not to bring food, cell phones, or other things that might serve as a distraction, they arrived with them anyway. It was always such a nuisance to have to do a retake because of an interruption from someone in the audience, but we'd grown used to it.

While the hair and makeup folks worked their magic on my cast, we did a quick run-through with stand-ins. By the time Kat, Scott, Brock, and the others emerged in front of the live audience, there was an electricity in the air I hadn't sensed in a while. Yes, this episode was definitely going to be magical.

We set up the first scene, and with my heart in my throat, I called, "Action." The cameras began to film, and we were on our way with the first shot in the elevator. My actors' performances went above and beyond my expectations, and the response from the audience was energizing. I hadn't heard this much laughter in ages. Perfect.

Well, mostly perfect. We had to do a second take of the last minute or so because I started sneezing. Great.

With the first shot behind us, I set up for the next. Then the next and the next. A couple of shots had to be redone, but we sailed through them the second time around. By the time we ended, Kat and Scott—as bunny-clad Angie and

Jack—were holding a real, live baby boy in their arms, and the audience was celebrating as if the whole thing had been real. And the sandwich-wrestling scene had been the very best part! Thank goodness I'd left it up to the guys.

See, Tia? You don't have to direct everything.

The celebration continued long after the audience members left. I'd never seen my cast and crew so ecstatic over a performance. I checked in with Jason to make sure we didn't need to do any retakes, then—after his assurance—dismissed the children for the day. Suddenly I felt like celebrating. Eating chocolate. Drinking sugar-filled soda. Wrestling sandwiches with the hunkiest cameraman in town.

Instead, I quietly crossed the set and took a seat on the sofa next to Kat, still decked out in her bunny suit from head to toe. "Girl, that was the best acting job I've ever seen. You actually looked like you were in labor."

She smiled and rubbed the stomach of her costume. "Felt like it too. I've been having those crazy Braxton Hicks contractions. They're a pain. Literally." She laughed. "Anyway, I'll be glad to get out of this getup and home in a tub. My back's giving me grief today."

I rubbed her tummy, and the baby lurched beneath my hand, startling me. "Yikes. Never felt that before."

"She's been pretty quiet today, actually. I was starting to wonder if she planned to sleep all day." Kat yawned. "That's what I plan to do—after a good, long bath, anyway."

"If anyone deserves a break, you do. I can't imagine working in your condition." A wave of emotion washed over me. "We're going to miss you around here over the next few weeks. I know we've got a great plan of action for the show, but it's just not going to be the same without you. Can't wait to have you back in the fall."

"Aw, thanks." Her eyes puddled. "I feel the same way. But

I know my time is up. This little girl has filled my dance card for the next few weeks. Things are as they should be. And the timing is perfect, what with the season coming to an end in a couple months."

"Yeah." I shrugged, not really understanding but pretending to.

Kat patted my arm. "You'll get it someday, Tia. A great man is going to come along and sweep you off your feet, and the next thing you know, you'll be married and expecting a little one."

"Can't imagine it." I shuddered. "Besides, I practically raised my younger brothers and sister, so my child-rearing years can wait, believe me."

"You'll change your mind." She gave me an encouraging nod. "Trust me when I say that my whole world has been flipped upside down over the past year or so. Life has a way of doing that to you." Her expression shifted, and she released a breath.

"You okay?" I asked.

"Yeah." She rubbed her midsection and sighed. "Just tight as a drum. You know how it is in the ninth month."

"Actually, I don't."

She laughed. "No, I guess not. Anyway, I'd better get out of this crazy costume and head home. You headed upstairs to watch the dailies?"

"Yep."

"Well, get some rest. You're looking exhausted."

"It's the house. I'm renovating." For whatever reason, I suddenly felt like sneezing. The "a-a-a-choo!" that followed was impressive, to say the least.

"Just more proof that you need to rest." She gave me a pensive look. "Have you been watching those home improvement shows again?"

"I record several of them, but I usually fall asleep late at night watching them. Between my work here and the renovations at home, I'm swamped."

"No time left over for a love life then?" She gave me a little pout.

"Hardly." My gaze shifted to Jason, who stood next to Erin and Brock on the far side of the room. He glanced my way and smiled.

Kat leaned my way and whispered her next words. "Having a career is great. Can't deny it. But Tia, one of these days you're going to wish you'd slowed down long enough to let love in."

Her words felt like a sucker punch. I tried not to let my feelings show, but she'd hurt me. Deeply. Did she think I didn't love people? Was I really such a workaholic that she thought I'd never find happiness outside the studio?

Would I?

The very thought left me reeling.

I managed to excuse myself and signaled for Erin to join me. As we made our way up the stairs to the room where I'd watch the film clips from today's show, I tried to put on a brave face. Still, I couldn't help but reflect on what Kat had said. Was I really so caught up in my career that I didn't have time left over for love? If so, could I go on living like that . . . forever?

As we entered the theater, I reached for my phone and noticed I'd missed a call from the doctor. After listening to his message, I scribbled down the name of the allergist he recommended. Maybe I could get these sneezing fits behind me.

"You okay, Tia?" Erin cast a concerned look my way.

"I'm . . . well, I'm a little tired. Aren't you? It's been a long day."

"Are you kidding?" She turned in a circle, nearly giddy. "I

feel like this is my home, the place where I was bound to end up. Don't you?"

"Hmm?" I glanced back at my phone then shoved it in my purse. "Oh, yeah."

"What made you want to be a director, Tia? Have you always wanted to do this?"

"I . . . I don't know. From the time I was a teen, anyway." I settled into one of the chairs.

Erin remained standing. "Do you think there's something inside us even as little girls that makes us want to tell others what to do?" She chuckled. "My mother says I was always a little bossy. What about you?"

"Oh, I'm not sure *bossy* is the right word. I've just always been one to take charge, especially when no one else would."

And trust me, in my world very few people were willing to take charge.

"Well, I for one love the whole idea of it, from start to finish. Taking a script and envisioning what it's going to look like through the eye of the camera. Helping the actors with their lines. Fine-tuning their inflections, rhythm, and so on. Helping them pace their lines with the other actors. Oh, and I love the idea of blocking a scene—deciding where everyone should stand and how the set should be arranged. And now I get to watch the dailies. I'll be the very first person to ever see what was filmed. Along with you, I mean." She sighed. "It's all so wonderful."

I nodded, though her enthusiasm did give me reason to pause. She reminded me of myself just after film school. Had I really become so jaded over the years? Nothing about this process felt as amazing as it once had.

Erin snapped her fingers. "I think I know why it sounds so magnificent." She clasped her hands together. "It's almost like we get to create our own world, one where funny stories come to life and everyone lives happily ever after. I've always loved happily ever afters. Haven't you?"

"I . . . I suppose I have." I thought about that. The resolution—the part of the story where everything worked out in the end—was always the part I fretted over the most. How many times had I sent a script back to the writers for a stronger resolution? But why?

Because the very idea of a happily ever after seems impossible to you.

The words flitted through my mind, but I could hardly believe them. Didn't every girl long for a happy ending to her life's story?

My heart twisted, and I realized the truth. With all I'd faced at home—watching my father break Mama's heart time after time—I'd given up on happily ever afters. That's why none of the endings felt real. I'd never seen one played out in the real world. So how could I possibly direct one?

"Tia?" Erin's brow wrinkled. "Did I say something wrong?"

"Hmm? Oh, no. I, um . . ." I glanced at my watch. "I think it's time to get going on these dailies. You ready?"

"Always! I live for this." She plopped down on the sofa and threw her arms back in dramatic fashion. "It's been the best day in television history. That whole experience was like going to Disney World. And the icing on the cake? I got to spend the day with Brock Benson. Every hour was like a minute. Every minute was like a second. Every second was like a nanosecond."

I put my hand up. "Okay, okay, I get it. He's pretty amazing."

"You can say that again." She sighed and leaned back against the sofa cushions.

"He's pretty amazing." I giggled. Before long, we were both laughing.

Rex joined us moments later, the soft wrinkles in his face growing more pronounced as he looked on. "You two okay?"

I did my best to get it together. "Um, yeah. We're fine. Just talking about . . ." I bit my lip to keep from saying what.

"Just talking about . . ." Erin echoed, then burst into laughter.

Rex shook his head. "Never mind. I have a feeling I don't want to know." He took me by the hand. "But it's great to see you smiling for a change, Tia."

Ouch. Smiling for a change? Was I really as somber as all that?

My giddy mood changed immediately as I pondered the words people had spoken to me today. First Kat hit me out of the blue with that line about being too focused on my career, now this?

Rex glanced at his watch. "I'll have to rush through the process tonight, ladies. I don't know if you noticed, but Lenora's not doing very well today. She's exhausted. Kat and Scott are going to take her to their place in a little while, but I don't want to leave her for long."

Erin looked his way with the sweetest expression on her face. "Rex, I think you're an amazing husband. I really do."

"Being married to Lenora is the easy part. Watching her struggle with her memory . . ." His eyes filled with tears. "Well, that's the tough part. But she's in good hands with Kat. I never worry when those two are together. But Kat's exhausted too. I can see it in her eyes. She needs to rest."

He pushed a button, and we watched as the bits we'd recorded played against the big screen. I found myself laughing out loud as I watched the delivery scene in the elevator. The writers would be tickled pink when they saw what a great job the actors had done with their script. Every single line, every single nuance was there.

About twenty minutes into the dailies, my phone rang. I

didn't recognize the number but answered, thinking it might be the doctor or allergist.

"Tia, we need you on the set." Jason's voice startled me.

"I'm up in the viewing room with Rex and Erin, looking over the dailies."

"I know, but that's going to have to wait." In the background, I heard the strangest sound—sort of a squeal. Or maybe panting.

"What in the world is going on down there?" I signaled for the film to stop, then sat up straight.

"I'm not sure you would believe me if I told you." His next words were rushed, laced with nervous energy. "You know how they say that life sometimes imitates art?"

"Sure." I smiled as I glanced at the screen, which had frozen mid-scene just as Kat, as Angie, held the baby in her arms for the first time.

"It's happening. Right now. In the studio. Kat is—" He was gone for a moment, then came back, sounding frantic. "We just called 911." Another pause followed. "Tia, she's asking for you. I'm not kidding. You guys need to get down here. She's having the baby."

9

All in the Family

I raced down to the soundstage with my heart in my throat. Rex rode my heels the whole way. So did Erin, who was oddly silent. We found Kat on the sofa of the living room set, still dressed in her rabbit costume, with Scott kneeling next to her. She was curled up in a fetal position, panting just as she'd done during our filming. For a moment, I almost thought it was an act. I wanted to shake her and say, "Ha! Funny one, Kat!" But this was no joke. As she turned to me, eyes wide, I realized just how quickly things had progressed in the short time I'd been upstairs.

Oh, help!

Jason rushed to my side. "The ambulance is on its way."

"Thank you." I glanced around, trying to think of what to do. Without a script to guide me, I had no idea how to manage the scene before me. For once, I'd met with something inside the studio walls that rivaled my life outside. Beat it, in fact.

"Where's Grandma?" Kat's words sounded strained.

"She just ran to your dressing room to get a pillow." Scott stroked her arm. "She wants you to be comfortable."

"I'll go get her." Rex turned on his heels.

"A pillow isn't going to cut it." Kat let out a whimper and began panting again.

I shook my head, trying to make sense of this. I looked at Scott, who appeared to be timing her contractions. "Why didn't you guys just get in the car and start driving to the hospital as soon as her water broke?"

Kat shook her head, tears now streaming. "I—I told him not to. I didn't think I could move just yet. The baby is—" Her eyes widened, and she began to pant once again. I had to admit, these contractions looked even better than the ones we'd filmed earlier.

Someone turn on a camera!

I heard Scott counting the seconds. When he reached forty-seven, the tension on her face eased a little.

"That was a long one," she whispered. She looked my way. "We never saw this coming, did we, Tia? I mean, I knew I was going to have the baby, but not in the studio." She leaned in and whispered, "I felt the baby drop just after my water broke. I honestly don't think we have time to make it to the hospital."

"What?" *Really? C'mon! You're exaggerating, right?* "I feel pretty sure you won't have the baby right here." *I hope.* "But in case you do, we've got the world's best delivery guy here." I pointed to Brock. Weird. What was he still doing here, anyway? I'd dismissed the cast half an hour ago.

"Can I get you guys anything?" Brock asked.

Scott chuckled. "I'll have one baby, well done, seven pounds, ten ounces."

That eased the tension in the room for about a minute . . . until Kat doubled over in pain. "Tia." Her wide eyes now reflected something more than pain, though I couldn't quite read them. "Can you get everyone out of here except you and Scott? And try to find my grandparents too, okay? If those paramedics don't get here quick, I'm going to need you."

"Ay yi yi."

I'm the director. I can handle this.

I called for all of the tech crew to sign off for the day and sent Erin and Brock packing too.

"Are you sure, Tia?" Erin asked. "What if you need my help?"

"You deliver babies too?" I asked.

She chuckled. "No. I meant need my help in some other way. I'm your production assistant." She pointed to Kat. "And this is quite a production, if I do say so myself."

"Tell you what." Brock reached into his pocket and came out with a set of keys. "You hang out with me for a while, Erin. Maybe we can meet up with everyone at the hospital later." He glanced Scott's way. "That okay?"

"Of course."

"We'll grab a bite to eat and see you after the baby's born."

Erin looked as if she'd won the lotto as she tagged along on Brock's heels to the parking lot. I could only imagine what my sister might've said, had she stuck around to witness all of this.

Within minutes the room was nearly empty. Scott hovered close to Kat, helping her with her breathing.

I caught sight of Jason gripping his script in his hands. I took a couple of steps toward him, and he grabbed my hand. "I'm going to wait outside for the paramedics. I'll stay out of the way, I promise, but I can't leave until I know you're—I mean, Kat's—okay."

"Thanks." I gazed into his eyes, noticing how much calmer I felt afterward. He had that way about him, for sure.

As soon as he left, Kat cried out in pain. A few seconds later, she glanced my way. "Tia, where are my grandparents? Why aren't they here?"

"I'll go find them." Scott took a couple steps away from the sofa.

"No." Her eyes widened, and she shifted her position on the sofa. "Don't go anywhere. Please. I need you." She glanced my way. "You too. Please don't leave."

"You . . . you need me?"

"Yes." A frantic look took over. "Tia, this baby is coming soon. She's not going to wait. I'm going to need help. I can't do this by myself."

"Oh no. No, no, no." I began to pace, then dove into a lengthy dissertation—in Spanish—about how that would never do. Turning her way, I managed a few words in English. "I'm completely to blame for this."

"You're completely to blame . . . for this?" She pointed to her belly, then winced. "How so?"

"It's all that panting I made you do. Maybe it was really causing something to happen." Suddenly I felt a little woozy.

"Tia, that's silly." She groaned and pulled her knees up. "Or maybe not. But either way, babies come when they want to. And obviously this little girl is determined to make her entrance, even though she's not due for another few weeks."

Still, a wave of guilt washed over me. I'd been guilty of a lot of things in my lifetime, but never throwing a woman into labor. My directorial skills were apparently much stronger than I'd realized.

Thank God the paramedics arrived before I could give it another thought. Otherwise I felt sure I'd be personally responsible for delivering the baby. And though I'd conquered the art of floating and taping Sheetrock, I felt sure bringing a child into the world would require skills I did not have.

Lenora and Rex came rushing into the room, pillows in hand, as the paramedics loaded Kat on the stretcher. Lenora appeared completely discombobulated, even more so than usual. "Why are those men taking my granddaughter away?"

"Kat has to go to the hospital, Lenora." Rex pulled her close and kissed her on the forehead. "Remember? We talked about this." He glanced my way and whispered, "Sorry. That's what took so long. She just couldn't make sense of this."

"Why the hospital?" Lenora's face paled. "Whatever is wrong with her?"

"She's having the baby, honey." Rex held her tight. "But don't worry, she'll be just fine. She's in good hands now, so we can rest easy."

"But KK already had the baby earlier today . . . right? I watched her. In the elevator. It was a boy. I heard them say it, loud and clear."

Oh, yikes!

"That was just a scene from the television show, Lenora." Rex stroked her arm. "It wasn't real. But this is. She's having the baby now."

"But that didn't look like KK at all. I thought it was a rabbit. A very tall rabbit."

As the paramedics wheeled Kat out, with Scott following, Lenora continued to ramble nonsensically. She grew more agitated by the second. I felt horrible for Rex, who led her out to the car. I followed them, still confused about what to do. Should I follow the ambulance to the hospital? Go home and paint the living room? Work on next week's script?

Thank goodness Jason met me at my car and gave me pointed instructions. "We'll take my car. I told Brock and Erin we'd meet them for a quick bite to eat before going to the hospital. That sound okay?"

"Huh? Oh . . . oh, yeah." Sure. Sounded like a good idea. I certainly didn't want to horn in any more than I already had.

"We're going to Pink's to kill some time. Hope you're hungry. I know you're not much for food, but I think it's a good idea. You need the carbs, frankly."

I looked his way. "Hungry. Pink's. Hospital. Carbs. Okay."

He looked at me and chuckled. "You sure you're up for this?"

I shook my head, and tears began to flow. "D-don't mind me. I a-always cry on d-days like this."

"You've had other days like this?" he asked. "Because this is a first for me."

I nodded then shook my head. Then nodded then shook my head. "No. I mean, I've had weird days, but nothing exactly like this."

"Me either. Never seen a woman have a baby twice in one day before. And the rabbit costumes are just the icing on the cake. You saw that Scott was still wearing his too, right?"

I just shook my head, unable to think of an appropriate answer. I hadn't noticed, but then again, I hadn't been looking at Scott.

"Good thing I'm driving." Jason took me by the arm and led me to his car. Seconds later I was strapped into the passenger side of a sexy BMW Z4 with a head-turning driver leading the way. Or, would that be a head-turning BMW Z4 with a sexy driver leading the way? Either way, we were on our way to meet Erin and Brock at Pink's, one of Hollywood's most famous hot dog stands, then on to the hospital.

We'd made it only about halfway when I got a call from Rex.

"Tia, it's a girl!" He rambled on and on, giving me the baby's stats, but most of it was a blur. He'd lost me at the part where he said the baby arrived in the ambulance. I couldn't seem to think clearly after that. The tabloid writers would have a field day with this one. I could almost see tomorrow's headlines now. What would that do to the show's ratings? Send them soaring or cause them to plummet?

I ended the call, drew in a deep breath, and then delivered—pun intended—the news to Jason. He stared, open-mouthed, when I told him that six-pound, nine-ounce Katherine Lenora Murphy had arrived en route to the hospital.

"Oy."

"Yeah."

"Poor Kat. Probably not the way she planned it."

"This is all my fault. I caused all of this." I leaned back against the seat, completely defeated.

"Clearly you missed that class in seventh grade where they told us how babies are made. Otherwise you would know that you have nothing in the world to do with this."

"No, not that. I mean . . . oh, everything else." The sting of tears caught me off guard. I refused to dab at my eyes for fear he would notice.

Jason chuckled. "Tia, you're a hoot. You know that?"

"I am?"

"You are. And I like seeing you like this."

"Like what?" As I looked his way, a lone tear trickled down my cheek.

"*Vulnerable.*" He spoke the word and then quirked a brow.

"Ah." Well, I didn't like it. Not one bit.

With his right fingertip, he gently wiped the tear from my cheek. "You're cute when you're vulnerable." He gave me a little wink and my heart stirred.

Okay, maybe I did like being vulnerable, if it meant Jason would look at me like that. And touch me like that. A delicious shiver ran through me.

"You've got your guard down," he whispered.

I nodded, feeling a bit numb. Jason reached over and

grabbed my hand, giving it a squeeze. "Good. Leave it there. I like you this way."

"O-okay." I'd leave it there, all right. Couldn't very well pick up my guard right now, anyway. Instead, I leaned back against the seat, closed my eyes, and wondered why I suddenly felt like laughing. All the cares of the day suddenly drifted away on the breeze. I was soaring along in a hot car with a very cool guy. And for the first time in nearly a year, I couldn't care less about anything work-related. All that mattered now was this moment, this opportunity . . . and the two of us. Well, the two of us and the birth of a brand-new baby girl. In an ambulance. With her mother dressed as a rabbit.

We arrived at Pink's in short order and enjoyed both the food and the company. In fact, I couldn't remember ever laughing or talking more. Brock and Erin were a blast to hang out with, but my focus—for the most part, anyway—was on Jason. His teasing and flirting continued as we made our way to the hospital. By the time we saw the baby for the first time, I had passed "vulnerable" and was pretty much an emotional wreck. Something about peering into that baby girl's face melted me like sweet, creamy butter.

Leaving the hospital was another story altogether. By nine o'clock, nearly every reporter in town had gotten wind of the news. The hallways were packed with reporters, some waving cameras madly at anyone who even looked like a doctor.

"Can we get a statement?" a guy with a baseball cap asked as I rushed down the hallway, clinging to Jason's arm.

"Oh, I, um . . ." Now what?

Jason put his hand up, and we kept moving toward the parking lot, where we were met by a FOX affiliate news truck pulling in.

"Is it true that Kat Murphy gave birth in an ambulance, wearing a rabbit costume?" the reporter called out.

With Jason's help, I just kept moving, giving no response.

Jason opened the passenger door to his BMW—a gentlemanly gesture—and I climbed in, happy to have survived the chaos.

"You can't blame them," Jason said, once inside. "They're excited about Jack and Angie having a baby."

"You mean Scott and Kat?"

"Yeah. Them too." He laughed. "See? I'm the cameraman for the show, and even I get things mixed up."

By the time we arrived back at the studio, I was half asleep. Jason gave me a hand getting out of the car, and we lingered for a moment in the darkness before saying good night. I wasn't sure what to expect next. After all of the flirting and teasing, I thought he might very well try to kiss me.

Would I let him?

Instead, he ran his finger along my cheek as we stood close. Then the night watchman happened by, interrupting the moment. Figured.

We said our goodbyes and I got into my car, my thoughts now tumbling madly. Had this crazy day really happened? Was it really just this afternoon that Kat had told me to make room in my life for love?

I somehow made the drive home, though my exhaustion nearly got the better of me. When I walked in my house, I felt like singing and dancing all at once. Carlos and Humberto had finished the entryway. Finished. Finito. Painted. Trimmed. No beer cans on the stairway. Sheer perfection.

Oh yes! This was a glorious day, one to be celebrated!

Well, until I climbed the stairs and discovered they'd somehow disabled my plumbing. No way. I needed a bath—a long, hot bath. I reached for my cell phone, groaning when I saw the time. Ten o'clock. Too late to call Carlos. I'd have to go to bed dirty . . . and then what?

I sent him a quick text, then somehow found the energy to change into my nightgown and slide under the covers. My eyes drifted shut. In that safe place, I replayed the movie of today's events from beginning to end. Well, on fast-forward, anyway. About halfway through, when I got to the part where Jason reached for my hand, I paused the tape to run it in slow motion. No point in missing the good stuff.

I hadn't imagined it all, had I?

Oh well. If I had, it'd been a whopper of a story. With grogginess easing me into slumber, I decided I'd just have to wait till tomorrow to see how it ended.

10

Brothers and Sisters

Friday morning I awoke feeling anxious and unsettled. Yesterday's events replayed in my mind, especially the part where Kat told me that I might have to help deliver the baby. Thank goodness I'd avoided that. I should send those paramedics a present. Something to show my gratitude.

I remembered the feelings that had passed over me as Jason ran his finger across my cheek. A delicious shiver ran over me as I relived the moment.

I rose and headed to the bathroom to brush my teeth, only to remember that the water was turned off. Ugh. Glancing down at my cell phone, I realized I'd missed a text from Humberto. *Sorry about the water. Long story.*

Great.

I made my way downstairs to the kitchen to fetch a bottle of water and groaned when I found a half-eaten plate of food inside my refrigerator and a sink full of dirty dishes. Did my brothers ever clean up after themselves? And what was the deal with all the beer cans? How many times did I have to tell Carlos I didn't want him drinking in my house?

I reached for a bottle of water, raced back upstairs, and brushed my teeth. A girl just hasn't lived until she's brushed her teeth with ice-cold water.

Now for the tricky part. I poured about half the bottle of water into a washcloth and went to work on my face. Then I used the rest to give myself a sponge bath. Ick. Not exactly a hot shower, but it was better than nothing. Unfortunately, I could do nothing about my hair, so I swept it up in a ponytail. Folks at work would be stunned, no doubt, but what did it matter? After what they'd witnessed yesterday, a director in a ponytail would be small potatoes. Besides, Fridays were mostly crew and writers, anyway. Hardly anyone would see me like this. I dressed in a pair of jeans and a simple gray blouse.

As I hit the 405, I waited for the phone to ring. Strangely, Mama didn't call. Again. If I went to her house tonight for tamales—as I did every Friday night—I would likely find my father seated next to her on the sofa. I would smile and act like nothing was out of the ordinary, just like I always did when he came back home.

Actually, nothing would be out of the ordinary. His comings and goings were as much a part of my life as anything else, I supposed.

Instead of talking to Mama, I turned on the radio and caught the tail end of a great worship song. I began to have that familiar longing as the words washed over me. I experienced that same feeling on Sunday mornings when I stood in church, eyes closed, listening to the worship music. Strange how worship could transport you out of your everyday life and make you feel like you were getting a little taste of the next. Kind of like being in the studio, only this felt more real.

This particular song kept me in a calm state of mind—until the guy in the car behind me laid on his horn and I realized I was driving too slow to please him. The worship ended and reality kicked in. The Hollywood version, anyway.

I sighed, wishing that for once I could just enjoy my morning drive without the angst of L.A. traffic.

The rest of the drive I was deep in thought about yesterday's strange turn of events. If I'd been writing the script, I would have made sure Kat's baby came not in an ambulance but during the actual delivery scene we'd been shooting. Wouldn't that have been something? And as for the stuff with Jason afterward . . . I wouldn't change a thing. Except maybe I would have added a teeny-tiny kiss at the end. Maybe just one on the cheek. Or the tip of my nose. Or my hand.

Was it getting hot in here? I reached over and turned on the AC. Crazy, running the air conditioning in April, but I couldn't help it.

When I arrived at the studio, I gave myself a quick glance in the rearview mirror and groaned. The ponytail was lopsided, and my makeup job left something to be desired. The dark circles under my eyes seemed to be saying, "Next time remember to use concealer, you goober!" Well, next time I would. Today I had work to do.

Into the soundstage I went. I found the set empty except for a couple of janitors who worked alongside each other. I stood in the quiet, relishing the aloneness. Rarely was this room so peaceful. Without the hum of children's voices, without the laughter of the older cast members, without the heat of the lights overhead, it was just a shell of a room, filled with unused cameras, gels, and fake set pieces. All glitz and glam when the cameras were rolling, but plain and empty otherwise.

There would be no chatter of children today. I'd dismissed

them for the day. In fact, I'd instructed the whole cast to take the day off. We'd gotten every take yesterday. Besides, after the trauma we'd been through, they needed a break. I, on the other hand, needed to meet with the writers, and the sooner, the better.

Once I entered the hallway, I heard familiar laughter coming from the writers' room. Nothing thrilled me more than hearing our writers laugh. If they thought the script was funny, the audience would too. There was no death sentence like a script that the writers couldn't laugh at.

I peeked inside their room to discover Benita sitting with them, heels up on the coffee table. She looked my way and grinned. "Hey, Tia."

"Beni?" Just one word, but it spoke volumes. "Aren't you off today?"

"Just came in to tidy up the makeup room. Got a little distracted."

Clearly.

I soon noticed the object of her affections, at least for today. Bob sat next to her on the sofa, laptop in hand. "She's been helping us with next week's script," he said. "Your sister's a hoot, Tia. Really. You should hear the stuff she's coming up with. It's priceless."

Benita? Funny?

"Okay, okay." She rose and stretched, revealing her mid-section. "I guess I've been funny enough for one day. I need to clean up the salon."

"Salon?"

"That's what she's calling the makeup room now," Athena explained. "I kind of like it. Gives the place a lot of class."

"That's what we need around here," Stephen said between bites of Greek pastries. "Class."

As Benita rose and gave Bob a wink, my stomach churned.

I looked at Athena and Stephen. "You guys ready to meet with me? I'm dying to see the script."

"Oh, we, uh, well . . ." Athena glanced at my sister, and I knew in an instant what she would have said if she could. Benita had served as too much of a distraction, so they hadn't gotten the script finished yet. Go figure. Well, I'd better get her out of here, at least for a while, so they could work.

"Beni, you want to show me how things are going in the hair and makeup area? Things have been so busy this week I haven't stopped by to see how you and Nora are getting along."

"Oh, we're doing great." Benita rose and took a few steps toward me. "She told me yesterday after seeing my work on Kat and the others that she feels sure you guys picked the right person." My sister's smile charmed me. "Made my day."

"Awesome. Well, let's go have a look."

As I followed her down the hallway, she talked almost non-stop, giving me a fascinating dissertation about Scott Murphy's thinning hair and Kat's bad pores. Then she dove into a story about Brock Benson and what fun she'd had, holding him captive in his makeup chair yesterday before filming.

Mental note: have a talk with Brock about my sister.

She turned into the makeup room and I followed her inside, a little confused when I saw the new decor on the wall. Apparently she'd already added her touch.

Benita flipped on the lights and the whole room came alive. I'd been in here a million times before, but usually to talk with one of our show's stars before a taping. Seeing the room empty right now made me feel a little sad. Still, the new decor helped. Added some Hollywood pizazz.

"You've done a nice job," I said. "I see your touches all around."

"Thanks." She pointed to one of the makeup chairs. "Have a seat in my chair, Tia."

"What? Why?"

"We need to talk." Her stern look let me know she wasn't messing around.

I eased my way into the chair like a schoolgirl in the principal's office. "Talk about what?" I noticed the look of concern in Benita's eyes, and my heart rate increased. "What's happened? What has he done now?"

"Who?"

"Dad. What's he done to break Mama's heart this time?"

"Oh, nothing that I know of. I want to talk to you about your eye shadow." Without warning, she swiveled the chair so that I faced the mirror.

"W-what? Are you kidding?" I stared at my reflection, realizing how bad I looked under these lights, particularly with the ponytail and rushed makeup job from earlier. Not that I could have done anything about it.

"I've been trying to work up the courage to talk to you about this for weeks now, but I've been scared." She whipped out a beauty apron and fastened it around my neck.

I stared at her, trying to figure this out. "You've been scared to talk to me about eye shadow? Beni, are you on drugs or something?"

"No, silly." She pulled out a compact and smeared lipstick across her bottom lip. After smacking her lips together, she glanced my way and released a slow breath. "I don't want to hurt your feelings, but you could use a few lessons from the master."

"What are you talking about?"

She waved her lipstick my way. "I've been to cosmetology school. I could help you . . . you know . . . get a man."

"Get a man?" Okay, now my blood began to boil. "What is this, some sort of primitive ritual where you doll me up to suddenly become attractive to the very men who just yesterday didn't know I existed?"

"Well, yeah." She giggled. "Isn't that the idea?"

"Definitely not. If they can't see me for who I am right now, then they're not worth it. Besides, I don't really need that much work." A pause followed as I thought it through. "Do I?"

"Oh, don't get so defensive, Tia. You've always been hyper-sensitive about your looks, but I've never understood why. You're the prettiest one in the family."

I'd just started to stammer a thank-you when she added, "Without makeup, I mean. But once I get my face painted, where do the guys look—at you or me? I'm an artist, I tell you. My work should be hanging in the Louvre."

I wanted to tell her that I wasn't interested in the kind of guys who'd been looking her way. I realized that at least one of them—Jason, to be precise—had spent quite a deal of time looking *my* way last night, and he hadn't been put off by my lack of makeup skills.

I turned again to face the mirror, noticing how sallow my skin looked. These lights didn't lie. They exaggerated every flaw.

Benita reached to take my face in her hands. "Tia, just let me work my magic. Then you'll come into work on Monday and the guys on the set will flip at the new and improved you. Trust me."

I paused just long enough for her to get the idea I might be interested. She pounced, reaching for her makeup bag then signaling me to sit up straight. "It won't take long, I promise. And besides, what do you have to do today? The filming went great yesterday."

"Yes, but I have to go upstairs to meet with the editors at some point, and the writers are counting on me to look over the script for next week, and—"

"Tia." She put her hand up. "I don't mean to be rude, but

you're on my turf now. It's time to stop acting like the boss and start trusting that someone else around here actually has a handle on what they're doing too."

"But—"

She turned the chair away from the mirror. "I don't want you to see this until after I've worked my magic. I think you're going to be surprised at the change in your appearance."

"No doubt."

Fifteen agonizing minutes later—after plucking stray eyebrow hairs, slathering me in concealer, highlighting my cheekbones, rippling on some brownish-purple eye shadow, and painting my lips—she turned me around to face the mirror.

The gasp that followed had little to do with my sister. I hardly recognized myself. Gone were the bags under my eyes. Gone were the tiny blemishes on my right cheek. Gone were the sallow spots on my cheeks. In place of all those things—a work of art. Hang me on the wall with a strong hook and let the viewers have a field day!

Heavens. If I'd known I would look this good, I would've asked for her help sooner.

I suddenly felt like a new person. And while it had felt like a lot of makeup going on, somehow she'd made me look almost natural. Weird how she'd accomplished that.

I leaned forward, noticing how the perfectly placed eye shadow brought out the deep brown of my eyes. And who knew my lashes were that long? Had she somehow glued on fake ones? I blinked extra hard to make sure. Nope. They were mine, in all their exquisite glory.

"Hmm." She crossed her arms at her chest and gave me a pensive look. "On the other hand, I don't think it's a very good idea for you to show up at the studio like this."

"Why not?"

"Because. " A sly grin lit her face. "None of the guys will

even notice I'm here." She giggled. "Not that it matters to you. You've already implied that you're not interested in guys looking at you *that* way. Right?"

"R-right." I glanced back at the mirror, pondering the reality of my reflection. Would it really be so bad for men to find me attractive? Was that so awful? "I guess I could try it once and see if anyone notices."

One of her thinly plucked brows elevated. "If anyone notices?" She laughed. "Honey, everyone's going to notice. Can't wait to see what Mama says. You're coming for tamales tonight, right?"

"Oh, I don't know. I . . ." A sigh followed. How could I argue that I needed to fix the plumbing in my house when I knew nothing about plumbing?

"You've got to come. Mama will love this."

I tried to rise from the chair, but Benita pushed me back down. "Oh no you don't. I'm not done with you yet."

"You're not?"

"No. That hair . . ." She shook her head. "I don't mean to hurt your feelings, but you look like you're thirteen with that ponytail."

She began to tug at the rubber band, and I winced. "Ouch. Could you be a little more gentle?"

"Sorry, Tia. *Gentle* and *beauty* are two words you will never find me using in the same sentence. There's nothing gentle about becoming gorgeous." She sighed. "Ask me how I know."

I started to say, "How do you know?" just to be sarcastic, but decided against it. Instead, I sat as she spent the next fifteen minutes curling and styling my hair in the cutest updo I'd ever seen. It had that trendy, messy look—like I hadn't spent all morning trying too hard. Yet it had a sophisticated edge to it too. Very Hollywood glam girl. And with the makeup in place, I looked downright . . .

111

"Wow, Tia. You look amazing."

I turned as I heard Athena's voice. She stepped into the room and walked toward me. "Is that really you?"

"It's me." I turned back to the mirror just to make sure.

"Benita, you've made her look prettier than ever. That makeup job is to die for, and I love her hair like that."

On and on she went, talking about me in third person as if I'd stepped out of the room or something. But I was sitting right here, listening to every word.

"That lip color is great against her olive skin," Athena said. "But I'm blown away by her eyelashes. I never knew Tia's lashes were that long. Or thick. They're amazing."

Okay, enough conversation about my physical appearance. I'd never been one for ranting and raving over such things. I rose and pulled off the beauty apron, then turned to my sister with a smile. "Thanks, Benita. You've been really sweet. But I need to talk to Athena and the other writers now, so—"

"No, that's what I came to tell you." Athena shoved a script into my hands. "We're ready for you. We've made all those changes you asked for."

"You rewrote that scene where Scott and Brock are at NASA with the kids?"

"Yep."

"And you added the scene where the guest star accidentally misplaces one of the kids?"

"Sure did. It's all done, Tia." Athena gave me a reassuring smile. "So our meeting won't take long. Then you can rest easy."

"Oh, I can't do that. I've got a meeting with Rex to talk about our plan of action without Kat. There's so much to do."

I rose, and Benita's gaze narrowed as she glanced down at my jeans and shoes.

"Wait a minute." She put her hand up. "Before you go, I have to ask you about one more thing."

"What's that?"

"Your clothes." Benita gestured to my jacket.

"My clothes? What about them?"

"That shirt is gray."

"Okay. So what?"

Why is everyone commenting on my gray clothes all of a sudden? Did someone stick a "bland and boring" sticker on my back?

"I've noticed it too." Athena crossed her arms and gave me a funny look. "This is just a thought—call it analysis—but I wonder if maybe you're wanting to go backwards in time to a kinder, simpler era."

"What in the world?"

"Watching you in these outfits is kind of like watching reruns of TV shows from the fifties and early sixties. Safe. Maybe a little too perfect."

"And very, very gray," Benita added.

"I happen to like gray," I said. "It's a nice color on me."

"It's a nice color on nuns," Athena said. "And flight attendants and lab techs. But definitely not on a hot tamale like you."

"Wait, a what? What did you just call me?"

"A hot tamale. That's what you are, Tia. Look at yourself."

I glanced in the mirror once again, getting a pleasant jolt at the reflection. Maybe I was a hot tamale. My spicy exterior had been cleverly buried underneath mounds of gray clothing.

"Come with me." Athena grabbed me by the hand. "I have the best idea ever."

"W-what?"

"Ooo, I'm coming too!" Benita followed on our heels as Athena pulled me out of the room and into the hallway.

Within seconds we were standing in the wardrobe room. Benita looked around, her eyes widening. I could read the glee on her face. "Oh, I've died and gone to glam-squad heaven!"

"You know that most of these outfits just get shuffled back and forth from one wardrobe department to another on the lot," Athena said. "It's fine to borrow whatever's in here. Jana has given us free reign."

"Well, yes, but—"

"You're long overdue for a loan, Tia." Athena picked up a soft blue blouse and held it up to me. "This would be great, but it's not perfect."

"I have wonderful, expensive clothes," I argued. I pointed to my gray blouse. "I bought this from a store on Rodeo Drive."

"I've never questioned that. I can tell your clothes are beautifully tailored. Maybe too beautifully tailored. They're just so . . . so stiff. And proper."

"And gray," my sister threw in.

Athena headed to the back of the room and began pushing clothes on the rack one at a time. She stopped when she got to a gorgeous teal blouse. I had to admit, it made my eyes pop. "Ooo, this is amazing." She held it up. "And can you even imagine that color against your skin? It's going to be like the waters of Grand Cayman lapping the sandy shore."

"Spoken like a writer." I grabbed it and turned toward the mirror. "Let me have a look at that." The gorgeous color did made my skin look really pretty, especially with the new hair and makeup. "Okay, I'll try it. But I'm not making any promises."

A half hour and seven outfits later, I'd been transformed from head to high-heeled toe.

Benita wiped tears from her eyes as she looked at me again. "I'm calling Mama. She's going to be thrilled."

"Don't." I shook my head. "I'll just surprise her tonight at dinner."

I walked out into the hallway and bumped straight into someone. Papers went flying, and I realized I'd hit Jason. We knelt to collect the papers, then rose. The moment he saw me—my hair, my makeup, my blouse, the bright-colored heels—the man was rendered speechless. He tried to move his lips, but no distinguishable sounds emerged.

"You okay?" I asked.

He nodded. "Yeah. I . . ."

I felt the heat rise to my cheeks. Without even trying, I'd flustered him.

Not that I minded. Flustering a handsome man gave me quite a rush, in fact. And the way he looked at me made me feel like I'd somehow grown up overnight.

Yes, a girl could get mighty used to this.

How Do I Look?

As Friday afternoon passed, I felt like I'd somehow invaded someone else's body. Felt a bit odd wearing the colorful clothing. And every time I glanced in the mirror—which I did more than usual, out of curiosity—it felt like I was looking at a stranger. The makeup job was flawless. Perfect. Definitely not something I could have pulled off on my own.

I could hardly get over Athena's reaction to my new look. She kept going on and on about it. "Tia, you should be in front of the camera, not behind it. You've always been a beauty queen, but add a little color and *zing!*" She giggled. "You come to life!"

Interesting. So color was the magic formula to bring the once drab and gray Tia to life. I didn't know if I should be flattered or offended, especially since I'd paid top dollar for that gray wardrobe.

Nah, from the smile on Athena's face, I could tell her words were only meant to make me feel good. Why not enjoy the attention and do just that—feel good?

Even Bob and Paul gave me a second look—and possibly a third—as we worked together on the script. Rex had quirked a shaggy brow at me when he entered the room for our meeting, but the craziest reaction of all was Jason's. He just kept staring at me like he'd never seen me before. Made me feel . . . what was the word? Mysterious.

Tia, woman of intrigue.

Ha! I could hardly stand it. The giggles wanted to overtake me. Then again, my giddy state might have had something to do with my lack of sleep.

Late afternoon, we all wound down for the day. No point in sticking around now that we'd settled on the final script, so I headed out of the studio toward my car. Off in the distance, Jason got in his car to leave. He glanced my way and gave me a little wave. Seconds later he disappeared from view. Weird that after last night, he hadn't spent more time with me. Then again, with Athena and Benita hovering like the rings around Uranus, how could he?

As I drove home, I found myself toying with the idea of calling him. Would that be presumptuous? Maybe I could invite him to church Sunday. Yes, that would work. He could meet my family.

Oh wait, no. He already had his own church. And did I really want him meeting my family? Not just yet. Maybe I should ease him into the idea one family member at a time. I'd start with the sanest in the bunch.

Hmm. Coming up with someone who qualified turned out to be more difficult than I thought. Maybe Humberto. Yes, Jason would surely like easygoing Humberto.

I stopped by my house to check on the progress and figured out the guys had turned the water back on. This was an easy deduction because I found my upstairs tub overflowing and the water seeping through the downstairs ceiling. Just when I thought life had finally taken a turn for the better.

"Carlos, did you not see this?" I pointed to the mess with the Sheetrock.

"Yes." He groaned. "We just got the water back on twenty minutes ago. It took me ten minutes to find the shutoff for the tub. It's buried in the wall. Didn't realize the faucet was on. I never touched it."

I sighed. How could I blame him, really? I'd tried to turn on the faucet late last night, hoping to bathe, but the handle had broken off in my hand. I tried to screw it back on, but with no water running, I'd apparently left the handle turned the wrong way. Go figure. At least he'd caught it before too much damage was done.

Once we got things calmed down, Carlos looked at me again, his gaze narrowing. "Something's different about you today."

Humberto studied my face. "Let me guess. Benita got her hooks into you?"

"Yeah. But I think she did a fine job." I gave a little twirl to show off the new blouse and jeans, then fussed with my hair.

"You look great. Mama will be happy." Humberto paused, brow wrinkled. "She's always talking about how you never wear any color."

I groaned. Had everyone on the planet already analyzed this? If so, I must've missed the memo.

"You are going to Mama's tonight, right?" Carlos asked. "She said it was going to be a special night, whatever that means."

"I can only imagine."

Carlos reached for a hammer and a container of nails. "Maria and the kids are meeting me there. Maria thinks

Mama must be up to something. She's been too quiet this week."

I put my hands up, grateful someone else agreed. "I've been thinking the same thing. She hasn't returned my calls all week, and that means only one thing."

"Dad's home." Humberto sighed, pulled off his baseball cap, and ran his fingers through his dark, wavy hair.

"Yeah," Carlos said. "So what?"

Humberto and I both looked at him like he'd grown an extra head.

"You think it's okay for him to come and go like that?" I asked. "Bounce from woman to woman and then come back to Mama and expect her to forgive him?"

"Didn't say it was okay. It's just not surprising." He shrugged. "But I don't think Maria was just referring to that. She thinks Mama's up to something else, something that involves you."

"Me?"

"Maria heard her talking about you to Benita. Something about a guy."

"O-oh? A guy?" Visions of Jason danced through my mind. Benita had told Mama about Jason? When? And why?

"Don't know. I'd just be on the lookout for odd happenings tonight. I have a strange feeling. And you'd better prepare yourself for the inevitable. I'm pretty sure Dad will be there too."

"Hopefully it will turn out to be nothing. And if Dad's there, I'm pretty sure I'll just act like he's not."

"I can't figure our parents out." Humberto sighed as he went back to work. "Half the time Mama's acting as weird as he is. One minute she's happy, the next she's sad."

"Ah." I nodded. "Well, she's been through a lot with Dad, but there's more going on than that. Mama's in her fifties. She's going through the change."

"Please." Carlos glared at me. "I've been hearing that excuse since I was in elementary school. Every time Mama was in a bad mood, Dad would say, 'Don't mind Mama. She's going through the change.'" Carlos hesitated. "There were times when I wanted to say, 'Change already.'"

Humberto laughed, but I didn't feel like joining in. "Trust me, she might be going through menopause, but it's more likely we could call it man-opause. One man in particular."

"Dad." We spoke the word in unison.

Humberto placed a nail on a piece of Sheetrock and started hammering it in place. Suddenly I felt like doing the same. No wonder construction workers were such even-keeled guys. They pounded out all their frustrations on the job.

My brothers worked a few more minutes, then left to head over to Mama's place. I cleaned up the overflow of water in my bathroom, but that left no time for a bath. I'd have to go in my current state. Oh well. With just the family there, who cared anyway?

When I got to my parents' house, I parked and stared at it. In my thirty years of living on the planet, I'd never known another home but this one—until I bought my place in Bel Air West, anyway. The contrast between the two homes—and the two worlds—was pretty remarkable. This one, an adobe bungalow, had been due for a paint job fifteen years ago. Dad always said he was going to get around to it. He never did. And Mama . . . she wasn't the sort to swing a paintbrush. A blush brush, sure. But a paintbrush? No way.

Oh well. Nothing I could do about that now. I couldn't even keep up with my own place, hard as I tried.

I gave myself another once-over in the mirror, smiling as I saw the new and improved face smiling back at me. Mama would flip . . . in a good way. And I was starting to get used to it too. In fact, I really liked the way I looked. And I loved the way it made me feel.

Benita met me at the door and gave me a thumbs-up when she saw my makeup still intact. She led the way into the living room, where I saw Mama seated on the couch watching *Jeopardy*.

"Mama," Benita said in a singsong voice.

"Not right now." Mama waved a hand, then shouted at the television, "What is *Beauty and the Beast*!"

Ironic.

"Mama, we need you for a minute."

She glanced our way, then began to squeal as she took in my appearance. She rose from the sofa like a phoenix from the ashes—arms extended, praising God in fluent Spanish for the transformation she was witnessing.

Good gravy. You would've thought I'd started the day as a troll.

"It's not that big of a deal, Mama," I said. "I'm wearing a little color, that's all."

"It's a huge deal. Color changes everything." She pointed to the walls of the living room, which Carlos had painted deep purple years ago. "You see? It sets the tone. Gives hope. Vibrancy."

"Well, it's not like I earned the Nobel Peace Prize." I settled onto the sofa, and her Chihuahua jumped into my lap. Suddenly I felt the urge to sneeze—and so I did, not just once but three times.

"You're sitting in Angel's spot." Mama gave me "the look," and I scooted down a few inches to accommodate the mongrel.

I turned to face her—Mama, not the dog. "So, I have a question."

"What, Tia-mia?" She gave me a cursory glance, then looked back at the television, hollering, "What is *Days of Our Lives*!"

"Beni says Dad is back."

121

"Ah." Mama's cheeks turned red, her eyes riveted to the television once again. "He is. Yes."

"If he's back, where is he now?"

"Working late." She shrugged. "A business meeting, I think he said." She looked at the dog and whispered, "Angel, come to Mama." The Chihuahua sprinted into my mother's waiting arms. "See there?" Mama said. "Always stays close. Never leaves me."

"Creates messes all over the place," Humberto said as he entered the room from the kitchen.

Just like Dad.

Mama began to cuddle and coo the little monster, now speaking to her in Spanish. Behind her back, Humberto mouthed the words, "Devil dog!" and I did my best not to laugh.

Still, as I watched my mother with the dog, a shiver ran down my spine. I wanted to tell Mama what a huge mistake she'd made taking Dad back. How he'd pull the same stunts he always did. Still, I managed to keep my mouth shut—a real feat considering the circumstances. Instead, I just sneezed.

After a few moments of listening to the game show, Mama finally turned my way. The tears in her eyes surprised me.

"*Al desdichado hace consuelo tener compania en su suerte y duelo,* Tia."

I knew the old expression: *Two in distress makes sorrow less.* How could I argue with those words? A rush of emotions threatened to overtake me. In spite of my feelings about my father, I had to admit that having someone to share life's tough times with would certainly make things easier.

Unless it made things worse. Which, in my father's case, it usually did.

Mama dried her tears and headed to the kitchen to start the tamales. I tagged along behind her, as always. There were two things I could do blindfolded—direct a television show and make tamales. She worked on the masa while I prepared the pork filling. My itchy nose continued to bother me, and the sneezes kept coming.

About fifteen minutes into the prep work, the doorbell rang. Strange. No one in this family rang the bell, so it threw me a little. I gave Mama a curious look and she shrugged. "You better go get it, Tia. My hands are dirty."

Mine were too, but I rinsed them off.

As I reached the living room, I noticed someone new standing near the entryway—someone tall, dark, and handsome. Sort of a cross between Mario Lopez and Jeremy Valdez. His dark eyes reminded me of espresso beans, and his olive skin was the most beautiful color imaginable. He looked like he'd walked out of a movie set. Wow. Definitely leading man material.

I probably should have said something. *Hello. How are you? Welcome to our home.* But I couldn't.

Benita brushed by me and whispered in my ear, "Happy birthday, Tia. He's meant for you."

Huh? First of all, it wasn't my birthday. Second . . . what? No way. This gorgeous hunk of manhood . . . was meant for me?

Clearly Mama was up to her tricks again.

12

Glee

Okay, so the guy standing in front of me was gorgeous. Beyond gorgeous, really. But honestly . . . *Mama! How could you do this to me? You promised to lay down your matchmaking efforts after the last fiasco!*

Before I could consider it further, my mother swept into the room, her face lighting up as she saw our visitor. "Oh, you made it. I'm so glad. What a wonderful evening we're all going to have." All of this in Spanish, of course.

"Thanks for inviting me." The rich Hispanic voice oozed sex appeal. Not the Hollywood version, mind you. This was the real deal. A true Latino heartthrob. In the flesh. In our living room. Intended for me. Whatever that meant.

Mama looked my way, and I could read the excitement in her eyes. She had probably spent days planning this, and all for poor Tia, the troll. "We've got a guest tonight, Tia. Have you been introduced?" She nudged me in Romeo's direction.

124

He didn't seem to mind. I, on the other hand, couldn't seem to get my thoughts to stop tumbling around in my head. Mama had set me up on a date with some strange guy she'd met . . . where?

"Julio, this is my daughter, Tia. She's a television director. Doesn't she look pretty in that color?"

"*Espléndido.*" He reached for my hand and kissed the back of it, then held on a bit longer, giving me a lingering gaze.

Mama began to elaborate about my job, going on and on about *Stars Collide* and the people I worked with. I did my best not to sigh aloud as she introduced me by my credentials. Whatever happened to "This is my daughter. She's so great"? Now she jumped straight to my work credits and the color of my clothes.

Julio didn't seem to notice. His deep brown eyes gazed at me with enough intensity to raise the temperature in the room. "Nice to meet you. I've been hearing about you for months now."

"You . . . you have?" *Where? How? When?*

"Yes, every time your mother comes in to pay her car insurance, she stays to chat." He gave my mother a playful wink. Awkward.

"Mama?" I turned to face her, hoping she could read my mind. *You've fixed me up with your insurance agent?*

She offered an innocent smile, one that almost won me over. "I adjusted my policy, honey. Put your father back on."

"Wait, you added Dad back to the policy?" I felt another sneeze coming on. "Is he back home for good this time?"

Mama went off on a tangent about the tamales, totally ignoring my question. Benita flashed me a smile—a fake, "gotcha" smile, and suddenly the whole day made sense. Her behavior at the studio. Her insistence that I put on makeup and new clothes. She and Mama had arranged every bit of this. I'd been duped—into a new face, a new wardrobe, and a new . . . .

I stared at Julio. A new guy. Only, I didn't want a new guy. The only guy I wanted was probably sitting in a mansion in Newport Beach, talking to gorgeous girls with names like Tiffany or Justine. He was not standing in an old, chipped adobe in South Central, looking like he'd won the lotto as he gazed at my snug blouse.

Suddenly I felt sick, inside and out.

Somehow I made it through dinner, though I found myself singing worship songs in my head to avoid the way I felt when Julio looked my way. Not that he wasn't the handsomest thing in the world. I'd have to be blind not to notice the broad shoulders and muscular arms, which he was happy to flex for my younger sister on at least one occasion—make that two. The guy was definitely hot. Just not my speed. Well, not when I already had my sights set on someone else.

Granted, that someone else had spent the last year of my life making things miserable for me. But we'd both changed. Right?

I stared at Julio—that fresh, perfectly chiseled face—and sighed. Likely we had nothing in common. Nada. Zip. Nothing. Well, except insurance, but who could spend a lifetime talking about that?

From across the table, I glared at my mother, sending her unspoken signals with my eyes. What was she thinking, fixing me up with someone without warning me first? The whole thing was awkward at best. And embarrassing. I could feel the eyes of my younger siblings on me throughout the meal and could almost read their thoughts: *Poor Tia. Can't even get a date. Mama has to go out and find a guy for her.*

A guy who was obviously more interested in my sister than

me, from the looks of things. Every few minutes, I caught him sneaking a glance at Benita, who gave him playful winks. Go figure.

He finally looked my way. "I noticed the BMW. That yours, Tia?"

"Mm-hmm." I swallowed and nodded.

Within minutes, Romeo—er, Julio—and I were deep into a tedious discussion about insurance rates. So much for a match made in heaven. Looked like this whole thing would turn out to be an insurance arrangement, not a romantic one. An adjustment to my policy, not my love life.

Mama finished eating and reached for the empty tamale plate. "I'll be in the kitchen washing dishes. Tia, you tell Julio all about your job, hear?"

I gave her a lame nod.

She'd no sooner left than Julio cracked a smile. "Sorry, but I can't hold this in any longer." He shifted to Spanish, his lyrical voice still as sexy as ever. "Did you guys know your mother changes her insurance policy at least once a month?"

"I had no idea." Benita shook her head.

"People at our office have a name for her. They call her the revolving door." He went off on a tangent in Spanish about how funny he thought she was. Great, a guy who made fun of my mother behind her back. Just one more reason to toss him out on his rear.

I shrugged, unsure of how to make this any better. "I'm sorry she's created so much work for you."

"I'm not." He wiggled his eyebrows. "It's good for business. It's just that she comes in every time her situation with your dad changes."

"Then she must be there every day." I attempted a smile.

"No, but at least once a month or so. She'll come in and drop him from the policy—which causes the rates to drop.

Then she'll come back in a few weeks and add him back. It's kind of crazy, really."

"Tell me about it." Okay, I'd had enough. I went into the kitchen to help Mama with the dishes.

"So, what do you think, Tia-mia? He's one handsome devil, right?" She winked. "I might be old, but I'm not blind."

"He's handsome, Mama. No doubt about that."

"And he has a steady job. He's been at the insurance firm for six years. I see him every month. A good, handsome Latino boy like that needs a pretty wife."

My face must've reflected my displeasure at that comment. Not that I had anything against Latino guys. No way. But a certain sandy-haired Newport Beach guy had caught my eye instead. For a half second, I wondered how Mama would take that news. Jason was no Julio, that was for sure. And why did it sound like she'd already promised my hand in marriage to this sexy insurance adjuster? I'd just met the guy.

"He's not my type, Mama. Definitely not my type."

Her gaze narrowed. She put her hands on her hips and stared me down.

"What?" I asked.

"Tia, you should be ashamed. Sometimes I think you're ashamed of your heritage."

"My heritage?" I stared at Mama, completely dumb-founded. "Where did that come from?"

"Just stating the obvious. Julio's not good enough for you, is that it?"

"No, I didn't mean that at all. He's not my type, but . . ." I felt my nose begin to itch and fought off another sneeze.

"Your type." She made a grunting sound. "He's a good, handsome Latino man, just not good enough for you?"

"Huh?"

"You're too high and mighty. The way you dress. The way

you speak. I hardly recognize your voice anymore when you call. You don't even talk like the old Tia."

"Well, I'm a professional now, Mama. They taught us in film school to always present ourselves—"

"You were taught at home to be yourself, not someone else. When I'm on the phone with you, I barely know who I'm talking to."

I shook my head, trying to make sense of this. "I love my heritage. I would never turn my back on it."

"Honey, I'm not trying to be tough on you. I know you work hard. You've come a long way in the industry. You were nominated for an Emmy, for Pete's sake. And I'm the only mother in South Central who can say she has a daughter with a Golden Globe."

"Well, yes, but—"

"I think you find value in your work, like a lot of people do. And there's nothing wrong with that up to a point. But your work doesn't define you."

"I never said it did."

"You didn't have to. The way you waltz in here wearing your expensive gray clothes from Rodeo Drive, and your hair and fancy car . . . you just radiate this sort of standoffishness."

I felt the sting of tears. Great. My own mother was turning on me. Accusing me of acting like I was better than everyone else in my family. And again with the gray clothes?

Okay, so I did usually wear gray clothes. But what was with this accusation that I thought I was better than everyone else in my family?

Hmm. Maybe a few words of explanation could make this right.

"Mama, this isn't what you think. We had a rough upbringing, but I'm still proud of my heritage. What I'm not proud of . . ." The lump in my throat would need to shift so that I could finish. "What I'm not proud of," I finally said, "is the fact that my father is a jerk. If I'm distancing myself from anything, it's not my heritage. It's him."

"Your father's a piece of work," she said. "But even so, you're thirty years old, Tia. A grown woman. I'm not saying you don't have a right to be angry at him. Heaven knows I've been mad a thousand times, and rightfully so. But you can hang on to bitterness for only so long before it eats you alive. Or freezes you over like a block of ice."

Ouch.

The door to the kitchen swung open, and as if on cue, my father walked in. Perfect. Just what I needed to end an already too-perfect day.

"What?" he called out. "Did I miss the tamales?" He slipped his arm around my mother's waist and drew her close, giving her a kiss on the cheek. "Ah, no! I see a hot one right here!"

She giggled.

I wanted to holler, "Where were you? Why didn't you show up for dinner?" But the roses he handed Mama distracted me from the speech I'd planned to give.

"*Rosas bellas para una bella dama,*" he whispered. "Beautiful roses for a beautiful lady."

Her cheeks turned pink. "Oh, Gerardo." She giggled and threw her arms around his neck. "You remembered how much I love red sweetheart roses. They're my favorite."

"Of course. Do I ever forget anything about the woman I love?"

A rhetorical question, I hoped. There had to have been at least five or six women he'd loved in the last three years alone.

Mama got busy putting the flowers in water, gushing over how my father shouldn't have purchased them for her, then gushing some more over how happy she was that he had. I took that opportunity to sneak away.

My mother's words from earlier still held a surprising sting. I truly felt like I'd been slapped. How dare she insinuate that I thought I was too good for people? That wasn't it at all.

Or was it?

I slipped back into the living room, wondering how in the world I was going to avoid Julio, only to discover he'd gone missing. Strange. So had Benita. I peeked out the front window and caught a glimpse of the two of them standing next to each other on the walkway. I pulled around the corner and watched as she got into his car and left with him. No way. She was going out with my blind date? Without even telling me?

Humberto appeared beside me. He slipped his arm over my shoulder, and I leaned into him. "You didn't want him anyway, Tia. Trust me. I know that guy. You're too good for him."

"Try telling that to Mama." I sighed. It wasn't that I'd wanted him. No way. But to dump me—in my currently made-up state—for my sister? In my mother's home? With my cheating father present? Everything about this felt wrong.

"So, what's going on in the kitchen?" Humberto asked.

I pointed out the window at Julio's car. "Pretty much the same thing that's going on right there. Schmoozing. Typical macho baloney. Except Mama kicked it off with a guilt fest about how I don't appreciate my heritage."

We both sighed, and I returned to the sofa, where I focused on the television. Not that I really paid much attention. No, my thoughts were on what my mother had said in the kitchen. Did she really see me as too high and mighty? Maybe that's why she'd picked out a guy like Julio—completely puffed up. Maybe she thought we'd be a matched set.

I didn't need a guy who was puffed up—macho on the inside and out. And I certainly didn't need a guy who paid more attention to other women than me. What I needed was . . .

Memories of the conversation in Jason's car flooded over

me. What I needed was a guy who took the time to get to know the real me, not the illusion. Not the image I presented but the true person underneath.

What I also needed was a hot soak in my tub and a good night's sleep.

Ugh. Thinking about the tub reminded me of the fiasco that my overflowing bathtub had caused at home. Whenever I thought about going back there to face the mess, I felt sick inside. So instead, I decided to spend the night at my mother's house. First time in six years. I climbed into my childhood twin bed, pulled the covers over my head, and with the roar of voices coming from the other room, fell into a deep sleep.

13

To Tell the Truth

Saturday morning dawned clear and bright. Mama woke me with a rap on my bedroom door and a cheerful "Wake up, Tia-mia! I made pancakes."

I didn't need the carbs—who in Hollywood did?—but I joined her at the breakfast table anyway.

My little brother Gabe gave me a curious look as he chowed down on his plate of syrup-covered pancakes. "You spent the night?"

"Mm-hmm."

"I thought you took off with that Julio guy." He rolled his eyes.

"No, that would be your *other* sister."

For whatever reason, I began a sneezing fit.

Mama sighed. "Beni called me this morning. Said it couldn't be helped. The chemistry between them was unavoidable."

My father entered the room in his boxers, immediately

causing me to feel uncomfortable. "I know a little something about chemistry." He waggled his thick brows as he looked at Mama. "How else do you think we ended up with five kids?" He kissed my mother on the forehead and her cheeks flamed pink.

Ick. Exactly why I lived in my own place. And exactly why I needed to get out of here right now. I mumbled a quick goodbye, grabbed my purse, and headed back to my house, where I hoped to find my brothers and a couple of their friends hard at work. Unfortunately, no one had arrived yet, except a teenager named David who stopped by to try to sell me a magazine subscription. No thank you.

I put in a call to Kat but she didn't answer, so I tried Scott's phone. He answered on the fourth ring.

"Scott, this is Tia. I wanted to come by and see you, but I didn't know if you were up to company."

"We're going through a mess over here," he said. "Some reporter got Kat's number. Don't ask me how. I don't know."

"Oh no."

"Yeah."

"You guys still at the hospital?"

"Trying to figure a way out of here. We need to take her home. The doctor's already released her, but getting past the mob in the lobby is going to be the issue. We're working on a plan right now. Last I heard, it involved going through the emergency room exit in an ambulance."

"Ironic." I chuckled. "At least baby Katherine will feel at home."

"True. Hadn't thought of that. Except this time her parents won't be dressed as Mr. and Mrs. Easter Bunny." He sighed. "I love my job, I really do. Wouldn't trade it for anything. But at times like this, I'd love to be anonymous. You know?"

Actually, I did know what it felt like to be anonymous. I'd

felt that way last night as Julio left with Benita. I skipped all that, however, and just said, "I'm praying for you guys. Can I come by the house later, or would it be better if I waited a few days?"

"Hang on. Let me ask her."

He returned a moment later. "Tia, she wants you there. She also wants Rocky Road ice cream. Do you mind stopping at the store to pick up some?"

"Of course not. I'd love to. In fact, I'll make you guys a home-cooked dinner tonight. How would that be?"

"Sounds awesome. We haven't had a real meal since lunch yesterday."

"Okay. I'll prepare a feast."

I hung up the phone and panic swept over me. What had I just promised? Other than tamales, I couldn't cook. Not a thing. Just one more problem to deal with on an already crazy day.

Carlos and Humberto finally showed up, and we got to work on the house. I helped them pull down the wall between the tiny master bath and the large walk-in closet. Expanding the bathroom space was key, so I worked alongside them, using every bit of strength in my petite body to make that wall disappear.

Something about kicking the wall down did something to me—something positive. I took out my frustrations with each kick. Carlos looked on with an admirable "Wow," and even Humberto got a laugh out of it.

"You're stronger than you look, Tia." He gave me a second look. "Should we name that wall Julio, perhaps?"

"No." *Call it Beni*. I gave it another kick. There. That felt better. *And call this one Dad*. That kick brought down another section. Yep. Much better. "Okay, now I'm ready for Julio." I gave the wall a final kick.

135

My brothers laughed until I thought they would give up on their work. Fortunately, they continued, taking down the framework of the wall and completely exposing the new space. Looking at the bigger room, I had to admit the truth—space was a good thing. A very good thing. Especially in a room with a beautiful jetted tub.

The guys worked until four, at which point I handed them each another check and sent them packing. With my plumbing now intact, I finally got to take a bath—my first in two and a half days—then dressed to go to Kat and Scott's.

I stopped by the grocery store and picked up a variety of things—chicken breast, veggies, stuff to make salad. Surely I could handle this, right? I'd already paid for my items when I realized I'd forgotten the Rocky Road ice cream, so back into the store I went. I bought several containers of the yummy stuff, all pint-sized.

As I made the drive to Beverly Hills, I thought about how hard I'd worked today. Something about physical labor felt good, really good. Who needed an aerobics class? Just flip your house!

I arrived at the Murphys' home around five and pressed the buzzer at the gate. Scott's voice came on the line. "Tia, thank goodness. She's dying for that ice cream."

"Your wish is my command."

The gate swung open, and I entered the grounds. Stepping inside the large house moments later, I immediately felt at home. Everything was beautiful, no doubt about it. But they'd somehow managed to take a home in Beverly Hills and make it look comfortable and inviting, not show-offish.

Suddenly my mother's words hit me again, hard and fresh. She'd accused me of acting like I was better than everyone else. Okay, so I did have friends with beautiful homes in Beverly Hills. Yes, I worked for a major studio. And true, I lived in a nice house. Well, a house that would one day be nice, if my brothers ever finished it. But I worked hard. And I took care of my family, better care than most of them did themselves. How could anyone fault me for following after my heart, my dreams?

I shook off her words and handed the groceries to Scott, holding back one container of ice cream. He brought me a spoon, then I headed upstairs to see Kat. The moment I laid eyes on her, every bit of frustration I'd been feeling was swept out to sea. She looked like a queen propped up against the pillows with the baby in her arms. A queen holding a princess, all decked out in pink.

See, Tia? Girls come into this world wearing color.

"Oh, Kat." For a moment, it felt like stepping into their room was equivalent to crossing into hallowed territory. This was truly a place where mother and daughter dwelled in perfect God-given harmony. After all the drama I'd had with my mother, I hardly felt worthy to cross over.

Yet cross over I did. I took a few steps toward the bed.

"Sit with us, Tia." Kat gestured to the spot on her left.

I eased myself into the spot next to her, still holding tight to the Rocky Road, and leaned over to look into the baby's face. The most awestruck feeling came over me as I took in her pink cheeks and wispy lashes. "Oh, Kat. She's even prettier than she was Thursday."

"Well, she had a rough day Thursday," Kat said. "We both did."

"Have you forgiven me yet?" I asked.

She laughed. "Tia, you're hopeless. You had nothing to do with that. Just how much power do you think you have in that director's hand of yours, anyway?"

"Very little, actually." I laughed too. "But speaking of things in my hand . . ." I fumbled with the ice cream, trying to decide how to go about giving it to her.

"You want to hold the baby for a few minutes?" Kat asked.

"Can I?"

We made the switch, and I stared down into that precious face, fully engaged in the moment. "She's like a little doll. I don't think I've ever been around a baby this little before."

"You saw her Thursday night, remember?" Kat pulled the top off the ice cream, shoved the spoon inside, took a bite, and leaned back against the headboard, a look of content-ment on her face.

"Thursday wasn't real. It was . . . nuts. But today she's dressed in this beautiful little dress and all curled up looking like a little burrito. She's . . ." I was suddenly overcome with emotion. Did I have motherly instincts? The very idea sent me reeling. Then again, I had pretty much raised my younger siblings, hadn't I? I'd walked my little brothers to school, done the laundry for Benita, and helped Gabe with his homework.

"You ladies decent in here?" Scott called out. He stepped into the room, and I almost gasped aloud when I saw Jason standing next to him. My heart suddenly gravitated to my throat and a shiver ran through me. If I'd known he was coming, I would have put on something other than these jeans and this shirt. Still, he didn't seem to notice. His warm smile captured my heart.

"Now there's a picture of perfection." Jason gestured to the three of us sitting on the bed.

"Oh?" I said.

"You two and that baby." He held his hands up, making a frame with his fingers. "Wish I could film this. I'd start with a wide shot of everyone, then narrow down to the baby's face."

I put my hand up. "You'll never film me. No way."

"How come?" He took a couple of steps my way. "Camera shy?"

"No. Yes. I don't know. My sister's the one who always

liked to have her picture taken. I was the one in the background, trying to blend into the furniture."

"Trust me, you don't blend into the furniture."

That prickly, warm feeling traveled up my arms, and I bit back a smile so he wouldn't see how strongly his words had affected me. This day was supposed to be about Kat and the baby, not me.

Kat looked my way and quirked a brow as if to ask, "What's going on with you two?"

By way of response, I slid off the bed, handed the baby to Scott, and smoothed my jeans. Then I mumbled something about how I'd better get busy making dinner. Jason and Scott stayed put with Kat and the baby, and I rushed down the stairs and into the kitchen.

Moments later, I fumbled my way around the spacious kitchen, wondering why I'd ever agreed to cook in the first place. A sane person would have driven through KFC or Taco Bell. But not me. Oh no. I'd promised a home-cooked meal, and a home-cooked meal they would have.

Only, now I was cooking for Jason too. If he stayed.

Hopefully he would stay.

"Something smells good in here."

I turned, and the onion I'd been holding rolled out of my hand and across the floor as I stared into Jason's eyes. "Oh, I, um, haven't started cooking yet."

"Ah." He grinned and reached down to pick up the onion. "That doesn't change what I said, though."

My cheeks grew warm as I realized he was talking about my perfume. Suddenly I was very glad I'd taken the time to spray it on.

"So, what are we cooking?" he asked.

"We?"

"Sure. I'm pretty good in the kitchen, or so I've been told.

I grew up with a great cook who considered me her prodigy. I know a thing or two."

No doubt he knew a lot more than I did. Well, maybe I'd take advantage of that. Swallowing my pride, I looked him in the eye. "Okay, here's a confession. Other than tamales, I can't cook a thing."

He looked at the array of food products spread out on the counter. "Then what's all this?"

"I don't know." I sighed. "I guess I thought if I bought all the right stuff, I'd figure it out. I was sure it would all come together somehow."

"Mm-hmm." His eyes narrowed into slits. After a moment, he reached down to pick up the onion and started peeling it. Then he prepared the chicken breasts, coating them with seasoning and dropping them into a skillet with a bit of olive oil.

Within minutes the room filled with the most delicious aroma. Go figure. The guy could run a camera and cook up a feast too. Our kids would never go hungry.

Our kids? Where in the world did that come from?

I must've slipped and hit my head for such a crazy notion to latch on to me. In all the time I'd known Jason Harris, I'd seen him only as an adversary. He'd irritated me, challenged me, frustrated me . . . and based on the fluttering sensation in my stomach as I now gazed into his gorgeous green eyes, completely mesmerized me. Why not just relax and see where the afternoon would take us? I had a feeling we had a few tasty hours ahead.

14

What I Like about You

I did my best to ignore the butterflies in my stomach as I watched Jason cooking. Thankfully, he lit into a story about surfing, which seemed to steady my breathing. A couple minutes later, Scott stuck his head in the kitchen door. I turned on the water at the sink and stuck my hands underneath, trying to look busy.

"Wow." Scott grinned. "You two have outdone yourselves. And you're just in time. Lenora and Rex are here. Hope you've made enough for a crowd."

"It's chicken cacciatore," Jason said. "There will be plenty for everyone."

Fascinating. What we were making actually had a name. He really was good.

"Well, I'm grateful," Scott said. "Because Athena and Stephen might be stopping by too. They're bringing a bunch of stuff from her parents' gyro shop, but we'll save that for tomorrow."

If only I'd known, I could have skipped cooking altogether. Then again, that would mean missing out on this time with Jason. Oh no, I wouldn't take that back for anything. Kat could wait until tomorrow for Greek food. Today it was Italian all the way.

Jason passed a bell pepper my way and said something about chopping it, so I got right to work. He looked through the pantry, coming out with a bag of pasta, then put some water on to boil.

"Something smells yummy in here!" Lenora's warbling voice rang out.

I looked up from the red pepper, trying not to gasp as I took her in. She wore the most fabulous black and white gown I'd ever seen in my life. Something about it seemed strangely familiar. And that hat! *Exquisite* didn't begin to describe it. It took a minute, but I finally realized where I'd seen this ensemble before.

"Oh, I know who you are!" I stood, mouth agape. "You're Eliza Doolittle from *My Fair Lady*."

"Yes, honey, I am the one and only Eliza Doolittle." Lenora smiled. "You got it right. And it's been quite a day at the races, let me tell you. That handsome professor, Henry Higgins, really showed me a lovely time. He's been such a nice chap to take me in after the rough life I've led as a flower girl. Not many a man would take a girl from such a rough background."

Ironic.

The door to the kitchen swung open, and Rex entered.

"Well, here he is now." Lenora giggled as she looked Rex's way. "Didn't we have a wonderful time at the races, Professor?"

"Um, yes." He pursed his lips and appeared to be thinking. "When a man is with the prettiest lady at the event, how could he help but have a wonderful time?"

"Still, those other women were a bit snobbish, if you don't mind my saying so. But I didn't pay them any mind at all."

"I only had eyes for you, Len—Eliza." He took her hand and gave it a gentle kiss.

Her smile broadened and she began to sing, "Just you wait, Henry Higgins, just you wait!" Then she gave him a playful wink, and he swept her into his arms, planting kisses in her hair.

Jason looked at me, his eyes twinkling. Apparently he enjoyed watching the little scenes that Lenora and Rex played out.

I, on the other hand, always felt like I was invading their private space. So, back to work I went, chopping the red pepper. As Lenora stepped beside me, I looked her way and smiled. She grabbed a piece of the pepper and popped it into her mouth. "Mmm. Can't wait for dinner. All they fed us at the racetrack were those little cucumber sandwiches. I need a real meal."

Looking at her ever-thinning physique, I could only agree. She did need a real meal. And we would give her one.

"It should be ready in about half an hour," Jason said. The look of confidence on his face gave me hope that we really might have dinner ready in half an hour. Right now I would simply continue to follow his lead.

Interesting. The director following someone else's lead. Not that I minded. It felt good not to be in charge for a change.

"Lenora, have you been upstairs to see Kat and the baby?" I asked.

"Baby?" Her eyes took on a faraway look as she nibbled on the pepper. "There's a baby?"

I swallowed hard and didn't say anything. Surely she hadn't forgotten her own great-grandchild.

Jason piped up. "Yes, she's beautiful. Looks just like her mommy."

Lenora finally snapped to attention. "Yes, my little girl does look like me, doesn't she? Everyone says so. She's got my blue eyes for sure. And my wrinkled skin."

Huh?

Rex shook his head and slipped his arm through Lenora's. "Come along, Eliza dear. We've had a wonderful day at the races, but it's time for family now."

"Ooo, family. Such a wonderful word. I've always longed for a family."

They disappeared out the door together.

Once we were alone in the kitchen, Jason looked my way and sighed. "It's getting worse."

"I know." In the time I'd known Lenora, her forgetful spells had grown more noticeable. "I'm so glad she has Rex."

"I think he's glad to have her too."

The exchange between the two left me feeling a little misty. I used the back of my hand to swipe at my eyes.

"You okay over there?" Jason asked.

"Yeah." I pulled up a bar stool and sat to finish cutting the pepper. "I think my defenses are down because I'm so worn out."

"It's Saturday. People are supposed to rest on Saturday."

"Humph."

"What?" He looked my way. "Don't believe in rest?"

"My house is being renovated, remember?" I finished cutting the pepper, then looked his way. "You should see the mess. We tore down a wall this morning. And repaired the fiasco from a water leak yesterday."

"Wow." He gave me a curious look. "Tia, do you ever stop?"

"Stop?" I put down the knife.

"To smell the roses. To sleep. To relax." He flipped the pieces of chicken in the skillet, then began to add tomatoes and other vegetables. "I mean, you work all week and all weekend too? You need to take a break."

"Oh, sure. I stop. When I'm sleeping. But it just seems like there's never enough time to get everything done. I'd like to get this house-flipping thing behind me."

"Why are you so set on getting the house done so quickly?" Jason asked. "Sounds like you're exhausted. Give it a rest for a few days—or weeks even."

"Easy for you to say. You don't have to live in it."

"Part of the fun of flipping a house is the experience itself. You know?"

"That would be great." *If I had someone to enjoy it with.* I sighed. "The whole thing has been complicated by some family drama. It's probably better if we don't talk about that, though." I grew silent.

After a moment's pause, he looked my way again. "I've noticed something about us, Tia."

"Oh?" *Us?*

"Yeah. We start conversations but don't finish them. I'm interested in hearing about your family drama. And the house . . . and everything."

I started to respond, then stopped. No point in letting him know all of my personal stuff just yet. Some things were better left unspoken.

He sat on the bar stool next to me. "I'm not trying to be nosy."

"Oh, it's not that. I'm just not comfortable talking about things that I can't do anything about."

An uncomfortable silence rose up between us.

Jason finally broke the silence. "Tia, sometimes I get the feeling that if I could see into some sort of invisible realm, I would find walls higher than Jericho built around you."

"W-what?" I did my best to look him in the eye. "What makes you say that?"

"It's just a feeling. We can be in the middle of a conversation about something and making progress, then all of a sudden—bam. Conversation over. It's like you reach a certain point and just shut down. You hit a wall."

"As I said, I'm not comfortable talking about some things, that's all. Especially where my family is concerned." I shrugged, hoping he would change the direction of the conversation. "But I wouldn't say I have walls up." In that moment, conviction grabbed hold of me. I somehow managed to keep sitting straight, but my insides began to quiver.

"Tia . . ." Jason put his hand on my back. "I wouldn't take the time to share all of this with you if I didn't care about you. I want to see you happy."

"I—I am happy."

"I'm talking about the kind of happiness that comes when you've let go of the things that keep you bound up. That kind of happy. It's not going to come until you kick that wall down."

I felt the sting of tears in my eyes. Brushing them aside, I turned to face him. "You don't understand. What's on the other side of that wall isn't pretty. If I kick it down, I'll have to face it, and I don't have the energy to right now. I really don't. Maybe after the house is done. Or maybe after this season ends. But not now."

"When you face it, you'll probably go through pain, but the only way you'll ever experience true freedom is to look it in the eye."

I thought about the wall I'd kicked down just this morning. Relived how good it had felt to get rid of my angst. If I could do it physically, maybe God could tear down the walls I'd put up emotionally. Still, I hadn't planned on a therapy session right here and now, in front of Jason of all people.

Before I could think any more about it, he slipped his arm over my shoulder. I felt genuinely comforted by his touch.

"I want to know more, but if you're not comfortable talking about your family, then let's talk about your house."

"What about it?"

"I see you dragging into the studio in the morning, worn out from working through the night. You think I haven't noticed the drops of paint in your hair?"

My hand instinctively went to my hair and he chuckled.

"Not today. But I've seen it. Somewhere in the house, you've got a light tan theme going."

"That would be the living room."

"And a light gray."

"Ah. The bedroom."

"You're painting your bedroom gray?" He shook his head. "Anyway, I've noticed. And I see how tired you are."

"I don't really know much about home repair except what I've seen on HGTV and the DIY network. I've watched my brothers, but they're not exactly experts."

"Why not hire contractors? They could knock out the job a lot faster, I bet."

I couldn't help the sigh that escaped. "I know this is hard to understand, but I do things for my family to help them out financially. I'm really the only one . . ." The pause that followed felt like it lasted forever.

"Ah." He nodded. "Gotcha."

"I'm the only one who can take up the slack." I put my hand up. "I know, I know. Before you say it, let me just agree with you in advance. I'm in a codependent relationship with my family members, especially those with financial woes. I'm too softhearted."

His laughter caught me off guard. "Sorry, but *softhearted* isn't exactly the word I'm used to hearing where you're concerned."

I leaned back and closed my eyes. "Guilty as charged. But

I try to be extra tough on the set because it's the only place where people seem to take me seriously. I have to come across that way. I'm the director."

"Oh, I'm not asking you to change. As directors go, you're one of the best I've worked with."

"R-really?"

"Really."

"But I lose it . . . a lot. Which is hard, because I like people to think I'm poised."

Confusion registered in his eyes. "You are poised."

I shook my head. "Did you see me trying to get through that one rough scene on Tuesday? I was anything but poised. I lost my cool a dozen times at least. It's embarrassing, but more than that . . . it's a sign that I lose control."

"Don't we all?" He shook his head. "Really, Tia, I think you're too hard on yourself."

I sighed. "Yeah."

"Seriously, do you *ever* give yourself a break?"

"I'll try. Starting now. Well, when I have some free time, anyway."

"Promise?" he whispered.

"Yeah."

We stood for a lovely moment or two, just enjoying the quiet as we returned to our work.

"If you had the free time, what would you do with it?" Jason asked.

"No clue. Other than sleep, you mean?"

"Yeah. Think of something you've never done before." He snapped his fingers. "I know. Have you ever been surfing?"

"Surfing?" I shook my head. "No way. Not my thing, trust me."

"There's something so freeing about it. When I'm out on

the water, I have no choice but to let go . . . of everything. Trust. That's what it's all about."

"I don't know, Jason. Sounds . . ." *Terrifying.*

"Okay, well, what about parasailing? Ever sailed across the sky over the ocean waves below?"

I sighed. Clearly he didn't see the bigger picture. "Look, the few times we went to the beach as kids, we couldn't afford to do things like that. We just played in the sand and the water."

And considered ourselves fortunate enough to get to do that.

My poor upbringing apparently didn't faze him. He snapped his fingers again. "Okay, parasailing might be a bit much. Let's go back to that surfing idea. One of these days I'm going to take you surfing. There's no place to let go of your inhibitions like on the water. I'm telling you, it's very freeing." He reached over and took my hand. "You watch and see, Tia-mia. Those walls will come down one at a time. God can do it if you let him."

He'd lost me at "Tia-mia." How in the world did he know to call me that? No one outside of my family knew that name.

Unfortunately, I never had the chance to ask. Athena and Stephen entered the room, gushing over how beautiful the baby was and how wonderful the kitchen smelled. Within minutes they'd invited themselves to dinner. Looked like we were having a real party. I didn't mind the interruption. Not at all. Jason had managed to put a little chink in my wall, already making me feel too vulnerable.

Still, as I looked into his eyes, as I contemplated all of the things he'd said to me, I could only conclude that the walls in my life—physical or otherwise—were destined to fall sooner or later. If I could work up the courage, I'd march around Jericho seven times, blow my trumpet, and watch them tumble to the ground.

15

Family Matters

Sunday morning I met my family at church, as always. With my father seated next to me, I was distracted from worship, and all the more so as I witnessed his tears during our pastor's sermon. Not that my father's tears were unusual, but something about his current emotional state seemed more genuine than before.

Out of the corner of my eye, I caught a glimpse of Mama, who dabbed at her eyes with a tissue. No doubt she had a lot of emotions to work through. I thought back to my conversation with Jason yesterday about the walls I'd put up. If I had so many, I could only imagine the ones my mother needed to tear down.

For the first time in a while, genuine compassion rose up for her situation. I couldn't deny that most days, I got that "Don't talk too long, please. I'm really busy" feeling where she was concerned. But not today. Today I wondered what it would feel like to walk a mile in her shoes. To be wounded by someone you loved. The Lord gripped my heart with an empathy that surprised me. I reached over and took Mama's hand and gave it a squeeze. She looked at me, eyes widening a bit, and squeezed back.

The calmness in my spirit lasted all day Sunday. And by the time I arose on Monday morning—thirty minutes later than usual—I was determined to have a better attitude . . . about everything.

I rushed through the process of getting ready and headed out the door. I waved at my neighbor, who was out walking his dog—the same dog who'd yapped all night—then climbed into my car and headed to the studio.

From inside my purse, my cell phone rang out the melody of "My Heart Will Go On," the theme from *Titanic*. Seemed appropriate for how I felt. I managed to reach beneath the receipts, wallet, breath mints, and keys to fetch the phone by the third ring.

"Hello?"

I expected to hear my mother's voice but did not. "Tia Morales?" The woman on the other end of the phone sounded like she was in a hurry.

"Yes?"

"This is Michelle from Dr. Kennedy's office. We got your phone messages over the weekend about coming in for allergy testing."

"Yes, I need to schedule an appointment. The sooner, the better."

"Dr. Kennedy had a cancellation this morning. Would you like to come in now?"

"Now?" I glanced at the clock. Eight twelve. Ack. How would I manage the roundtable reading? "How long will it take?"

"Oh, not that long. You'll just be coming in for a consultation. Dr. Kennedy will schedule the actual allergy testing for a later date. We can probably have you out of here no later than 9:30."

"I see." Hmm. Maybe if I hurried, I could accomplish this.

I agreed to leave right away and ended the call. Then I called Erin's cell phone. She answered on the third ring and said she would help out by corralling the cast members into the roundtable reading room at nine o'clock, along with the writers, who would share their vision for the script. If all went as planned, I'd be in my chair by 9:45, just in time to start the read-through. Perfect.

I exited the freeway, did a U-turn, and headed to the doctor's office. The allergist, Dr. Kennedy, talked me through the process, explaining the tests she had scheduled for the following week. She sat at the computer, typing madly. "I would guess, based on your symptoms, that you're allergic to dust and mold. You said you're flipping your house?"

"Yes." The sneeze that followed was more coincidence than anything.

"Mm-hmm." She paused to type something else. "Well, I'll check for other things too, but I'm pretty sure those triggers would be enough to cause all of this." She gave me a pensive look. "And what about your stress level? Stress can definitely exacerbate allergy symptoms."

"My stress level?" I repeated her words, unable to think of an easy answer. "Oh, well, you know. I live and work in Hollywood."

"What do you do?"

"I direct a television sitcom."

She stopped typing and turned my way. I could read the curiosity in her eyes as she asked, "Which one?"

I'd no sooner responded than she dove into an explanation of why *Stars Collide* happened to be her very favorite show on television. "It's one of the funniest shows I've ever seen. I can always count on it to cheer me up when I've had a bad day."

"Thank you. That's the goal. There's nothing like humor to get you through the rough patches." I thought about my words, wondering why I hadn't applied them to my life.

Before I left, Dr. Kennedy gushed a bit more about the show, focusing on Scott and Kat. She smiled. "Hey, I read in the paper that Kat Murphy had her baby. A girl, right?"

"Yep." I nodded. "She's a doll."

"Oh, I'm sure. And how interesting that Kat's character, Angie, is going to have a boy. I read that just this morning."

"Ah." So much for hoping our studio audience wouldn't leak the news to the papers. Oh well. It was inevitable, I supposed.

"I think the best part is what they're naming the baby." Dr. Kennedy chuckled. "It's perfect."

This certainly got my attention. We'd worked hard to protect that secret. Even our own cast and crew didn't know. We'd deliberately left the name out of the episode we'd just filmed.

I felt myself getting nervous. "O-oh?"

"Little Ricky. Priceless!" She laughed. "I think it's such a great tribute to *I Love Lucy*. You know, I've always felt that Lucille Ball would have loved *Stars Collide*. It's her kind of show—quirky, slapstick, filled with real humor, not the twisted stuff you see on those comedy channels."

She went off on a tangent about comedy shows, but she'd lost me at "Little Ricky." Rex was going to kill me. Well, not me exactly, but someone.

"If you don't mind my asking, where did you read all of this info about the show?"

"It's all in *The Scoop*." She giggled. "I can't believe I just confessed to reading that gossip rag. You won't hold it against me, will you?"

"Of course not." Still, how and why had they run that story? And who fed them the information in the first place?

Suddenly all of the frustrations I'd worked so hard to get rid of over the weekend came back in full glory. I somehow managed to muster a smile, then paid for my visit and left. My drive up the 405 was faster than usual. My foot felt like it weighed a hundred pounds as I headed toward the studio.

I arrived in record time, whipped into a parking space, and stormed inside, then kept moving until I got to the conference room. My cast members looked my way as I popped my head in the door, but I couldn't break my train of thought. "Rex?"

"Yes?" He glanced at me, his brow wrinkling the moment he saw the concerned look on my face. He rose and took a few steps my way.

"We need to talk," I whispered.

With a nod, he joined me at the door. I turned back to Erin. "Erin, do you think you could handle the roundtable reading until I get back?"

"What do we do about the Lesleigh thing?" she asked.

Rex looked my way. "You know that scene where the kids are with Scott at NASA and the tour guide is supposed to accidentally let them on board a real shuttle?"

"Yeah?"

"Well, Lesleigh Conroy was doing a guest appearance as the tour guide."

"Right . . ."

"Apparently she's got some sort of stomach bug and can't be here today. We just got a call from her agent."

"Hmm." I paused to think things through. "Well, it's no big deal. It's only Monday, right?" I glanced back inside the

154

room. "I'll have a courier run a copy of the script to her house. In the meantime, Erin, would you mind reading for her?"

Erin's eyes grew wide, but I didn't give her a chance to say no. Instead, I slipped back out into the hallway. Knowing her aim-to-please mentality, I hoped she'd dive right in.

Rex and I took a few steps away from the room, and I faced him, ready to get this over with. "Rex, I hate to tell you this, but someone is leaking information to the media."

"Leaking information?" He looked confused. "What sort of information?"

"The news is out that Jack and Angie's baby is a boy. Came out in the same article with the news about Scott and Kat's baby being a girl. My doctor told me all about it."

"I'm surprised it took this long. But it's not that big of a deal, Tia."

"They know the baby's name, Rex."

"No way. No one knows that but the two of us and the writers." He paced the hallway, saying nothing for a moment. "It's got to be someone from the inside. Maybe the scripts are going out to the media somehow." He released a slow breath. "Let's go talk to Athena and the others to see what they have to say."

Ugh. I hated to have to do that. No doubt they would think we were accusing them in some way.

We arrived in the writers' room to find them hard at work, already laughing over next week's script. Paul was pacing, and Bob was seated on the sofa with his laptop. Stephen nibbled on a piece of baklava while Athena sat at the desk, pen and paper in hand.

"Hey, guys."

Athena turned to look at me. "Well, hello, strangers. Aren't you guys supposed to be in a roundtable reading or something?"

I noticed the tray of baklava on the coffee table and took a couple of steps that way.

"Help yourself," Athena said with a smile.

I did. Between bites, I explained what had happened. Athena paled. "This is awful." She sat on the sofa, shoulders slumped forward, then turned to face Stephen. "What do you think happened?"

"I have no idea. We're so careful. Don't have a clue how someone could've leaked information that wasn't even written down. You know?"

"It is written down," Athena said. "It's in the script they're reading right now."

"But they just got it this morning," he argued.

For whatever reason, we all happened to look at Bob and Paul at the same time. Bob threw his hands up in the air. "Wasn't me. I promise."

"You guys know me better than that." Paul grunted. "Besides, I need my job too much. I would never risk that."

True. None of them would. Still, someone had leaked the story.

"What are we going to do?" Athena asked.

Stephen shook his head. "Only one thing I can think of. We get the scripts back at the end of each day."

"The actors have to be able to memorize their lines," I said. "Besides, I'm sure they're not to blame. We can trust them."

"Even the guest stars?" Bob asked. "I'm not saying anything against Brock, just wondering if we're safe letting those scripts go out to people we don't know very well."

"I know Brock, both by reputation and in person," Rex said. "He's not behind this." He turned to face me. "I want you to keep an eye on people in your department, Tia. I've got a strong suspicion about this. It's definitely an inside job. So we watch and wait to see when the person strikes again.

Watch is the key word. Keep an eye on everyone and everything, okay?"

"Okay." I shook my head, unable to process this. What kind of person would do something like this?

I did my best to push my concerns aside as I headed back to my office, where I spent a few moments of alone time just thinking things through. Surely we'd figure this out in time.

Now back to work. I checked my appearance in my compact mirror, noticing how tight my face looked. I did a couple of deep breathing exercises and tried to relax. No point in letting my cast and crew know I was worried about something. They would certainly pick up on it if I didn't watch myself.

I headed back to the conference room just in time to find everyone taking a break. Jason lingered, probably concerned by my earlier interruption to the process.

"How did Erin do?" I asked.

"She was great." He nodded. "Very businesslike, but kind with the kids too. A couple of times she had to help them through their lines, but she did a fantastic job with the cast. She's a natural leader."

"I asked her to fill in for Lesleigh Conroy. Did that part go okay?"

"Yeah, she sounded like the part had been written for her." He gave me a pensive look. "So, what's up? What's going on? It worried me a little the way you called Rex out." He shrugged. "Not that it's really any of my business, but I'd like to know what's bothering you."

I hesitated. Did I really want to share the information with him? Shouldn't I be careful?

"Oh, c'mon, Tia. Don't be neurotic. It's me, Jason, for Pete's sake."

I touched his arm, for the first time noticing the solid biceps. "I—well, we've got a problem."

"Obviously. But what?"

"Someone is leaking information to the media. *The Scoop* carried a story this morning, naming Jack and Angie's baby."

"No way." He shook his head. "I don't even know the name of the baby."

"Right. Hardly anyone does. Or, rather, hardly anyone *did*. Apparently everyone who reads *The Scoop* knows now. So our element of surprise is gone. And once that's gone . . ." I shuddered to think of what might happen next. We needed to keep our audience guessing. That was half the fun of pulling off a great sitcom—challenging the audience.

"Do you guys think it's someone from the inside?" Jason asked. "Could be someone we've overlooked. A cleaning lady. Someone from the studio who comes to replace the overhead lights. Someone in hair and makeup."

As he spoke those last words, a shiver ran down my spine. Not once had my sister's name entered my mind . . . till now. Surely Benita wasn't capable of something like this. Was she?

She'd been hanging out with Bob a lot, hadn't she? Was it possible that last Friday she'd somehow gotten a copy of this week's script and given it to the tabloids? The possibility suddenly seemed very real.

Calm down, Tia. That's just nuts. Why would she do something like that?

I could suddenly think of a thousand reasons, and all of them easy to spend.

My thoughts reeled. I was reminded of the necklace I'd seen her wearing Friday night. Those new, expensive shoes. She made a decent salary, but those shoes cost a pretty penny.

"I'll be right back. Do you mind waiting?"

"Of course not. But where are you going?" Jason's brow wrinkled.

"Just need to check something out."

I turned on my heels and headed to the hair and makeup department, where I found Benita fussing over a tray of eye shadow. She looked up and winced when she saw me.

"Hey, Tia. Still mad at me?"

If you tipped off the media, yes.

"Mad at you? What for?"

"The whole Julio thing, of course. I was just telling that girl Jana in the wardrobe department all about him." Her eyes took on a dreamy look. "It couldn't be helped, I promise. I tried to resist the temptation, but . . ." She sighed. "He's pretty irresistible. You have to admit that."

"Yeah. Irresistible."

"Hey, what's up with your makeup?" She pointed to my face and I flinched. She clucked her tongue in disapproval. "I don't believe it. What about that makeup lesson I gave you on Friday? Was it all in vain?"

Hush, Beni. We don't need everyone on the set listening in.

She drew close to look at my eye shadow job, then sighed. "You're hopeless."

"Not hopeless, just very, very busy. Do you know what kind of weekend I've had?" I paused, realizing that I was biting my lip. "Beni, I have a question for you, but I'm going to ask you in advance not to take it personally."

"O-okay."

"You've been hanging out with the writers."

"Yeah. They're great. I like them a lot." She blushed. Weird, I'd never seen Benita blush before.

"You were there on Friday to hear about this week's episode."

"Yeah." She shrugged. "I even helped them come up with a great bit about NASA."

"You know that our scripts are top secret until filming, right?"

"Top secret?" Her eyes grew wide. "What are you saying?"

159

"I'm just saying that if you have any information about upcoming episodes, you would keep it to yourself, correct?"

She flinched, and her pause worried me. "S-sure, but who cares?"

"I do." *This is important.* "This is not an accusation. I just found out that someone leaked information about this week's episode to the media. It's got to be someone on the inside. Obviously."

Her eyes narrowed to slits. "Oh, perfect. Just because I steal your date, you think I'm the kind of person who would sabotage my own career by blabbing to the media? What kind of person do you think I am?"

You really don't want to get me started, Beni.

She rolled her eyes. "Mama was right. You've changed, Tia."

Her words stopped me cold. I stared at her. "What did you say?"

"You've changed." Her expression tightened. "You used to be really sweet. Well, maybe not really sweet, but nicer than you are now. I don't even recognize you anymore."

I wanted to say, "The feeling is mutual," but I didn't.

She pointed her finger at me, snagging the attention of Lenora, who appeared in the doorway looking a bit lost. "I know what it is too. Ever since the Golden Globes, you're just . . . well, full of yourself."

A thousand things went through my mind at once, but not one of them could I say aloud in front of Lenora, who now stood within ten feet of us, a puzzled expression on her face.

"As far as I'm concerned, you can put that award where your heart ought to be."

The craziest wave of anger passed over me. How dare she say such a thing when I'd never been anything but good to her or the others in my family? I'd just opened my mouth to let her have it when a girlish giggle from behind us startled me.

160

"Oh, I know that one!" Lenora said. "Bette Davis, *All About Eve*. 1950." She sighed and gazed directly into my eyes. "I always loved Bette, didn't you?"

Before I could answer, Benita opened her mouth. "My sister wouldn't know love if it jumped up and bit her."

Lenora looked stunned at this proclamation. Just as quickly, her smile returned. "Would one of you sweet girls point me in the direction of the ladies' room? I need to powder my nose."

Benita pointed down the hallway to the left, and Lenora bounced her way in that direction, rambling about Bette Davis and what a fine job she'd done in that movie. I couldn't get past her comment about Benita and me being "sweet girls." There was nothing sweet about the conversation we'd just had.

I turned on my heels and marched out into the hallway, running straight into Jason.

"Well?"

"I asked if she knew anything about it, but she denied it."

"Maybe she's telling the truth." He shrugged.

"You don't know her, Jason. If you did . . ." I stopped myself from saying the rest. No matter what I thought of my sister's character where men were concerned, I had zero proof that she'd sabotaged me by going to the media. In fact, the more I thought about it, the more ashamed I became. My accusation now seemed presumptuous at best. But how could I take it back?

"It's okay, Tia." Jason rested his hand on my arm and smiled. "In a week or so, none of this will even matter. Take it in stride."

Take it in stride. Now there were a few words to live by.

Oh, if only I could.

16

Curb Your Enthusiasm

By Tuesday morning, I'd resolved that we would have to change the sex of Jack and Angie's baby to a girl, just to keep the viewers guessing. When the episode aired, we wanted them to be surprised.

On the other hand, we'd already announced the sex of the baby in the final scene of the episode we'd filmed last week. Of course, that episode hadn't aired yet. It wouldn't for another week. Hmm. Maybe we could get Kat back in here to do a voice-over and then somehow dub the rest.

No, we couldn't get Kat back in here. She was happily curled up at home with a new baby—a real baby—in her arms. I wouldn't wrestle her back to the studio for anything in the world.

Maybe we could go to her. Maybe we could take a camera, some microphones, a—*Tia, what are you thinking? Have you gone crazy? Of course we're not going to her house.*

That would be asking her to go above and beyond the call of duty. The only people who needed to live like that were the director and the producer. And sometimes the actors, but not right after giving birth.

When I arrived at the studio, I tried to put the problem out of my mind. Unfortunately, my sister seemed bent on making me feel bad. I should have just apologized first thing, but the sour expression on her face let me know I needed to keep my distance. She must've somehow tipped Bob off to my suspicions, because he seemed to give me the cold shoulder too. Was it my imagination, or was he really snubbing me?

By midmorning, my nerves were on edge. Gone was the peace I'd felt during the Sunday morning service. In its place, raw nerves, exposed and aching. And my sister's erratic behavior did nothing to calm me down. She seemed to be playing to my suspicions, hovering around Bob and giggling like a schoolgirl.

I approached her, ready to get this apology over with. But as soon as I came over, she reached for Bob's arm and gazed into his eyes, batting her lashes like a helicopter approaching liftoff.

He gave her a coy smile. "Beni, I had the craziest dream last night."

"Oh?" She giggled and glanced my way, likely to make sure I was watching.

"Yes, I dreamed I was kidnapped by cannibals."

My sister's eyes widened. "Ooo, what happened?"

"Well, they took me away to the Amazon rain forest, to their leader."

"What did he do?"

"She." Bob slipped his arm over my sister's shoulder.

"What did she do?" Benita's voice grew more animated.

"That's up to you." Bob gave her a wink and pulled her close.

"Huh?" My sister's little giggle reflected her confusion.

"She looked just like you, so I figured the dream would pick up when I got to work. So, now that you've caught me in your lair, what are you going to do with me?"

Suddenly I felt sick. At least I had to give it to him—Bob could come up with a great story. That's why we kept him on the payroll.

Benita finally got the joke and giggled. "Oh, you're so cute." She slapped him on the arm. She turned to me, gave me a charming look, and said, "Isn't he just the sweetest thing, Tia? I mean, really, who could say no to a great guy like this?"

"Music to my ears." He squared his shoulders. "So will you go out with me?"

"Well, I'm kind of seeing this other guy. Julio." She looked my way again, as if to rub it in.

My stomach churned. *Why are you doing this, Beni? Enough already. Can't you see I came over here to apologize?*

She released an exaggerated sigh. "He's the most handsome man God ever put on the earth. We're perfect for each other."

You would've thought this would hurt Bob's feelings, but he didn't look terribly downcast. "Look, I'm a writer. We can have Julio's character killed off, no problem. That just leaves me. So, what about it? What say the two of us go to a movie this Friday night?"

"Ooo, a movie?" She sighed. "I've been dying to see Brock's new movie. It releases this weekend, right?"

"Yeah." Bob nodded. "It's a date then?"

"Sure. The idea of sitting in a theater staring at Brock Benson's gorgeous face gets me all tingly inside."

Bob shrugged. "As long as I'm the one holding your hand while you're tingling."

Gross.

She leaned over and gave him a little kiss on the cheek. I thought he might fall over. He put his hand on his face and sighed. "I'm never washing this cheek again."

As she rose, I noticed the searing glance she shot my way. It could've burned holes through me if I'd let it. Clearly her flirtatious scene with Bob was meant for me, but why? Seeing them together only strengthened my resolve to end the feud sooner rather than later. I could put an end to all of this with, "I'm sorry, Benita. I don't know what I was thinking." Only, now she took off across the room, headed straight for Brock. Great. I couldn't apologize in front of him.

Not that I had time, anyway. Glancing at my watch, I realized we needed to get this show on the road.

I heard Lenora's voice ring out behind me. I turned, somewhat surprised to see her carrying an open umbrella and wearing a black coat over a long, gray skirt. She also appeared to be carrying a large carpetbag. Odd.

Well, odd until I heard her singing "Supercalifragilisticexpialidocious." Then it all made sense.

"Ooo, I always loved that movie," Athena said as she passed by. "But I could never figure out how Mary Poppins got all of that stuff into her bag."

"That's for me to know and you to find out." Lenora winked and headed off down the hall.

Yep. Just another day on the *Stars Collide* set.

Our resident diva child, Candy, entered the room with her mother on her heels. The youngster had proven to be quite a handful, but Mama Bianca was far worse. I dreaded the days when Candy was featured in an episode, because it meant dealing with the world's worst stage mother. And I could tell she had something on her mind this morning.

"Tia, I'm not happy with Candy's costume for this NASA shoot. She doesn't look good in gray."

Interesting. Apparently neither do I.

"I would like her in a blue shirt. If you look at her contract, you'll see that it stipulates a list of colors that she can be filmed in. Gray is not on the list. Frankly, I don't see how anyone could think that gray is even a color."

Are you kidding me?

"I tried to talk to Jana back in wardrobe, but you know how she is."

Yeah, I do. Sweet. Kind. Gracious.

"So I must come to you once again to make things right." Bianca gave me a half smile, albeit sarcastic. "You're the boss, after all."

Funny. I didn't much feel like the boss today.

"I'll take care of it, Bianca." I forced a smile. "Candy will look beautiful, I promise."

With a curt nod, the irritable stage mom turned and headed back to the wardrobe department.

I was just about to gather the cast and crew when Rex approached, worry lines etched in his brow.

"What's happened?" I whispered. "Something else with the media?"

"No." He shook his head. "It's Lesleigh Conroy. She's still sick. Erin's going to have to do the run-through for her."

"Ah." Man. When Lesleigh arrived tomorrow, we would have to double our efforts to bring her up to speed. In the meantime, I called for Erin. She approached, eyes sparkling.

"G'morning, Tia."

"Good morning to you too. Would you do me a little favor?"

"Of course. Anything. Your wish is my command."

Perfect. "I need you to fill in for Lesleigh again today."

Erin's mouth opened. "Oh. You mean in the run-through?"

"Yes, do you mind?"

"I guess not." She shrugged. "I'm a little out of my element, but I'll do my best."

"I know you will, Erin. You always do."

Clapping my hands, I managed to gather the cast and crew. "All right, everyone. We're going to run through this thing scene by scene." I explained that Erin would be filling in for Lesleigh, and everyone seemed to take the news in stride.

Well, those who were paying attention, anyway. I was slightly distracted by Bianca and Candy, who argued with Jana off in the distance. I would have to remedy this at once. Bianca would win, of course. Candy would wear blue. What did it really matter, anyway? Some things weren't worth fighting for.

Unfortunately, the morning seemed to be going every direction but the right one. Things got off to a rough start right away as I argued with Brock about—of all things—his characterization. If someone had told me a year ago that I'd be standing in a room with Brock Benson, directing a scene, I would've swooned. Ironic that I used the opportunity to chew him out.

"I'm not sure you're understanding me," I said. "I think your portrayal of this character is a little weak. You could give it more."

"More what?" he asked. "I'm not clear on that."

"You have to actually become the character. Have you spent much time with Greek people?"

He shrugged. "A few."

"Well, get to know Athena and Stephen, our writers. They can give you all the advice you'll ever need and will help you with the accent and mannerisms." To cheer him up, I added, "And they'll feed you the best gyros in town while they're doing it. Athena's dad owns Super Gyros."

"Ooo, I love that place." He licked his lips.

One crisis averted.

We'd just gotten into the scene again when Scott's cell phone went off. "So sorry," he said. "This is Kat. I've got to take it."

"Understandable."

Two minutes later he announced to the cast and crew that baby Katherine had apparently smiled for the first time.

"It's gas," Jason whispered, leaning my way. "Trust me. Babies don't smile when they're this young."

I buried my laughter and kept going. We'd almost made it through the first scene when the nastiest aroma filled the room. *Gag me.* Out of the corner of my eye, I caught a glimpse of Joey with a wicked grin on his face. Next to him, Candy began to squirm. Her nose wrinkled and she turned to face him, ready to interrupt the scene.

Don't do it. I shook my head just in case she happened to look my way. *Don't do anything to stop this scene, or . . .*

Ack. The odor now permeated the room. A teeny-tiny giggle erupted, but Brock and Scott continued their lines, thank goodness.

We made it through the second scene, and I marveled at what a great job Erin did. She was actually the strongest of all of them. From there, we dove into the toughest scene of all, the one involving the kids. Unfortunately, they were on their worst behavior today. From the sidelines I watched as Bianca tried to give Candy direction. I hated when the parents did that. Did they not trust me to do my job?

I got so aggravated that I had to stop. With my hands on my hips, I turned to the kids. "Let's try that again, okay? Candy, you stand on Joey's right this time."

"But . . ." She looked at her mother, not at me.

I shook my head. "No buts. Just do as I say."

Bianca's mouth tightened, and I felt sure I would hear from her after rehearsal. We plowed through the scene, my directing skills taking a beating every step of the way. I watched as my sister looked on from a distance. She rolled her eyes, and I could almost read her thoughts: *You call yourself a director?*

Yes, thank you very much, I do. And if you'll get out of here, I'll do my job.

Unfortunately, she didn't leave. And during the fourth scene, I managed to lose control of the cast altogether. Lenora, who was supposed to appear stage left, was MIA. Rex went off to find her, finally locating her in the costume department. She couldn't seem to remember any of her lines, so we fed them to her one by one. Her mental state—always fuzzy—was far worse than usual.

In fact, everything was far worse than usual. And though I did my best to maintain my composure, keeping in mind Dr. Kennedy's warning about my stress level, I could not. By the time we hit four in the afternoon, I was ready to snap like a twig. Everyone in the room could sense it, from the looks of terror on their faces.

I caught a glimpse of Jason, who gave me a compassionate look. I marveled at how much things had changed between us over the past few weeks. Why, just a few months back, he would have been the first to roll his eyes at me. Not now, though. No, all I saw coming from those eyes today was genuine kindness.

When five o'clock rolled around, we'd gone through each scene multiple times, and I felt a little better about our situation. Still, there were details to be worked out. Candy's costume situation. Brock's characterization problems. Lenora's inability to remember lines. Gathering my cast into a cluster center stage, I gave some final instructions, tried to look encouraging, and then released them to go home.

Benita marched past me, her nose in the air. The others

left with their heads hanging low. *Great. Love it when I have that effect on my cast.* Despite my best efforts, I'd managed to end the day on a sour note once again. So much for having control inside the studio. And so much for thinking I could leave my stress at the door.

I half expected Jason to hang around and chat, but he seemed to be in a hurry tonight. Was it my imagination, or had he hurried off after Benita? The very idea made me sick. Well, why not? Hadn't she already stolen my blind date? Why not take the only guy I was interested in too?

Calm down, Tia.

I waited until the others had left, then worked out the costume issue with Jana in the wardrobe department. Afterward I headed to my car, ready to hit the road. Though it wasn't on my agenda, I found myself stopping off at Kat and Scott's place to see the baby one more time. This time I found Kat in the living room, nursing Katherine.

"Okay to come in?" I asked.

"Of course. Come on." She pulled the little baby blanket over her shoulder and gestured for me to sit in the wingback chair. "How did it go at work today?"

"Rough."

"Scott said it was a little shaky. You're missing Lesleigh Conroy?"

"Yeah, she's really sick."

"Oh no. What did you do?"

"Erin filled in for her. She's amazing. One of the strongest actresses I've seen in ages." Too late I realized what I'd said and clamped a hand over my mouth.

"Oh, don't be silly. You can't possibly hurt my feelings." She gazed at the baby. "Besides, who knows? Maybe I won't go back to acting now that Katherine's here. I'd be perfectly content to sit in this room and take care of her . . . forever."

A ripple of fear ran through me until I realized that all new moms probably felt this way. Give Kat a couple months, and hopefully she'd be ready to come back.

"You can bring the baby to work."

"Oh, I know. Scott and I have hired a full-time nanny. She's been with me every step of the way, and she'll come with me to the studio. I'm sure it'll be fine. But my figure . . ." She groaned. "I hope and pray I'm back in shape by the time I come back in the fall."

"Don't worry about it, Kat. If I've learned one thing, it's that you just have to be yourself."

"You've learned this lesson, eh?" She smiled. "And you had to go and learn it while I was away?"

"Yeah."

She gave me a pensive look. "Tell me why you really stopped by."

I released a sigh. "I went to the doctor."

"You've been sick?"

"Well, I've had some allergies. At least, I thought I had allergies. Now I'm not so sure. They're going to do tests."

"What do you mean?" Now she really looked concerned.

"The allergist thinks I'm overworked and overstressed."

"Well, yeah." She chuckled. "What else is new?"

"She says the stress is causing my immune system to not function as it should. Go figure."

"Well, God designed us to rest, Tia. Even he took a day off."

"Everyone keeps telling me that. I take the weekends off."

"Do you?"

I sighed again. "Well, I try. But my house is under construction."

"I know you've heard the old expression about burning the candle at both ends, so I won't bore you by going into detail." Kat gazed down at her baby. "And trust me, after years of nonstop working, I'd be a hypocrite to say I'd led by example. But sitting here with this little girl every day—seeing how peaceful she is in my arms—has been a wakeup call."

"Oh?"

"Yeah." She stared at the baby, the most contented look on her face. "Peace. Quiet. Rest. They're all key ingredients to a happy, healthy life." She looked my way and shrugged. "I know you can't quit your job, Tia. And I'm sure that wouldn't solve the problem, anyway. You'd still find something to keep you busy."

"True."

"I just think you need to take some time every day to relax. Get a massage."

"A massage?" Hmm. How many years had it been?

"Maybe a pedicure too. And a manicure."

I could feel my body relax as she spoke. The tension in my shoulders lifted.

"But most of all, you just need to get alone with God. Pour your troubles on him. Ask him to carry that stress for you." With tears in her eyes, she smiled at baby Katherine. "I really think the Lord wants us to be this relaxed in his arms." She nodded at the bundle in her arms. "See how calm she is? How peaceful?"

"Do you really think it's possible in Hollywood?" I asked.

She gazed into the baby's face and whispered, "I do."

I felt a sense of ease come over me as she spoke. For the first time in weeks, I truly felt like I could let God take all of this anxiety from me. All I had to do . . . was let it go.

17

Extreme Makeover

Tuesday night, after visiting with Kat, I had what Mama liked to call a "come to Jesus meeting." No one else attended—just Jesus and me. I'd been through a few of these before—mostly in my teens—so I knew the drill. He laid a few things bare, and I responded with lots of tears and a bit of fussing and fuming. The end result? I would take it easy. Kick back. Be more relaxed. Let him play the role of director in my life . . . willingly.

Would it happen overnight? No. Would I make a deliberate effort to let go of my anxiety and trust him to handle the things I could not? Well, I'd give it my best shot. And if I failed, I would pick myself up, dust myself off, and try again. What I would *not* do was stress. Not as a first choice, anyway. In thirty years of living, I'd already stressed enough for ten or twelve people.

That night I slept like a baby. Somewhere in the middle of my

173

dreams I must've come to the startling conclusion that I couldn't fix the issue with the tabloids, because I woke up completely at peace about it all. We would leave the recorded episode exactly as it was. Little Ricky would be Little Ricky. So what if the viewers knew his name? Maybe they would feel that we cared enough about them to entrust them with the news. And I would make my apologies to Benita, doing my best to unravel any existing issues between us. She was, after all, my baby sister.

Whew! Letting go of things actually felt good. Who knew?

Since I'd gone to bed at a decent hour, my body didn't feel the usual early-morning tenseness. I rolled over in bed, then sat up and reached for my Bible, determined not to let the moment get away from me. No rushing here and there to get ready. That could wait a few minutes. I had some business to take care of first.

Not that it felt like business. No, as I lingered in God's presence, I actually felt—possibly for the first time—that meeting with him wasn't something to check off of my to-do list. Turned out it was a privilege. A blessing. I enjoyed it so much, in fact, that I continued my conversation with him as I showered and fixed my hair. Just for kicks, I decided to wear my hair loose around my face, not overcombed, but soft and a little messy. I'd never done the messy look before, but maybe it was about time.

When it came time to dress, I picked out a soft pink blouse with ruffles, which I wore over a pair of relaxed jeans. My heels were a perfect complement to the belt. And just for fun, I wore dangly earrings. That would throw people off, no doubt. I'd never worn anything other than my usual diamond studs before.

When it came time to leave for work, I found myself looking forward to the day ahead. In spite of any troubles yesterday, today would be a great day. No matter what happened, I would maintain the right attitude. Once again my professor's words ran through my mind: *They're following your lead. You set the stage for the attitude on the set. The director directs not just the filmed action but all the action.*

Today we would experience the best possible in-studio experience. I would lead the way.

I pulled onto the 405 and pressed the button on the steering wheel to call Mama. She answered on the second ring. "Tia, is everything okay?"

"Of course."

"Oh." I could hear her breathe a sigh of relief, then mutter "God be praised" in Spanish. "You're calling me on your way to work."

"I always talk to you on my way to work."

"Well, yes, but I always call you. At 7:45 a.m. You called me at 7:39 a.m. So I had to think maybe something terrible had happened. Nothing terrible happened, did it, Tia-mia? Oh, don't tell me. I'm already upset enough about this nonsense with your sister."

"Ah, she told you. Well, don't worry about that, Mama. I plan to apologize to her."

"I'm not saying you have to be the one to apologize, Tia. I don't know what to think. I just hate to see my girls not getting along. It's so hard when there's a strain in a relationship. We've seen so much of it in this family. I just want everyone to love one another."

"I do love her, Mama, and I'm going to do what I can to make things better."

"I'm glad to hear it, Tia. Honestly, I just don't know what to do with that girl sometimes."

"Oh?"

"Yes, there's always so much drama where she's concerned. Where all of your siblings are concerned, really."

Interesting.

Mama opened up and talked about her concerns—about Benita, Carlos's drinking, and even Gabe's struggle with ADHD. Who knew? She actually did see her children's flaws.

I pulled into the drive-through at Starbucks, ended the call with my mother, and ordered a Grande Earl Grey tea, heavy on the cream, with two Splendas. Of course, it was too hot to drink. By the time I arrived at the studio, I'd hoped it would be cool enough to sip. No such luck. Oh well. Just one more thing *not* to get upset about.

When I got out of my car, I realized I'd parked next to Jason. He took one look at me in my pink ruffled blouse, and I thought the boy's eyes would pop right out of his head.

"Wow." A delicious smile lit his face. "You look . . ." He raked his fingers through his hair. "Amazing."

"Thank you." I felt the edges of my lips curl up in a smile. A girl could get used to being greeted like this in the morning.

I closed the door to my car, and the doors automatically locked. Slipping my Prada handbag over my shoulder, I walked alongside Jason. He dove into a story about a movie he'd seen the night before, and before long he had me smiling. Oh, how I loved this kind of attention. If I had my way, we would skip ahead a few pages in the script and get to the part where he told me I was the greatest thing that had ever happened to him.

"Tia?"

"Hmm?" I looked at him, realizing I'd gotten lost in my thoughts.

"You still with me?"

I felt my cheeks grow hot. "Oh, yes, I . . ." *Quick, Tia. Think on your feet.* "You know, I hate to cut this short, but I need to find my sister. I really need to talk to her."

"Ah. Okay. Well, I'll see you later then."

I practically took off running toward the soundstage. Once inside, I hid my purse in my office, then went off in search of Benita. I found her in the hair and makeup room, taking inventory of her products.

I took a couple of steps in her direction, and she put her hands up. "What did I do this time?"

"Nothing." I sighed and sat in her chair. Turning to face the mirror, I stared at both of our reflections. Strange how much we looked alike today. She happened to be wearing pink too. "That's not why I'm here."

Little creases appeared between her brows. "Oh?"

"Beni, I came to apologize. I don't know what came over me. I'll admit, the thing with Julio totally threw me—hurt my feelings a little—but not for the reasons you think. He wasn't my type."

"Tell me about it." She rolled her eyes. "Mama totally botched that up."

Okay, I don't know if you're insulting me or just stating a fact, so I'll just smile and keep talking.

"Anyway, to suspect you of sabotaging the show was just plain stupid." I gave her a sheepish look. "Will you forgive me?"

She waited awhile before answering. "Just so you know, the thing with Julio was not really my fault. He's a handsome guy. Very handsome."

"Agreed."

She sighed. "I think maybe I was blinded by the heavenly glow surrounding his face. It drew me in like a magnet. I don't know any way to explain it other than that. He cast a spell on me with his looks, and I'm hooked. Just reel me in and fry me up in a pan. I can't help myself when I'm in the room with a gorgeous guy."

It wasn't the first time she'd been swayed by a handsome

face, and I knew it wouldn't be the last. "Well, if it's all the same to you, I'd like to put both of these things behind us. Can we do that?" I turned away from the mirror and looked into her eyes.

Again, she didn't answer right away. When she finally spoke, her words surprised me. "I love my job here, Tia. This is the best job I've ever had, and not just because I get to put makeup on people like Brock Benson." Her eyes misted over. "I . . . I'm learning a lot. About the industry. About how sitcoms are made. About what the writers go through." She shrugged. "Even what you do for a living. I never got it before, but I do now."

"I'm glad." I rose and gave her a warm hug.

"Everyone here respects you, Tia," she whispered. "I've never known what that felt like . . . to be respected."

Whoa. Her words caught me totally off guard.

"When you speak, everyone listens," she said. "And you're loaded with great ideas to make the show even better than it already is." She paused. "Makes me want to be the best I can be too."

I hardly knew what to say. After stumbling through a couple of responses, I finally gave up and threw my arms around her neck, giving her the tightest squeeze I could. "Thank you," I whispered. "That means a lot, coming from someone in the family."

When I released my hold, she took a close look at my blouse and hair. "You look great, Tia. Where did the blouse come from?"

"I bought it ages ago on a whim."

"Then you need to buy more things on a whim. This color is great on you. And these ruffles . . . " She reached to touch the sleeve of the blouse. "I just can't get over the fact that you're wearing ruffles."

"Well, I was in a ruffly sort of mood today."

"Interesting." She grinned, then turned me around so that we both faced the mirror again. "Look how pretty you are."

I stared at my reflection, more amazed at the relaxed expression on my face than anything else. Being a changed woman—giving up stress—had actually softened my appearance. Who knew?

I ran into my first opportunity to prove that I was a changed woman just moments later when Rex appeared in the doorway, concern etched into his brow. "Houston, we have a problem."

"What's that?" I rose and met him at the door. He gestured for me to join him in the hallway, so I headed that direction.

"Remember I told you that Lesleigh had the stomach flu?" he whispered.

"Yeah?"

Rex sighed. "It wasn't the flu. It was her appendix. She's just been admitted to the hospital, and doctors are prepping her for surgery as we speak."

"Are you kidding me? Tell me you're kidding."

Deep breath, Tia. This is one of those moments you rehearsed for, remember?

"Not kidding." Rex took a few steps toward the soundstage. "She's out, and we're looking for an actress to take her place. Pronto."

I began to pace the room. As the show's director, I should've had a backup plan. I stopped pacing and shrugged. "We'll have to talk to Athena and Stephen and see if they can rewrite that scene, I guess."

"I thought of that. It's just a lot to ask of them, and they're already working on next week's script. Not to mention that was a really funny scene. It affects everything else in the episode."

"You're right." I crossed the room and took a seat in my director's chair. I could usually think more clearly here.

Off in the distance, Erin played with the kids, her laughter ringing out. Looked like our answer was already here, right in front of us.

"Follow me, Rex. I have an idea." I rose and walked across the studio, calling out Erin's name.

Erin turned, all smiles, as usual. "What's up, Ms. T?"

"Erin, let me ask you a question. You're in film school, right?"

"Sure am." She squared her shoulders and smiled. "Gonna be like you when I grow up."

"Would you, just this once, consider being like Kat when you grow up?"

Her jaw dropped. "You want me to have a baby?"

"No, silly. I'm asking you to be an actress. Have you had any acting experience? Besides filling in for Lesleigh, I mean."

"Oh, sure." She waved a hand. "I did some school plays, and even played Guinevere last fall at a community theater. Just did it to give myself exposure and get to know others in the acting community. You never know when it might come in handy."

"Like now."

"Huh?" Her brow wrinkled. "What do you mean?"

I decided to speak to her, director to director. "Erin, did you ever see the movie *42nd Street* with Ruby Keeler?"

"Did I?" She laughed. "We studied that movie in film school. It's a classic. Loaded with great lines. And that Busby Berkley choreography was out of this world. He was ahead of his time."

"Remember how the star of the show broke her ankle and couldn't go on, so Ruby Keeler's character had to take her place at the last minute?"

"Of course. It was the opportunity of a lifetime."

"Exactly. Sometimes life gives us those."

180

To my right, Rex grinned.

"Tia, what are you saying?" Confusion registered in Erin's eyes.

I released a breath, then spit out the whole explanation: "Lesleigh Conroy's appendix is about to burst, so she's going into surgery and won't be here today, and we need you to take her place. Not just today for the final run-through, but for the filming tomorrow too. We're going to turn the little chorus girl into a star."

Erin turned white as a sheet. "I . . . I think I need to sit down." She did. Finally, she looked up at me, bug-eyed. "There's no one else?"

"Nope. It's just you, kid. So, what do you say? Can we go over the lines one more time so I can give you some direction?"

"I—I guess so."

I passed a script to her, instructing her to turn to page seven. She glanced down at the script and started to read.

Turned out I didn't have to give any direction at all. Erin had every nuance right, even the facial expressions. And best of all, she'd somehow already memorized the lines. After the first couple, she barely looked at the script.

"Good gravy." Rex paused and shook his head. "This is something else. I don't believe it. Haven't seen anything like this since '57 when Elvis and I auditioned for the same part in *Jailhouse Rock*." A sheepish look came over his face. "He got the part, obviously. Not me."

Erin chuckled. "The world will never know what it missed, Rex."

"Oh, I remember Elvis," Lenora said, joining us. "I did a movie with him once." She went off on a tangent about what it was like to work with the King, but I turned my attention to Erin.

"I can't thank you enough."

"Ugh." Erin's nose wrinkled. "I know I'm pretty rough."

"Rough?" I laughed, suddenly feeling very carefree. "Oh, Erin."

A flush ran up her neck and into her cheeks. Time to put her out of her misery.

"Erin, you've always stayed behind the camera."

"Sure." She shrugged. "I love it there. Anything to be in the studio."

"I know, but the camera is going to love you. And your acting skills are pretty amazing. You're a natural."

"I am?" She looked stunned at this proclamation.

I put my hand on her arm. "Don't you sense it when you're acting? Every now and again I see a rare gem like you—someone who's gifted in such a natural and obvious way—but most of those people have trained for years. With you, it's just an unpretentious, God-given gift. No other way to describe it."

"Wow. Thanks." Her cheeks flushed pink again. "I'll admit, acting is a lot of fun, but I'm not really into the glitz and glam side of Hollywood. I'm the one who wants to make sure the camera angles are right and the cast is prepared to do the best job possible." She shrugged. "I'm not trying to say I want your job, Tia, but one day I want to have a job like yours. It's something great to aspire to."

"I think that's awesome, and I hope you get whatever your heart desires. But in the meantime, thank you for doing this. It means the world to me."

"Oh, you're welcome." She smiled. "I'm sure it will be fun too. It's all fun."

"Yes, it is." *When you have a great attitude like that.* "Now get yourself over to hair and makeup and make sure they age you a little. You've got to look like you're thirty, not twenty-two."

"I remember when I was twenty-two," Lenora said. "Seems like just yesterday."

Erin still looked half stunned, half thrilled. "This is really happening," she whispered.

"Carpe diem." I squeezed her hand. "Seize the day, Erin."

"Oh, I know that one," Lenora said with a wave of her hand. "Robin Williams. *Dead Poets Society*."

"1990," Rex threw in.

"No, I think it was '89," Erin said. "But I don't suppose it matters."

"I've always thought Robin Williams was such a funny man." Lenora giggled. "I met him once when I did a guest appearance on *Mork and Mindy*."

I turned back to Erin with a smile. "I know I've put you on the spot, but let me remind you that you'll be playing the part of Brock Benson's love interest. And there's a kiss involved."

She tried to respond but could only manage a stammer.

"Exactly. Now get in there and let them figure out the hair and wardrobe thing. And count your lucky stars. Okay?"

"O-okay." She giggled. "Just wait till I call my mama. She's gonna flip."

As I watched her walk away, I couldn't help but be reminded of my years in film school. I'd taken enough acting classes to learn how to give instruction to my show's stars. I understood vocal inflection, characterization, tone, pitch, volume control. Only one problem—I couldn't act my way out of a paper bag. No way, no how. Still, it was clear Erin could, and I needed her now more than ever.

"Thank you, Lord. You sent the right person at the right time."

I turned and ran smack-dab into Jason, who offered me a broad smile. "Well, thank you. I'll take that as a compliment."

"Oh, I . . . well, I . . ."

Nah. What would be the point in explaining, anyway?

He gave me a wink, which caused me to lose focus. If there was one thing I'd learned over the years, it was that an out-of-focus director meant an out-of-focus cast.

Gazing into his beautiful green eyes, I had to conclude there were worse things to befall a director.

18

Life's Too Short

Our morning run-through went far better than I might've guessed, based on the prior day's rehearsal. And even though our regulars did a fine job, I had to admit there was something rather special about watching Erin at work, especially now that I knew she would be playing the role. Her comedic timing simply took my breath away.

We took a break for lunch around 11:30, but I had a lot of work on my plate, so leaving seemed out of the question. Jason had other ideas.

"I'm starving. Want to join me for lunch?"

Suddenly everything I'd planned to do during the lunch hour could wait. I gave him a smile. "Love to. Hang on, okay?" I turned back to scribble a few things onto a piece of paper. "Sorry, I had to get that down before I forgot."

We walked to the commissary as a tour bus approached. Several starstruck fans waved as if they thought we were movie stars. After years in the business, I still couldn't get over how some fans acted around famous people. Crazy.

"Whoa." Jason took hold of my arm and pulled me toward him as the bus ambled by. The protective gesture almost brought tears to my eyes. Most of the men in my world would've protected themselves first, then glanced back to make sure the rest of us were okay.

Inside the commissary, I ordered a club sandwich, fries, and a Coke.

Jason looked at me with wide eyes. "You eat? Something other than salad, I mean?"

"Yeah. I eat. And I kick down walls. And I wear pink. And ruffles too. And I apologize to people when I'm wrong." I sighed. "I'm a changed woman."

"I see. Well, don't change too much. I might not recognize you." He waggled his brows and laughter bubbled up inside me.

Off in the distance, one of the workers cleaned off a table. I nodded in that direction, and a couple minutes later we were seated together eating. It felt really good to be able to just be myself in front of a guy for a change.

Now that the opportunity had presented itself, I wanted to talk to Jason about something he'd said on Saturday. Hopefully I wouldn't botch this. I tried to figure out how to begin.

"What's up?" he asked after a couple minutes of silence. "You have something on your mind."

"Am I that obvious?"

He nodded and took a bite of his burger. "Yep."

"Okay." A deep breath followed. "I wanted to respond to what you said last Saturday, about having walls up."

"Ah." He took a swig of his Coke. "Hope I didn't hurt your feelings."

"No. Well, maybe a little, but you were right. I've always

had walls up. I . . . I don't really want people to know about my life outside the studio, so it's been a protective measure, I guess."

He stopped eating and leaned forward. "I want to know about your life, Tia. The things that bother you. The things that make you laugh. I want to know it all." His words were soft and took me by surprise.

I managed a lame nod. Brilliant. "I can't tell you the whole story over one short lunch, but there's a lot about me that people just don't know. Where I come from . . ." I shook my head. "Well, it's been a tough life. And maybe it's made me a little hard."

"Tell me." He took another bite and leaned back in his chair.

"You've met my sister, Benita. But you probably don't know I have three brothers. There are five of us, and I'm the oldest."

He gave me an admiring look. "I always wanted brothers and sisters."

"Not these." I paused long enough to repent for what I'd just said. "Anyway, I grew up in South Central."

"Where exactly? I'm wondering if it's close to the street church I've been working with."

"Closer than you think, but that's a story for later."

"Okay." He crossed his arms at his chest, his gaze penetrating.

"Anyway, I lived there until a few years ago. I grew up in a bungalow that was built in the twenties. One bathroom. Three bedrooms. My brothers had one room, my sister and I had another."

"Man."

"Yeah. And we're talking small bedrooms too. Most of my life I slept on the floor on a twin mattress with my little sister curled up beside me." The memories overtook me at this point. "My father was gone as much as he was home, so sometimes I slept in my mama's room. She would cry a lot because she didn't know where he was."

Jason squirmed a bit in his chair, and I could tell he was sorry he'd brought up the subject. "I'm sorry, Tia. I had no idea."

"You had no idea because I didn't want anyone to know. I made good grades in school and managed to put myself through film school, and now here I am."

"Wearing Kenneth Cole shoes and carrying a Prada handbag."

I drew in a deep breath and thought through my next words. "You think I'm covering up something with all that?"

"No. That never occurred to me. Just an observation that you've got great taste. I never would have guessed you were from such a rough background."

"It's not that I'm ashamed of my upbringing." The conversation with my mother washed over me afresh. "Well, some of it I'm ashamed of. Never knowing if my dad was coming or going. That part stunk. And watching my mama get her heart broken over and over again—that wasn't much fun either. But I learned how to be tough in the projects. And determined. That's where my backbone came from."

"No doubt." He gave me a curious look. "Can I ask a question?"

"Sure."

"I know you're a Christian. It's obvious. But how did you manage to hang on for the ride if your situation was that rough?"

"Ah." So the moment had come. "Remember I told you earlier that the street church you're working with is closer than you think?"

"Yeah."

"I didn't just mean physically close, though it is. They meet about four blocks from my house. But it's close to me in other ways too." I paused, trying to work up the courage to share. "See, I never really went to church as a little girl. My mother did for a while, but once my dad started coming and going, she gave it up. Then, when I was about eight, a group of people from a church starting coming down to our area on Saturday mornings to do street ministry for the kids. They called it Sidewalk Sunday School."

"Oh, wow. They still call it that. It's great."

"I know. And it was great. I'm sure it still is. I met some kind and loving people, and they took the time to really pour into me. Not just to pound the gospel into me, mind you, but to really, genuinely care for me. They made sure we had Christmas presents every year and even bought me shoes on a few occasions."

He sat up straight, eyes riveted on mine.

"When I got to my teens, I wandered a little bit, but they came looking for me. Before long, I was working alongside them, directing their dramas. It gave me a sense of purpose. And when the time came to graduate from school, I had no doubt what I wanted to do with my life: I was born to be a director. I never would've known it if they hadn't given me a chance."

"Tia, this is amazing."

I nodded. "They saw something in me that I didn't even see in myself. And they reached down and stirred up the gifts inside me. That's why I do what I do. I don't just direct these actors and actresses so that I can tell them what to do. I direct them so that I can stir up the gifts God has placed inside them. Sure, sometimes I'm hard on them. I want them to be their very best, not just so the show's ratings stay up, but so they can be proud of their performance. So they can say they've done their very best, given their all."

He gave me a curious look, one I couldn't quite make out. "Do you think I've been mean? Is that how I come across?"

"I'm not sure *mean* is the right word. I've heard people in the cast say . . ." His words drifted off. "It's all a matter of perception, anyway."

"I don't want anyone to have a bad perception of me. It's just so hard. I know the names they call me. But you have to understand. I grew up in a rough place. If you weren't tough, you could get killed. I was surrounded on every side by gang activity and shootings. That's my background. It's a part of who I am, even though I keep going."

"Wow." He took a sip of his Coke, then set it back down on the table.

"We don't have to talk about this if it makes you uncomfortable."

"Tia . . . " He leaned forward and took my hand. "This is exactly what I want to talk about. I want to know you, even the hard things."

Well, if that didn't give a girl courage, nothing would.

He looked at me with a smile so sweet I thought I'd melt into a puddle right there in the commissary. His expression shifted, and suddenly I read concern in his eyes. "Tia, before you say anything else, I have to tell you something."

"Oh?" My heart skipped to double time as I imagined what he might say.

"Until a couple of months ago, I was really hard on you. I don't know why, I really don't. Maybe because I'd already been here a couple of years before you took over as director. I had my own way of doing things and saw you as some sort of threat."

I sighed. "I came in like a lion, didn't I?"

"Yeah, but that's what directors do. They direct. They lead. I . . ." He offered a woeful shrug. "I saw you as a challenge to the way I'd always done things. But you made me think outside the box. I'm a better cameraman, thanks to you. In fact, I'm a better *man*, thanks to you."

"Wow." I hardly knew what to say.

He squeezed my hand. "I'm glad we're getting to know each other. I had no idea of all you've been through." He gave me the sweetest look. "If I'd known, I would have gone easier on you. And in case I don't say it enough, I'm really proud of you, Tia. You're an amazing woman."

"Th-thank you." I couldn't think of the last time I'd heard a man tell me he was proud of me, so his words genuinely touched me.

Jason's hand lingered in mine, and I was captivated by the tenderness pouring from his eyes. In that moment, I did the craziest thing. I released a giggle—a girlish, flirtatious giggle. Then, perhaps overcome by the sweetness of the conversation, I brushed a loose hair off my face—flirting à la Benita—and gazed into Jason's eyes, allowing the pause to last an extra-long time.

As our eyes met and held, I felt that little spark—that tiny bit of magic that happens in musicals, where the leading man suddenly sweeps the leading lady into his arms and takes her for a choreographed spin around the dance floor. I could almost see us now—me in my ball gown and Jason in his tuxedo, waltzing across a beautiful outdoor set near a lake. Nah, maybe I'd better stick to indoor. A ballroom. A grand and glorious place with exquisite chandeliers and a large wooden dance floor, where we danced like the Hollywood greats from days gone by.

"Tia?" Jason's voice startled me back to attention.

"Hmm?" My hazy dream came to an end. Fred and Ginger's dance ended abruptly.

"I want you to know something." A smile turned up the edges of his lips. "I really want you to know that—"

"What are you kids up to?"

I looked up to discover Lenora at our table. Her food tray trembled in her hand.

"Can I join you, or is this a private meeting?" Lenora's gaze shifted to the table, and I realized Jason and I were still holding hands.

"Oh, well, we . . ."

"I'm all alone today." The tray continued to tremble in her hands. "Rex had to stay in his office to work, but he told me to come and find someone to sit with."

"Please, join us." Jason released my hand, rose, and grabbed Lenora's tray. She sat and dove into a lengthy discussion about the price of Salisbury steak as he put her plate in front of her.

Looked like I would have to wait until another day to see what Jason had on his mind. For now, Lenora totally consumed the conversation.

I dabbed my lips with a napkin and gave her a closer look. "Lenora, that dress is divine. Who are you today?"

"Claudette Colbert. *It Happened One Night.*" She took on a faraway look. "Did you ever see that one, honey?"

"No, I don't think so."

"Oh, get to the theater and see it as soon as you can. There's something so magical about the interaction between Clark Gable and Claudette Colbert. They're both breathtakingly beautiful to look at, but it's not just that. They're meant to be together. You can see it in their eyes." She sighed. "I can always tell when people are supposed to be together."

"You can?"

She flashed a girlish smile, then looked back and forth between us. "Well, sure. I knew KK and Jack were supposed to get married as soon as I met him."

I decided not to correct her. If she wanted to call Scott by his stage name, so be it.

"And take you, for instance." Lenora chuckled. "You're such a funny little thing. Always acting so tough and all. But you're going to marry a man with a heart of gold, someone who would give his shirt to help another." Her gaze shifted to Jason, who, thank goodness, didn't react.

"I am?"

"Well, sure, honey. You just wait and see. God will use him to rub off those hard edges. Before long, you'll be smooth as a stone, inside and out."

I sighed. Even Lenora thought I was rough and tough. But at least she saw my heart. I couldn't say that about everyone.

Besides, the newer, softer me wouldn't get offended anymore. I would handle things—all things, good and bad—with grace and ease.

"I see that you're already wearing pink. That's a start." Lenora glanced at Jason. "Doesn't she look lovely in pink?"

"*Lovely* is the right word." He gave me a little wink and my heart fluttered.

Lenora took a bite of her Salisbury steak, then offered a contented sigh. "God's in his heaven, all's right with the world."

Something quickened inside of me. "Oh, I know that one. *Anne of Green Gables.*"

"Yes, such a sweet little thing, Anne." Lenora took a bite of her mashed potatoes. "I do hope our new baby grows up to be just like her—silly, sweet, and filled with spunk."

"Oh, I'm sure she will," Jason said. "She's got the best parents in the world."

Lenora smiled. "Oh, you'll be so happy to know I called Ted Holliday, one of my favorite reporters, to tell him all about the baby. He was so happy to get the news."

This certainly got my attention. She'd been talking to reporters? I wondered if Rex knew.

"You mean the *real* baby, right?" I asked, choosing my words carefully.

"Well, of course. The one KK had in the elevator. I told Ted all about it. He was tickled pink." She giggled. "Or would that be blue?" A look of confusion registered in her eyes. "She did have a baby boy, right?"

"You mean the real baby, or the one on the show?" Jason asked.

"Show?" Lenora shook her head. "I'm talking about KK's new baby. I was sure she had a boy. But then I saw the baby in her arms, and I could've sworn it was a girl." She sighed. "Oh, but it's the prettiest little baby in the world. Reminds me of my little one all those years ago." She went off on a tangent, but she'd lost me.

"Lenora, what did you say the reporter's name was again?" I asked.

"Ted Holliday, honey." Her eyes sparkled. "Oh, I could always count on Ted to cover a story with flair. You should have seen the write-up he did when I starred in *It Had to Be You* back in '57."

A reporter who worked for *The Scoop* back in '57 was still there today? I couldn't imagine it.

"So, you told Mr. Holliday about the baby." Jason looked her way and then glanced at me.

She nodded.

"Did you happen to mention the baby's name?" he asked.

Confusion registered in her eyes again. "Oh dear. Now I've done it."

"Done what?" My heart began to race.

"I . . ." Tears rose to cover her lashes. "I can't remember the baby's name," she whispered. "Isn't that awful?"

I patted her on the arm, doing my best to comfort her. "I forget names all the time, Lenora. Don't worry about it."

Her expression brightened. "Anyway, we have a new baby. And I remember now! She's named Anne with an *e* just like the little girl from *Anne of Green Gables*. I think that's what we were talking about, wasn't it? Or was it Little Ricky? I can't remember now. Oh, yes, I told that reporter the baby's name was Little Ricky." She flashed a contented smile. "I've always loved that name. Reminds me of *I Love Lucy*. Didn't Lucille Ball have the prettiest red hair?" She leaned in close and whispered, "Though I can assure you, it was Lady Clairol, not Mother Nature." A giggle followed, and she took another bite of her steak.

I didn't have the heart to tell Lenora that her granddaughter's name was Katherine. And I certainly couldn't tell her that she'd committed a grave error by going to a tabloid with news about the baby boy. It would probably also break her heart to know that Ted Holliday had likely passed away years ago. She had clearly talked with someone else at *The Scoop*, not him.

Jason gave me a knowing look, and I knew we were on the same page. My sister hadn't tipped off the media. Lenora had. And though she'd created all sorts of trouble for the show, none of us could tell her. Or blame her. Or hold it against her.

Still, I had to tell Rex. He needed to know . . . and the sooner, the better.

19

The Young and the Restless

As we walked back to the soundstage, Lenora rambled on and on about Kat's baby, Little Ricky. Before long, she was telling stories about Lucille Ball and what a great time she'd had getting to know her in the sixties when they worked together. At this point, I didn't know if her stories from days gone by were real or figments of her imagination.

All the while, Jason and I walked side by side. At one point he reached for my hand and gave it a squeeze. I couldn't tell if he was sympathizing with me for having to listen to Lenora's endless chatter about Hollywood past, or if the hand-holding spoke of more. Perhaps time would tell.

We joined the others for a final run-through of the show, then I sent my cast off to wardrobe to finalize their fittings while I talked through the more technical aspect of the episode with the camera crew. Jason led the way through this discussion, and I thanked God—albeit silently—for someone who really knew his stuff.

Jason walked me to my car after rehearsal, keeping me entertained with funny stories about his surfing days. The more he talked about being out on the water, the more appealing it sounded. In fact, the idea of getting away from the studio—getting away from house-flipping—held more appeal than I'd realized.

As we said our goodbyes, he reached for my hand once again and focused on my eyes. "I had a lot of fun with you today, Tia."

Wow. New words. No one ever told me that I was fun. Hardworking, sure. Tough as nails, yep. But . . . fun?

"I had fun with you too." His stories had been great, but our conversation over lunch had really made my day. Oh, if only Lenora hadn't interrupted us. I half expected Jason to finish the conversation now, but his cell phone rang, and he took the call, then waved his goodbye.

Not that I minded. I climbed into my car and pointed it toward the nearest mall. I had a sudden desire to shop for clothes with color.

And shop I did. I found the prettiest blouses in greens and pinks. My favorite, though, was the soft blue button-up shirt. I'd never worn anything like it.

As soon as I arrived at home, my new wardrobe pieces went into the newly repaired closet. I had to push back some of the gray items to make space, but I didn't mind a bit. In fact, I felt so good about things that I decided to cook dinner. Fumbling around in the freezer, I came out with a piece of tilapia, which I thawed and broiled in the oven. *See, Tia? You can cook.*

Fifteen minutes later, I ate the yummy fish, along with a salad. Then I headed off to take a long, hot bath. As I soaked under the luxurious bubbles, I thought about my conversation with Jason over lunch. I tried to imagine what he would've said if Lenora hadn't happened upon us.

I got so lost in my imaginings that I almost fell asleep in

the tub. Scrambling out, I dressed in a new pink nightie and headed straight for bed. By the time my head hit the pillow, I felt the lull of slumber.

The following morning I awoke feeling even more peaceful than the day before. Mama called me on my way to the studio, her happy-go-lucky voice like music to my ears.

"I won't keep you long, Tia," she said. "I know it's Thursday. You're filming in front of a live audience today."

"Oh, it's okay, Mama. I've got time to talk."

And talk we did. She shared a funny story about something my dad had done last night, then sighed with contentment. Interesting. Was it just my relaxed state, or were other people changing too?

I arrived at the studio to find Lenora dressed up as Glinda the Good Witch from *The Wizard of Oz*. Not exactly the costume I would've picked for her today, so I sent her off to the wardrobe department to dress for her upcoming scenes.

"You've got to admit, she looks pretty good in that dress she's wearing," Jason said from behind me.

"Just not in the script for this particular episode." I chuckled.

"You sure we can't send it back for a rewrite? Take out the NASA bit and add a *Wizard of Oz* scene?"

"This late in the game?" I asked. "I'm flexible, but not that flexible."

He crossed his arms.

"Okay, I'm not really flexible. But I'm working on it."

"Yes, you are." He leaned down to whisper, "And by the way, that color of blue is perfect for you."

"I like it a lot too." I giggled.

His breath was warm on my ear as he whispered, "I like a girl who knows what she likes." A wink followed, which sent my heart fluttering a thousand directions.

Suddenly I knew exactly what I liked . . . and it had nothing to do with sitcom scripts. I shoved the script behind my back, hoping he hadn't noticed the trembling in my hands.

A wiggle of his brows let me know he had. *What's happening here? I'm the one who's always in control. I don't let things inside the studio unnerve me.* But one look into his gorgeous eyes convinced me otherwise. I melted like an ice cube on a hot sidewalk. In that moment, he could have very easily pulled me into his arms and kissed me, and I would have given myself over to the moment. In front of an audience, no less.

Audience!

I looked up to see that the doors had opened and the first five rows were already full.

"Man." I looked at my watch and gasped. "Is it really that late? Our audience is here."

"Just so you know," Jason whispered, "where you're concerned, there's always an audience." He gave me a knowing look, then meandered away.

"Always an audience?" I spoke the words aloud, trying to make sense of them.

"He's nuts about you, Tia."

I turned to face Athena, who handed me the corrected script. "He is?"

"Of course. I'm a writer. I keep a close eye on things like expressions, body signals, and so on. He's been crazy about you since the day you arrived on the set."

I could no longer deny it, could I? Still, talking about it openly made it seem almost too real.

She leaned in to whisper, "Trust me when I say that he thinks you're the cat's meow. And yeah, he's always done a great job of acting tough—sometimes acting like he can't stand you, even—but on the inside he's a marshmallow. I'm glad he's finally showing you that softer side. And speaking of softer, you look great."

"Thanks." A shiver ran up my spine as I contemplated her words. Most of my thoughts about Jason over the past several months had been of a different vein: *How long can that guy go on irritating me before I smack him upside his handsome head?* Now suddenly I had to change gears and ponder the fact that he actually liked me? What an interesting twist. Then again, all good scripts were filled with interesting twists.

Another shiver sent my thoughts reeling. *Back to reality, Tia. We have a show to film. And an audience to deal with.*

Thankfully, the filming went great. When Erin and Brock finished the scene where they kissed, the audience went wild. From her flushed cheeks, I'd have to say Erin enjoyed the process. She seemed to enjoy all of it, actually. From start to finish. I'd never seen such a natural in front of the camera.

By the time the filming came to a close, I felt more than confident about the episode. In spite of the problems leading up to it, everything had come off without a hitch. Well, except for a few dropped lines from Lenora, but we were getting used to that.

After the audience members left, I dismissed the cast, thanking them for a wonderful day. Most headed off to wardrobe to get changed, but Lenora lingered near the cameras.

"You okay?" I asked.

"Oh, I, um . . ." She shrugged and gave me a sheepish grin. "I can't remember where I was going."

Rex appeared behind her and put his hand on her back. "Down the hall to wardrobe, sweet girl. It's time to get back into that beautiful gown you were wearing this morning."

"Gown?" She sighed. "I guess. But I'd rather just wear my flannel nightgown." She turned my way, shaking her head. "I simply don't understand why he won't let me wear my nightgown. It's the most comfortable item of clothing I own."

He stroked her arm. "I'll get you home right away, Lenora, and you can change into your flannel nightgown."

Her expression brightened. "The soft green one with the little roses on it?"

"Yes." Rex nodded. "I'll make us some hot chocolate and we'll watch an old movie together."

"Oh, that sounds wonderful."

He looked at me. "Looks like I won't be able to stay tonight, Tia. Can you handle the dailies without me?"

"Sure," I said, but I felt my insides turn to mush. I'd hoped to talk to Rex tonight, to tell him that Lenora had called *The Scoop*. Looked like it would have to wait till tomorrow.

He nodded, then took Lenora by the arm, guiding her down the hallway.

"That's love in action." Jason's voice rang out from behind me.

I turned, feeling the sting of tears in my eyes. "It is. I can only hope to have someone like Rex in my life, should I ever . . ." I didn't speak the words. I didn't dare. But to have someone walk alongside you through the really tough seasons would be incredible.

"He's amazing with her." Jason nodded. "And speaking of amazing, Erin did a great job, don't you think?"

"She was brilliant. Can't wait to head upstairs to watch the dailies." I paused, an idea coming to me. "Hey, Jason, I wonder if you could hang around and watch them with me. Rex has to take Lenora home, and Erin's got a meeting at school. She told me all about it this morning." I didn't want to tell him how much I hated hanging out in that dark theater alone, so I threw in a line of flattery to throw him off. "You've got a great eye."

He gave me a lingering glance and said, "Yes, I do."

My heart almost stopped beating right then and there.

"I'd love to join you," he added. "Just let me close up shop down here and I'll be right up."

"Perfect."

I stopped off at the dressing room to thank Erin for a magnificent job, but I found her too engaged in a conversation with Brock to realize I was there. Oh well. I'd tell her tomorrow.

When I arrived in the viewing room, I gave a few instructions to our editor, then settled back in my chair, waiting on Jason. He turned down the lights and took the seat next to me.

"Where's the popcorn?" he asked.

I laughed. "Yeah, we should probably keep some up here. Don't know why I never thought of it."

As we watched the various clips from today's show, our laughter rang out time and time again. Not everything was flawless, though. Looked like we'd have to redo both Lenora's scenes. I hated to have to tell Rex, but they would have to come back in tomorrow for a retake. Still, as Jason reached for my hand, none of the problems related to today's filming fazed me at all.

When we'd finished watching, Jason and I lingered in the dark room with only the glow from the frozen picture on the screen.

"I honestly think *Stars Collide* is the best sitcom on TV," he said. "I'm hooked on a lot of shows, but none of them has the heart and soul this one does."

"Can I tell you a little secret?" I whispered.

"Sure."

"I don't watch a lot of fictional TV, and I'm clueless when it comes to other shows. I keep up with the ratings and all that, but I honestly couldn't tell you who's in those other shows or even what they're about."

He gave me a funny look. "No way. You direct one of the most popular sitcoms on TV. How could you not watch the competition?"

I sighed. "The truth is, I watch mostly reality stuff. Competitions. Home renovation shows. I like to see things . . ." There was really only one word. "Flipped."

"Flipped?"

"Changed. Turned inside out. New leaf. Fresh start. I like shows where things—or people—start out one way and end up another. I'm a makeover-TV addict. I admit it."

"I see." He leaned a bit closer. "Is there a twelve-step program for this addiction?"

"In Hollywood? Probably. But I wouldn't have time to attend the sessions. Besides, a little reality TV never hurt anyone."

"Unless you happen to be the director of a non–reality show and need to stay on top of the competition." He crossed his arms. "But I'm confused. Didn't you direct a nighttime drama before you came to *Stars Collide*?"

"Yeah."

"*Give Me Liberty*, right?"

"Yes. I'll admit, I've directed other non–reality shows."

"You just never watch them."

I sighed.

He stared at me. "I used to love that show, by the way. Great exposé of life in the military. The stories were incredibly powerful . . . and the actors weren't shabby either." He paused. "Weren't you up for an Emmy for that one too?"

You had to go there.

"Yeah. I didn't win."

"But you were nominated. That's quite an honor."

"Can we change the subject?"

"Sure." His expression brightened. "I'll tell you anything you want to know about nighttime dramas. Or sitcoms. Or cop shows. I'm pretty much hooked on three or four of those."

"Not me. I grew up in South Central, you know. Every day

was a real-life episode of a cop show. I watch TV to escape, which is why I watch reality TV." After a pause, I added, "Guess I take after my mama when it comes to escapism. She's been hooked on *General Hospital* since the seventies. No joke. She can tell you every character's name, going back thirty-five years."

"What's the fascination?"

"I'm clueless. Those daytime dramas seem to drag the tiniest little things out for days. I truly don't understand the method to their madness."

"So your mom was inspired by soap operas. What did you watch as a kid?"

"Funny you should ask. I didn't watch a lot of regular shows even back then. I mean, c'mon. My mother and father weren't exactly Ozzie and Harriet. *The Love Boat* wasn't sailing out of port anytime soon in our neck of the woods. And *Beverly Hills, 90210* was just a TV show, not someplace I would ever live."

"Ah." He pursed his lips. "So you didn't watch any sitcoms?"

"Just one. *The Fresh Prince of Bel-Air*."

"Oh? You're a Will Smith fan?"

"Well, yeah, that too. But the idea of picking up and moving from the inner city to Bel-Air? It held a lot of appeal for a kid from South Central. I always felt like I'd been born in the wrong world."

"God knew what he was doing, dropping you into the heart of the city."

I sighed. "Therein lies the rub. If I admit that God knew what he was doing by bringing me into this world in the projects, then he and I need to have a long discussion about the reasoning behind that decision."

"So you're saying God made a mistake?"

Ugh. Did we have to go there? Really?

"God doesn't make mistakes," Jason continued.

"Easy to say when you were raised in Newport Beach." I slapped my hand over my mouth. Had I really just spoken those words out loud? Judging from the look on his face, yes.

"I don't want to preach. But just consider this one thing: an upbringing in a fancy house doesn't necessarily make for a happy life. And an upbringing in a home where you faced major struggles doesn't mean you'll have restrictions in life. How we end up . . . well, that's up to us."

"Right." I chewed on his words for a minute.

"I'm sorry, Tia. I didn't mean to hurt your feelings. I guess you've figured out I'm pretty good at speaking my mind, whether people want to hear or not."

"I like a person who speaks his mind." I rose and walked to the light switch. Before I could turn it on, however, Jason's hand stopped me. I turned to face him, curious.

"Before you do that . . ." He paused. "There's something I want to tell you. I started to say it at the commissary before Lenora showed up."

"Oh?"

For a moment, he didn't say anything. I could almost hear the wheels clicking in his head. "All my adult life, I've been told I have a good eye," he said at last. "You said it downstairs less than an hour ago. That's what I'm known for. Shooting great angles. Having great focus." He paused again. "But sometimes my eyes deceive me."

"What do you mean?"

"Sometimes I'm so busy with the narrow focus that I don't see the bigger picture—what's going on outside of the set, for instance. And sometimes I'm so distracted with what I see right in front of me that I don't realize the angle's wrong."

I couldn't figure out where he was going with this. "Are you admitting that you make mistakes?" I asked.

"Oh, I make mistakes every day, but some are bigger than

others." He drew closer. "I've been watching you out of the corner of my eye for nearly a year now, Tia, but you've deserved my full attention, not just a halfhearted glance."

Not exactly a line our writers would've written, but it made perfect sense to me and had just the right romantic angle. Strangely, I could only manage a one-word response. "O-oh?"

He leaned in and stroked my cheek with his fingertip. "You came tearing in here, ready to take the world by storm. And I'll admit, you got all of us riled up those first few weeks. You were hard as nails, but about the prettiest thing I'd ever laid eyes on. I called you the Spanish Spitfire."

"You did?" I couldn't help the sigh that escaped. "I'm pretty sure everyone hated me back then. Some more than others." As I stared into his eyes, that butterfly sensation wriggled its way across my stomach.

In that moment, I saw a pain in his eyes I'd never noticed before. Not anger. Something else entirely. "You—you think I hated you?" He slipped his arm around my waist and drew me to him. "You really think that?"

"I—I . . ." Now I wasn't sure what I thought.

"You're the toughest woman I've ever met, I'll give you that. Just because you're good at whipping people into shape doesn't mean I hate you. I . . . I respect you. I always have, right back to that first day."

"You did . . . you do?" Suddenly I felt discombobulated.

"Of course. And yeah, we butt heads, but that's because we're so much alike. I was used to working with a more placid director. You . . ." He gazed into my eyes, drawing me so close that I felt the air shoot out of me. "You're different."

"So they tell me." I couldn't help the little laugh that followed.

"They're right."

206

He reached to brush a loose hair out of my face, and a shiver ran through me. *What's happening here?*

"If I come across as angry to you, then it's just misdirected emotions. Trust me, it's not anger."

"It—it's not?" My heart started doing this strange twisting thing as he placed a couple of tender kisses on my forehead. Surely I must be imagining all of this. I gazed up into those beautiful eyes and sighed. "You're making it hard for me to be mad at you right now."

"Good. Because frankly, I'm tired of pretending like we're always mad at each other when we're really something else altogether."

"We—we are?" I never had a chance to say anything else because his lips blocked the way. Within seconds I found myself on the receiving end of the world's most passionate kiss. A spine-tingling, heart-throbbing, weak-in-the-knees kiss that would've made our sitcom stars swoon.

Talk about a shocker. In my thirty years on Planet Earth, I'd never experienced a kiss like this. Directed one—sure. Experienced one—never. As the kiss lingered, I sensed every emotion he'd been holding inside. Every question I'd ever had about Jason Harris was answered. In that moment, a thousand thoughts went through my head, none of which had anything to do with *Stars Collide.* He had me completely off-kilter, and I was loving every minute of it.

One of Mama's favorite phrases ran through my mind: *A la ocasion la pintan calva.* "Strike while the iron is hot."

The iron was hot, all right. And if I'd had any doubt in my mind, the kiss that followed only added more fuel to the fire. Yes, things were definitely heating up on the *Stars Collide* set, and I couldn't help but think the best was yet to come.

20

Law and Order

I somehow buzzed through work on Friday, trying not to let my happy heart become the subject of too much attention on the set. Since we had to reshoot both of Lenora's scenes, we ended up calling back all of the cast members involved. Brock and Erin didn't seem to mind. In fact, they seemed to be inseparable these days. And they were especially delighted to do a retake on the kissing scene. Go figure.

Afterward Rex asked to speak to me. I offered him my director's chair, and he sat.

"You heard that Brock got an offer to perform on *Dancing with the Stars*, didn't you?"

"No." I gasped. "Is he going to do it?"

"Well, it's next season's show, so we're talking next fall. By then Kat will be back on the set and everything will be back to normal between Jack and Angie."

I sniggered. "Since when has anything been normal on the *Stars Collide* set, Rex?"

He laughed. "Okay, well, you know what I mean. When Kat comes back, we can probably spare Brock, though I do want to keep him in the storyline the whole time. I'd be thrilled if he decided to stay on with us for years to come."

"I wonder if he can dance."

"I guess we'll see." Rex grinned. He paused, and I could tell he had something else on his mind.

"What is it?"

"Well, I didn't want to tell anyone, but they want Lenora to do the show too."

"No way."

"Yes. Apparently they've had quite a few senior citizens on the show in recent years, and the crowd has gone crazy for them."

"Yeah, you should've seen the year Cloris Leachman danced," I said. "And Florence Henderson. It was a lot of fun to watch. Oh, and Priscilla Presley was on the show one year too. She's in such great shape, though. I couldn't believe she was really in her sixties. She looks remarkably young. Then again, she was married to the king of rock and roll. I guess that'll keep you young."

His eyes narrowed. "You watch *Dancing with the Stars*, Tia?"

"Oh, well, I . . . doesn't everyone?"

He laughed. "Well, not me. And just so you know, I haven't told Lenora. I can't imagine she would be up to it. But Brock will probably do it. It'll be great for the show, and probably for his career too."

"Right."

"I just wanted to tell you because we'll need to think ahead."

"That's me, always thinking ahead." I saluted him.

"Oh, honey, are you auditioning for a military movie?" Lenora said from behind me.

"No, I was just—"

"Because if you are, you might want to know that you always salute with your right hand." She gave me a wink. "Just thought you'd like to know."

She did a funny little dance across the stage, and I looked at Rex and smiled. "Her dance skills are impeccable. You might want to reconsider."

"That blessed woman has already caused me to reconsider nearly everything else in my life," he said. "So why not?" He headed off to join her in the dance. I watched from a distance as they waltzed together around the set. They touched my heart with their tenderness toward one another.

The soundstage cleared, and Jason and I were left alone at last. He drew near and pulled me into his arms. That tingling sensation washed over me again.

"Missed you," he whispered.

"I was right here."

"I know. But I still missed you."

Well, if that didn't make a girl feel good, I didn't know what would.

He leaned in to give me a kiss I wouldn't soon forget. I got so wrapped up in the moment that I almost forgot we still had writers down the hall. Only when Athena cleared her throat did I catch on to the fact that we weren't alone.

I felt heat rush to my cheeks, and I took a giant step back from Jason, who had that deer-caught-in-the-headlights look on his face.

"I, um, well, I guess I'll just go on back to my office." Athena laid the script on my chair. "You can look at this, um, later."

She left, and Jason and I both dissolved in laughter.

"Guess our secret's out." He wiggled his brows. "I, for one, am glad."

"Me too." I gave him a little kiss on the nose.

"Good. Now that that's behind us, let's talk about food."

"Food?" I said. "What about it?"

"I need some. We skipped lunch."

"Oh, I was actually headed to my mother's place. It's kind of a Friday night tradition for our family. She's cooking . . ." I let my words drift off. Mama was doing her usual Friday night thing. Tamales. "Traditional Mexican fare."

"Homemade Mexican food?" I could practically see him drooling.

"You . . . you want to come?"

He nodded and reached for my hand. "Yes, but let's get something straight."

"O-okay."

"I'm not just coming for the food. I want to meet your parents. Your whole family, actually. That okay?"

My heart began that strange twisting sensation again, and I found myself caught up in his eyes. I wanted to respond but couldn't think of anything to say. He'd met my sister and survived. Surely we could get past meeting the rest of the family. I hoped.

"Anything I need to know before I meet your parents?" he asked as we headed out to the parking lot.

"Well, I told you they separated, and now they're back together."

"Right. What else?"

"My mother has a Chihuahua."

"One of those tiny little dogs that looks like a rat?"

"Please don't say that in her presence. She got him as a gift years ago from my father."

When he came home after several weeks of carousing with another woman, but I'll skip that part for now.

"Anyway, she's in love with that little dog. It's the most

211

annoying canine you'll ever meet—barks like a maniac when people come in the door and doesn't stop until you've been there awhile. I always like to tell people before they get to the house."

"Okay, what else?"

"Mama loves to be complimented on her cooking." I laughed. "Funny, I know. The mother can cook, but the daughter can't."

"Hey, I thought your chicken cacciatore was pretty good."

"Ha. Like I made that myself."

"You did. With a little help from a friend." He kissed me again, and I was swept away.

Jason offered to drive, so I left my car on the lot. He opened the door for me—a true gentleman—and I climbed into the passenger seat.

We arrived at Mama's house at six, and I half expected Jason to turn and hightail it back to Newport Beach as soon as he got a look at the neighborhood. But he kept his cool, even leaving his BMW parked at the curb without comment.

"So, who comes to dinner on Friday nights?" he asked as he opened the car door for me.

"Oh, everyone. All of my brothers and my sister. It's a tradition. Mama's been cooking all day, I can assure you. She lives for Fridays."

"And you're sure she won't mind that I'm here?"

"Oh no. She loves it when we bring people over. My brother Carlos will be here with his wife and kids. And Humberto— he's my middle brother—has a girlfriend who comes about half the time. I'm sure Beni's invited Julio. He's, well . . ." I decided to stop right there. No point in ruining a perfectly good Friday night.

"And your parents?" Jason looked worried. "Are they going to welcome me with open arms?"

"See for yourself." I pointed to my mother, who stood in the doorway of the house, a broad smile on her face.

"Who is this, Tia-mia?" She clasped her hands together at her chest. "A handsome stranger from Hollywood? A big star?"

"I'm no star, trust me, Mrs. Morales." Jason took several steps in Mama's direction. "Just a cameraman. Part of the tech crew."

Mama's dog began to yap and lunged forward to tug on Jason's pants leg. He managed to wriggle free.

"Well, if you're part of the tech crew, then you're a key player. That show couldn't go on without you, now could it?" Mama scooped up the ornery pup and turned to give me a "he's good-looking, Tia!" glance. She continued chattering, slipping into Spanish from time to time.

Jason didn't seem to mind. In fact, he managed to hold up his end of the conversation even when her English failed.

We made our way inside, and I introduced Jason to Humberto and his girlfriend, Kate. I started to ask him how things were going at my house but decided to skip it. That was a conversation for another day. Besides, I couldn't get past the fact that I suddenly felt like sneezing again. Odd.

Benita rushed through the room, pausing long enough to give Jason a curious glance, then headed off to the bathroom claiming she needed to touch up her eyeliner.

By five thirty, Carlos and Maria had arrived with their three kids. Gabe joined us minutes later. Mama brought a bowl of salsa into the living room, and we all dove in, devouring the chips she placed alongside the bowl.

"Jason, you try it." Mama pushed the bowl in his direction.

He stuck in a chip—homemade, of course—and his eyes glazed over as he bit into it. "This salsa . . ." He shook his head and pointed to the bowl.

"Too spicy?" Mama's brow wrinkled.

"No, not at all."

"Too mild?" she asked, still looking a little nervous.

"No, it's perfect. I'm not just saying this—it's the best I've ever had. Ever. In my life. Bar none." He took another bite, a contented look on his face.

Mama began to celebrate in fluid Spanish, likely forgetting that he probably understood every word.

"Come!" She grabbed him by the hand and pulled him from the sofa. "I'll show you how it's done. Then you and Tia can make it for your children."

Lovely. Now he'd have to marry me or face the wrath of my mother and her jalapeños.

We followed on Mama's heels into the kitchen, where she went to work chopping tomatoes, onions, cilantro, and peppers. Jason watched, even taking notes as she went along. When she squeezed the lime juice into the mixture, the kitchen came alive with the aroma.

We'd no sooner finished the salsa than the doorbell rang. I could hardly believe it when I saw Bob—writer Bob—on the other side.

"Hey, Tia." He straightened his collar. "Do I look okay?"

"Um, sure." I gestured for him to come inside, confusion registering.

"Beni told me to be here at six."

"Ah." Well, go figure. She'd invited him to dinner?

Benita walked in, took one look at Bob, and went into a panic. She grabbed me by the arm and pulled me back into the kitchen. "Oh, help!"

"What?" I grabbed another chip and took a bite, then leaned against the counter. "What's the big deal?"

"I totally forgot Bob was coming tonight. I invited him that day I was so mad at you. I . . . well, I didn't really mean it."

"So what? He's a great guy. Just spend the evening with him, then break his heart tomorrow." I finished off the chip and shrugged.

"You don't understand. I—" The doorbell rang again. Her eyes widened and I could read the terror in them. "That's Julio."

"Oops." I laughed, suddenly delighted to see my sister in such a pickle. She deserved this. Still, the girl looked like she might be sick.

"So play it off like you're all just good friends." I gave her a curious look. "You are good friends, right? You like Bob? He's a great guy, you know."

Her expression relaxed. "What's not to like about Bob? He's amazing. He's got the kindest heart. And he seems to know me even better than I know myself." She sighed. "But Julio . . . Tia, he's gorgeous. I'm not sure he remembers my name half the time, but with eyes like that, who cares?"

"You should care."

Did I really just say that out loud?

"Anyway, we'll just have a fun time. And when the evening's over . . ." She pursed her lips. "Hmm. Julio will probably want to go out and do something after. But I think I told Bob I'd go to a movie with him. That might be a problem." She gave me a hopeful look. "Take one of them off my hands, Tia? Bob, maybe?"

"No way. In case you haven't noticed, I have a guy of my own here tonight."

"Yeah." Benita's thinly plucked brows wiggled. "And in case I haven't mentioned it, Jason looks really hot tonight. That blue shirt is great. He's got amazing taste. And did you notice his car?"

I nodded. "Yes, he drove me here in that car. But just for the record, I would like him even if he drove a Ford Taurus."

"No you wouldn't."

I reached for a tissue to dab at my runny nose. "Bob drives a Taurus."

"Well, that seals it. I can't go out with him." She reached for a chip, dunked it in the salsa, and took a bite.

"I'm totally kidding. I have no idea what Bob drives. Just testing you."

"Okay, I failed that test," she said. "So sue me. You know I like nice things." She squared her shoulders. "Okay, here I go. Out to handle two men. If it looks like I'm drowning, throw me a life preserver."

Might be more fun to throw her a brick, under the circumstances. Watching her squirm between Bob and Julio would be entertaining, no doubt.

Except that I already had someone to keep my attention. I grabbed a can of Coke from the fridge and headed back to the living room, handing the drink to Jason with a smile.

"Now, how did you know I needed that?" he asked.

"Easy. You're eating salsa. Coke and salsa always go together." I released a trio of sneezes, and he offered a cheerful "God bless you."

We settled into an easy conversation with the others, and before long, my father arrived. I rose to introduce him to Jason, who shook his hand and offered a few polite words of conversation. Moments later, we were all seated at the table, eating tamales, rice, and beans. The first few minutes went really well, particularly the part where Gabe asked about Jason's job. As he talked about his role on the *Stars Collide* set, I focused on my father, who listened in silence.

My gaze occasionally shifted to Benita. In spite of the fact that she was seated between two guys of her own, she managed to flirt with Jason throughout the meal. Thank goodness he seemed oblivious. I was not. Neither was Mama. At least three times I caught her casting a warning look at my sister.

It didn't stop her. She continued to flirt and tease all of the guys. It didn't take much to keep Bob interested, but Julio seemed a little put off by her attentions. And Jason . . . well, he finally caught on and looked like he wanted to bolt from the room.

After dinner, I offered to help Mama in the kitchen. I needed time to cool down. Unfortunately—or fortunately—Benita decided to join us.

"Aren't we the luckiest two girls in town?" She giggled. "Three great guys and only two of us. What a dilemma!"

I looked her way, completely stunned. "You're hopeless."

"I am?" Confusion registered in her eyes. "How so?"

"You already have two guys to choose from—one of them really great, I might add—and you hit on the only one who's ever given me a second glance?"

She looked shocked at my outburst. "Tia, calm down. I wasn't hitting on him."

"You called him a hottie and complimented his eyes."

"So what?" She shrugged. "That's what I do."

"Well, stop doing it. What are you trying to prove, anyway? That you can have any man you like?"

"Good grief, Tia. I was just playing around. Stop making such a big deal out of it." She turned to Mama. "Mama, make her stop. She's being ridiculous."

"I don't think it's ridiculous." My mother stopped washing the dishes long enough to look Benita's way. "What you did in there was completely out of line."

"Oh, please." She rolled her eyes. "I was just messing around. I told you, it's no big deal."

"It *is* a big deal," I argued.

Mama shook her head. "Beni, what has happened to my sweet, innocent little girl?"

Benita's face contorted. "She grew up, Mama. And she's

ready for a little fun. Ready to turn a few heads. Nothing wrong with that."

"Everything is wrong with that." Where should I begin? By telling her that giving pieces of herself to a man was intrinsically wrong? That her willingness to split herself between so many people of the opposite sex was a flaw she'd gleaned from our father? That she didn't need to go looking for the love she needed . . . that God was ready to sweep her into his arms and show her the kind of love she'd been looking for elsewhere?

"You've always done things your way, Tia, and I've done them mine." Benita reached for her purse. "You win them over with your intelligence and directing skills. I win them over with my . . ." She shrugged, then gestured to her body. A feeling of nausea swept over me.

My father entered the kitchen, humming a song. Benita swept past him into the living room. I watched through the open kitchen door as she looked back and forth between Bob and Julio.

"Come on, both of you. Let's get out of here."

"But we haven't had dessert yet," Julio said with a pout. "Your mom made flan."

"And I wanted some of your dad's coffee," Bob said. "He just went into the kitchen to make it."

"We'll go to Starbucks." Benita opened the front door. "Anywhere but here. Come on." She stormed out, and the two guys looked at each other.

Bob's backbone remained intact. He shrugged and said to Julio, "You go on. I'm staying here."

"Weird. I was just about to say the same thing to you." Julio sighed and followed after Benita, calling her name.

Mama glanced at my father and sighed. "What are we going to do with that girl?" She looked Bob's way. "I'm so sorry."

He shrugged. "Coffee ready?"

My father gestured for Bob to join us in the kitchen. Poor Jason. We'd left him alone in the living room with my brothers and the kids. Hopefully he would forgive me. Right now I had to take care of something important.

With my hands on my hips, I turned to my mother. "Mama, she's impossible."

"*Borrón y cuenta nueva*, Tia."

I didn't want to let bygones be bygones. I'd tried that approach before. Right now I just wanted to put Benita in her place. As soon as I got this sneezing fit under control.

I managed to get calmed down after snuggling into the loveseat alongside Jason and drinking a cup of coffee. Afterward, Bob thanked my parents for a great time and headed off on his way. Carlos and his crew watched television until he fell asleep on the sofa, at which point Maria woke him up and offered to drive home. Humberto and Kate headed out to see a late movie. My parents disappeared into the kitchen to wash dishes, which left me alone with Jason in the living room.

"So, there you go," I said. "You've met the Morales clan."

He nodded. "I like them, Tia."

"Sure you do."

"No, I really do. I mean, your sister's a piece of work, but I think she's just . . ."

"Being herself."

"Yeah. Anyway, besides that, I had a really good time. Your mom is great, and I like Humberto a lot. And Gabe too. He's a great kid."

"Yeah. He is." I nuzzled up against Jason, ready to relax.

He leaned down and whispered in my ear, "You know how I told you that you have walls up?"

"Yeah." I sighed.

"I'm starting to get it now. Your life here—outside of the studio—is so different from your life inside the studio." He paused. "Out here, you're not in charge of everything like you are on the set."

"I know. It stinks. I'm pretty sure I could have done a better job directing the scene we just watched."

"Better than God?"

Ugh. "No, I mean . . . I don't know what I mean."

"Well, I get it. I really do. You can't control what happens in the real world like you can at the studio. And I'm sure that's got to bother you. Am I right?"

I hated to say yes, but what else could I do? He'd hit the nail on the head.

"I think I've figured out why you like being in charge. It gives you a sense of security. And there's nothing wrong with that . . . when you're on the set. But you're not on the set right now."

"I wish I was." A little sigh escaped. "Take me back now?"

"Really? You're ready to go?"

I nodded, feeling sick about everything that had happened. After tonight, Jason would probably run as fast and as far away as he could. Not that I would blame him. No, if the shoe were on the other foot, I would've already used it to jog out of South Central and back to Newport Beach.

21

Better with You

The rest of the weekend was—thankfully—uneventful. Jason called on Saturday to say that he had to go out of town for his uncle's birthday and would call when he got there. Unfortunately, Saturday rolled into Sunday, and I didn't hear from him. By the time I awoke on Monday morning, I decided he'd probably run for the hills. Who could blame him, really?

Besides, I had other things on my mind this morning. Allergy tests, to be precise. My eight o'clock appointment with Dr. Kennedy was first and foremost on my mind.

On the way to the doctor, I called my mother. I just needed to hear her voice. She answered on the second ring. "Good morning, Tia-mia. How's my girl today?"

I sighed. "Headed to the doctor for these allergy tests."

"Oh, I'd forgotten about that. You'll have to call me after to let me know how it went, okay?"

"Yeah." I paused.

"Everything okay, Tia?"

"It's probably better if we don't talk about me, okay?" I swallowed the lump in my throat and pulled onto the 405. "What's going on over there?"

"Oh, Dad's just working on the loose pipe under the kitchen sink. He noticed it was leaking last night. He's trying to get everything in the house fixed before the summer. He said it's his gift to me."

The summer. I'd almost forgotten. Summer was just a few weeks away. I'd been so caught up in the show that the time had slipped right by me. I found it interesting that my father had a sudden interest in home repair. For years he'd put off taking care of things around the house.

"He seems really different this time, Tia," Mama said. "I don't know how to explain it exactly, but it's almost like he's the man I married once again."

I paused, almost afraid to ask the question. "So, are you saying you think things will work out this time?"

"I don't know. I do know that he's been more attentive than ever." She paused. "Tia, I don't need to involve you in my situation with your father, especially after watching what your sister did to you the other night. You don't need all of my drama on top of what you're already going through."

"I'm interested in what you're going through. Maybe I haven't shown it in the right way, I don't know. But I've figured out that I can't fix it."

"Well, honey, I never wanted you to."

Her words took me by surprise. "You didn't?"

"No. Just needed someone to talk to, I guess. You're so grown up now and have such a way about you. I can tell you things I've never told anyone else. But I guess I've burdened you. I never meant to do that, Tia-mia. Forgive me?"

"Well, sure." I could hardly believe my ears.

"We both have a fix-it mentality, Tia. I don't know if you've noticed, but I've been trying to fix your father for over thirty years. It took me almost that long to figure out that it's going to take something—or rather, some*one*—bigger than me to fix this situation."

"I guess I do come by it honestly." I pondered the fact that I'd gone to school so that I could learn how to lead and direct. I really did come by it honestly. But somewhere along the way, I started thinking that I needed to fix everything—not just things on the set but things in my own life too.

Mama's voice jarred me back to attention. "You were always that way, Tia," she said. "From the time you were a little girl."

"Oh?"

"Sure." She chuckled. "Don't you remember the time your brother broke the thermostat and you tried to fix it? You wired it backwards and blew up the fan in the attic."

"Yeah." I sighed.

"And what about the time the rent was overdue and we thought we were going to lose the house? You're the one who put together a plan to raise the money."

Wow. I'd forgotten all about that.

"There's nothing wrong with having a heart for people. Yours is so soft that I think we sometimes take advantage of it. I know for a fact that your sister did the other night. And I've seen Carlos pull some stunts on you too. I can't believe you haven't knocked him upside the head yet."

I hardly knew what to say. She'd never told me I had a soft heart before, so that totally threw me. But what really got to me was the admission that people in my family took advantage of me.

"You're wiser than your thirty years, honey," Mama said. "You're so grown up that sometimes I forget you're still young." She paused. "So, tell me what's going on with you, Tia. I'm always telling you about my troubles, but I've noticed you never tell me yours."

Her words reminded me of the conversation with Jason last Saturday. I'd done my best to tear down those walls. Might as well come clean and tell Mama my troubles. Seemed like she was really interested.

"I have a lot on my mind. I've been trying to have a more laid-back approach to life. And there are days when I succeed. I really do. I hand things over to God and keep my hands off. But it doesn't seem to stick. One day goes great, the next is a mess."

"That's life. That's why we keep trying," she said. "But what's really bothering you? There's more to it than that."

"Most of it has to do with Jason."

"Ah, that handsome cameraman. Your dad and I really liked him, by the way. We hope you'll bring him back around sometime. He was awfully nice."

"I agree."

And I hope he'll come back around after the way Benita acted.

I opened up and shared my concerns with my mother. Like all good mothers, she gave me advice, most of it in Spanish. She even promised to pray. That meant more to me than anything.

We ended the call, and I felt like my spirits had truly been lifted. Sharing my struggles with someone else really did help. Maybe, if I could keep my guard down long enough, I'd get used to the idea of opening up and talking to people about the things that bothered me.

I arrived at the allergist's office, unsure of what to expect but ready to get this over with. The nurse came in and prepped me, then asked me to get undressed and into a gown. Soon Dr. Kennedy arrived, buzzing with excitement.

"You're here. I've been looking forward to this visit." She opened my chart, glanced at it, and looked my way. "Well, let's get this ball rolling, shall we?" She started by drawing blood to send to the lab, and then she began the process of testing me, using needle pricks on my back and arms.

Dr. Kennedy chattered throughout the process, going on and on about Scott and Kat Murphy and even Lenora. I tried to focus on the skin pricks. Though most of them caused a tingling sensation, they weren't really painful. Well, not terribly painful.

"This one's for mold." I felt a little stick on my back. "And this one is for cat dander. Do you have a cat?"

"No." But I sneezed just thinking about it.

"This one is for pollen."

On and on she went, doing the little needle pricks down my back and my left arm. Dogs, ragweed, a variety of foods and trees—she tested me for them all.

As she worked, she continued to pepper me with questions I couldn't avoid about the show. "Okay, I know the episode with Angie's delivery airs soon, but what comes next? How are you guys filling in the gap for the rest of this season? I'm assuming she'll be back in the fall, right?"

"Right." I fought the temptation to tell her about Brock Benson's new role on the show or his upcoming stint on *Dancing with the Stars*. That would surely send her over the edge. Instead, I talked about the children and the role they would play in wrapping up the season. That seemed to satisfy her.

Dr. Kennedy finished the testing, then told me to wait twenty minutes for the results. By the time she came back in the room, I would've given my left arm for a back scratcher.

"Interesting." She nodded as she examined me. "It's not just mold and dust. You'll need to keep your distance from dogs too, I'm afraid."

No wonder I always got hives around my mother's Chihuahua. I'd considered it an aversion issue, not allergies.

"I see several positive reactions here." She pointed to my arm. "No wonder you've been sneezing." Dr. Kennedy wrote out several prescriptions, instructed me to come back in a week to start allergy shots, handed me an allergy tablet to take ASAP, and sent me on my way.

The trip to the studio was miserable. Every square inch of my back itched. I found it maddening. I'd hoped the itching would resolve itself before I got to the studio, but it did not. I arrived inside, leaned back against the doorjamb, and scratched until I felt some relief. Finally I headed down the hallway to see if our writers had arrived. It was Monday, and Monday always meant baklava. Thank goodness Athena and Stephen had brought a large tray. I'd skipped breakfast.

"Wow, Tia." Athena laughed. "You must be in love."

"What?"

"Well, when I fell for Stephen, I couldn't stop eating."

"I thought it was the other way around. I thought being in love made you unable to eat." The itching in my back began again, and I squirmed.

Athena gave me a funny look. "I'm Greek, Tia. To not eat would be a curse, not a blessing."

"Ha." That got me tickled. Great. Tickled and itching. "Hey, I stopped by to ask a favor."

"Sure. What's up?"

"Erin did such a great job, so can we keep her character going?"

Athena laughed and looked at Stephen, then back at me. "It's so funny you should say that. We were just talking about how awesome it would be to keep up that relationship between Brock's character and Erin's. The viewers are going to love it."

226

"I read the final script over the weekend, but I really want to add Erin into it before the roundtable reading. Any chance we could pull that off?" I continued to squirm but did my best not to let it show.

"Watch me try." Athena reached for her laptop and dove right in.

I stopped off in the ladies' room to pull up my shirt and look at my back. I'd never seen anything quite like it. Rows and rows of blisters. Why hadn't that antihistamine kicked in yet?

Oh well. Maybe if I stayed focused on my job, the itching would subside. I went in search of Rex and found him in his office. I rapped on the door and he looked my way.

"Rex, I need to talk to you. Do you have a minute?"

"Sure." He swiveled his chair around and gestured for me to come in. "Something happen?"

"Yeah, I've been trying to get you alone for a while now to tell you."

"What's up?"

I released a slow breath, trying to work up the courage to share. "I hate to tell you this, but Lenora was the one who leaked the story about Little Ricky to the tabloids."

"What?" His eyes narrowed into slits and he shook his head. "How? And when?"

"She told me a few days ago that she'd called some reporter named Ted Holliday at *The Scoop*. I'm not sure when it happened exactly. Must've been right after the baby was born."

"Ted Holliday?" Rex sighed. "Tia, he died years ago. I tried to tell her that, but she doesn't remember."

"I figured. But she talked to someone there and told them everything—the sex of the baby and the name."

He pursed his lips and swiveled his chair back around. After a couple minutes of strained silence, he glanced back

at me. "I'm sorry it happened, Tia. But it's a wake-up call."
Another pause followed . . . so long that I finally slipped out
of the room to leave Rex alone.

By the time I made it back to the soundstage, most of my
crew had arrived. When I saw Jason approach, I held my
breath, wondering if he would talk to me.

"Tia." He reached for my hand.

"Are you still speaking to me?" I whispered. "I didn't hear
from you all weekend."

"Yes." He groaned. "I feel terrible that I didn't call you.
You're not going to believe what happened. We went to the
beach while we were at my uncle's place, and one of the kids
got ahold of my phone."

"Oh?" The itching in my back kicked in again, but there
was nothing I could do about it. I wriggled and twisted, but
nothing seemed to help.

He gave me a funny look, then dissolved into a dramatic
sigh. "Yeah. I didn't even realize it until after the fact, but she
got in the water with it. The whole phone was shot. That's
why I'm a little late this morning. I had to stop off at the cell
phone place on Sunset and get another one to replace it."

My heart wanted to sing at this news. To dance around
the soundstage and proclaim that he hadn't run for the hills
after all. I gazed into those beautiful green eyes and grinned.
"I'm sorry about your phone, but I'm glad you're still speaking to me. After Friday night, I wasn't sure you'd want to."

"Friday night?" He looked perplexed.

"Well, yeah. After all that stuff with my sister."

If this itching doesn't stop, I'm going to scream.

Jason chuckled. "I can't believe you were worried about
that. How could I possibly blame you for something one of
your siblings did?"

Whoa. Why those words hit me so hard, I couldn't be sure.

All my life I'd taken the blame—or would that be shame?—for the things my siblings had done. And now here stood a man telling me I didn't have to do that anymore. Quite a revelation.

"I've spent most of my adult life making apologies for things my family members have done. And I've gone overboard trying to make things better for all of them." I gave a little shrug. "I've always wanted things to get better."

"Maybe they will."

"I used to hope for it all the time. Every time my dad would come back home, I'd get my hopes up again. And then they would be dashed. So maybe I'm just jaded."

"This is Hollywood, Tia. Everyone is jaded." He gave me a little kiss on the cheek, and I didn't even mind that the rest of the crew was looking on. "Can I ask you a question?"

"Sure." I tugged at my collar, hoping the movement of my shirt against my back would help the itching.

"You wish you knew what was coming next with your parents, don't you?"

"Well, yeah. It would be nice."

"Are you saying you wish you could see into the future?"

Interesting question. "I don't know. I mean, no, I don't. Or yes, I do." I groaned. "I'm glad I can't see what's coming tomorrow, because what if I didn't like what I saw? It's probably a blessing that I don't know the bad stuff. But there would be a certain sense of security in knowing the hard things—the things I'm unsure about—were going to work out okay. Is that so bad?"

"Just one more question."

I shrugged. "What's that?"

"If you got your wish and could see that everything was going to work out, why would you need to have faith?"

"What do you mean?"

"I mean, there would be no need for faith at all if you already knew the outcome."

"Ah." I took a few steps toward my director's chair and sat down. "Never really thought about that. I'm just always thinking like a director. You know? A director *always* knows what's coming next. All I have to do is flip the page and read the dialogue and narrative. And if I don't like what I see, I send the script back for a rewrite."

"Tia . . ." He took my hand. "You can't send the script of your life back."

"I know." A lingering sigh followed. "That's the problem, don't you see?"

"I see one thing, Tia. I see a girl who's wrestling with letting go of the reins. And I don't claim to have a lot of expertise in this area, but I do know that it's always better to take your hands off of situations that aren't yours to control. Whether it's stuff to do with your family or things in your personal life, you've got to let go and admit you're not supposed to be the one directing the show."

"Mama and I were just talking about this. She says I've been a fixer ever since I was a little girl." I breathed a sigh of relief, realizing the itching sensation was finally subsiding.

"So it's going to be harder for you than most people. I get that." He gave me the sweetest smile. "But I can tell you, based on personal experience, that letting go—really letting go—will change your life."

At this point we stopped talking for a couple minutes while others—mainly Scott and Lenora—passed by. We said our good mornings, Jason commented on Lenora's costume of the day, and then I looked back at him.

"Sometimes I think it would be easier to be like Lenora, to have no memory of the things that happened yesterday."

"Tia, you don't mean that."

I bit my lip. "If you can't remember the horrible things that happened yesterday, then they can't hurt you."

"Okay, I'll admit that's true. But the past is what makes us who we are. It shapes our character."

"I feel overshaped."

He gave me a playful look. "I'm not going to respond, on the grounds that it could incriminate me."

His words lightened the mood.

"Promise me one thing, Tia." He gave my hand a squeeze.

"Sure. What's that?"

"When the weather warms up, you'll go surfing with me."

"S-surfing?" Was he kidding? I'd kill myself.

"Remember what we talked about that day in Scott and Kat's kitchen? About the feeling of freedom you get when you're surfing?"

"Well, sure, but we were just talking. Talking about it and doing it are two different things."

"Exactly my point. I want you to experience what it feels like to let go. To really, truly let go and just ride the wave. Let it take you where you need to be."

"I don't know, Jason." I stood and took a couple of steps away from him. "I would be so afraid—"

"Exactly." He grabbed my hand. "On the water, you have to admit your fear and give it up—all at the same time. It's a great rehearsal for life, Tia. And I promise you'll love it."

"You think?"

"I know. And you'll thank me later."

"You obviously haven't figured out what a control freak I am."

"Yes I have. But I see something else. I see a girl who's capable of forgiving and moving forward."

His words boosted my confidence, though that part where he agreed that I was a control freak did sting a little. "Hey, speaking of forgiveness . . ." I looked across the studio and saw that Benita had entered. "There's one more thing I have to take care of before we start the roundtable reading."

My heart felt heavy as I saw the sour expression on Benita's face. How many times would it come back to this? Were the two of us really going to be at odds—again?

Not if I could help it. While I didn't agree with what she'd done, I had to be the bigger person. Lead by example. Use a more laid-back approach.

Turning in her direction, I made up my mind to do just that.

22

The Wonder Years

After drawing a deep breath and ushering up a quick, silent prayer, I walked over to my sister and asked if I could speak with her alone. She looked like a nervous wreck as she followed me into the hallway. I grabbed her hand and gave it a squeeze. "Beni, there's something I need to say."

Before I could utter a word, her eyes filled with tears and she put her hand up. "Tia, don't."

"Don't what?"

"Apologize."

Actually, I hadn't planned to apologize this time. I'd just wanted to break the ice so we could get on with the day without all of the tension.

She sniffled. "I know what you're going to say, and you're right."

"I am?"

"I was flirting with Jason on Friday night. I admit it. He's a great-looking guy." She sighed. "You know my problem, Tia. I can't seem to help myself around hot guys. I can't."

"You can try."

"I should." She spoke the words as if this were the first time she'd considered that option. "Maybe I will."

"Beni, you know I love you, right?"

"Yeah. So why do I have the feeling you're about to chew me out?"

"I'm not going to chew you out. I'm just going to tell you something that came to me when I was praying for you last night."

"Wait. You were praying for me last night?" Her mouth rounded in a perfect O.

"Yes. Before bed. Anyway, it occurred to me that maybe the reason you're so drawn to guys is because you're trying to fill some sort of hole inside of you."

"Hole?"

"It's just a thought. After all the stuff Dad has put us through, I thought maybe you were looking for some sort of validation from men that you have value, since Dad never stuck around long enough to offer any."

Her eyes filled with tears, but she quickly brushed them away. "I never really thought about it. I just thought . . ." She shrugged. "I just like flirting."

Clearly.

"I know, but you've got to remember how pretty you are."

"Thank you." Her cheeks turned pink.

"I'm just saying it makes it harder for the guy to resist when the girl is a knockout. And it's not fair to the guy's heart either. Sometimes innocent people get hurt."

"Like Bob." She sighed.

"Yeah." I glanced across the studio and caught a glimpse of Bob standing with Paul and Stephen. "He's a great guy who deserves someone's full attention."

"He is pretty great. I think maybe I took advantage of his kindness."

You think?

"What happened after I left with Julio the other night? Did Bob cry?"

"Cry? No. He ate some flan, drank two cups of coffee, hung out with us for a while, had a few laughs, and then went home." I paused. "See? That's the great thing about Bob. He's easygoing and very forgiving. I've seen him get his feelings hurt by some of the cast members, and he always has a more humorous way of reacting. So even if he's hurt, I'm pretty sure he'll get over it. You two will probably be friends for years to come."

"I hope so." She bit her lip as she looked his way. "Because he's a really great guy." A pause followed, then she turned back toward me. "And just for the record, Julio's not that into me."

"He's not?"

She shook her head. "I couldn't believe it, but after we left the house the other night, we didn't go to a movie or anything. He spent the whole time talking about insurance rates and cars and stuff. It was so boring."

She glanced at Bob once more, then back at me.

"What's wrong, Beni?"

"Tia, do you think Bob is handsome?"

"I've loved Bob from the minute I met him. He's a great guy and an even better writer."

"Yeah, but that's not what I asked. I asked if you thought he was handsome."

I paused to think about it. Bob wasn't Hollywood hot, but he was relatively nice-looking. One of those boy-next-door types. Kind of a paunchy middle and thinning hair. But I'd never really considered his looks before. "I think he's a nice-looking guy." I shrugged. "Why?"

235

"I don't know." She paced the room, finally pausing to look my way. "Maybe I've been a little mixed up."

"What do you mean?"

"I've only ever looked at the really handsome guys."

"Like Julio?"

"Yeah. And you have to admit, they're fun to look at. But I'm starting to think . . ." She sighed.

"What?"

"Starting to think they're just superficial."

Whoa. Open up the earth and swallow me whole. For my sister—the one who couldn't even go out to check the mail without makeup on—to be having this revelation was truly shocking.

"Handsome is good, but I got to thinking . . . if I marry a really handsome guy, I'll always have to worry that some other woman will be trying to tear him away from me."

"In other words, you'll be like Mama?" I asked.

"Yeah. Never thought about that before." She leaned in close. "Have you seen pictures of Daddy when they first got married?"

"Yeah."

"Tia, it's kind of weird, but he looked a lot like Julio looks now. Tall, dark, and handsome. And I know he's still handsome—for a fifty-something—but see the price Mama's had to pay?"

"What are you saying, Beni? You suddenly want to marry an ugly man?"

"No, not an ugly man. But someone in between. Someone like . . ." The edges of her lips curled up in a smile. "Someone like Bob."

"You want to marry Bob?"

"Well, maybe not today. Or in a week. But I'd like to have a guy like that—one who makes me laugh, and who flatters me not just so I'll turn around and talk about how pretty he is too. If that makes sense."

"You don't want a pretty boy."

"Right."

"You want Bob."

She groaned. "I know. Sounds crazy, doesn't it? And I know what you're thinking: 'Poor Beni, she's so fickle.'"

Um, yeah.

"Maybe I am. But . . ." A little sigh erupted. "I only know how I feel when he's around. I could hang out in his office all day and just watch him work. He cracks me up. Makes me laugh. Makes me feel like I'm really smart and funny."

A new resolve took hold as I responded. "You asked me if I think Bob is handsome. I'd have to say yes. Because he's good inside and out. Remember how Mama used to say 'pretty is as pretty does'?"

"Mama never said that." Benita laughed. "Just the opposite, in fact."

"Well, you've heard the expression, anyway." I paused to think through my next words. "When someone is really good on the inside—especially someone who radiates joy like Bob does—there's a certain sheen on the outside too. I guess what I'm saying is a good heart equals handsomeness to me. When a guy has a great heart, I can't see beyond it to the color of his eyes or hair, or how muscular he is."

"You're totally making that up. Jason Harris is handsome outside and inside."

"Okay, maybe I'm still aware of those things, but they don't matter so much to me. I'd rather have an average-looking guy with an amazing heart for the Lord than have the handsomest guy in the city who sees nothing but himself. Does that make sense?"

"Perfect sense, actually." Benita's eyes got a little misty. "I've worked so hard to make myself beautiful on the outside, Tia. It scares me to think about how un-pretty I am on the inside."

"No, you're beautiful inside and out."

Her smile radiated a newfound innocence.

I glanced at the clock, stunned by the time. "We have to get going." I gave her a quick hug, then realized I still had something left to share. "Oh, one more thing. You know that whole thing about someone going to the tabloids with the name of the baby?"

"Yeah?"

"I found out that Lenora was the one who leaked the info to the media."

Benita's eyes widened. "No way."

"Yeah. We can't blame her, though. She doesn't realize what she's doing. I'm sure you've figured out by now that she's got Alzheimer's."

"I wasn't sure that's what it was, but I definitely knew something was up. The other day when I was putting on her makeup, she told me her new grandbaby's name was Anne with an *e*."

"Yeah, I heard that one too." I gazed into Benita's eyes. "Beni, I know I already apologized for this, but I'm really sorry for even suggesting it might've been you."

She groaned. "Tia, I never claimed to be a saint. I . . ." She shrugged. "The reason I knee-jerked like I did was because I felt guilty."

"Guilty? Why?"

"Because I told Julio the baby's name. That first night I met him, I mean."

"You did?" I couldn't believe it.

"Yeah. I don't know if he told anyone or not, but I shared private information with him," she said. "But to my credit, I didn't realize it was private till after the fact. No one actually made it clear to me that the scripts for upcoming episodes were secret until that day you and I talked. I was too scared to tell you because . . ." She sighed. "I'm such a screwup."

"What? What do you mean?"

"I can't even keep a job. I'm so . . . fickle. And I mess up everything, Tia. I'll never be like you."

"You don't want to be. For your information, I'm the biggest screwup there is."

She laughed. "We're a mess, aren't we? I can't even compliment you without you feeling bad. Do you think we'll ever get past all of this?"

"Yes. And I think it's going to be sooner rather than later."

"Good." She grinned, and for a moment, I saw the little sister I'd known in junior high—the one who liked to entertain me with her stories about how perfect life would one day be for the two of us. "Let's make a pact that we'll both be quick to admit our flaws, okay?"

"I'll do my best."

The itching kicked in again, and I turned, asking her to scratch my back. As she did, I told her about my visit to the allergist.

"Oh, Tia, you're allergic to Angel?"

"Mm-hmm." I nodded. "A little to the left, please."

She continued to scratch. "What are you gonna tell Mama?"

"I have no idea. I just know that I'll be on allergy meds the next time I come over, so if I'm talking like a drunken sailor, you'll know why."

Benita laughed. "Now *that* I would pay money to see."

I gave her a hug, and then we headed into the conference room. I felt like I'd lost ten pounds. The tightness in my shoulders had lifted. Something about getting through this situation with Benita had proven once and for all that coolheaded reactions really could dictate healthier, happier outcomes.

Jason met me at the door of the conference room, all smiles. "Ready to roll?"

"Yep." I smiled. "I have a feeling things are only going to get better from here."

"Oh, I do hope so," Lenora said as she came in. "It's about time things got better. It seems like I always get the fuzzy end of the lollipop."

I paused, unsure of her meaning. Then Jason snapped his fingers and said, "*Some Like It Hot.* 1958."

"That would be 1959, young man," she said with a wink. "Why, has anyone ever told you that you look just like Tony Curtis? He was in that movie, you know."

"Jamie Lee's father," Jason said with a nod.

"Ah, yes. I was there when that beautiful little girl was born." Lenora sighed. "But anyway, Tony, I would be so grateful if you would sit next to me at the . . . " She looked around the conference room. "What are we here for again?"

"Roundtable reading," Jason said, looping her arm through his.

"Yes, the roundtable reading. Though I've always wondered why they call it that. This table isn't round. It's rectangular."

She began to tell a story about the day Jamie Lee Curtis was born. I had no way of knowing if she'd ever met Jamie Lee, but I did know one thing—the man seated next to her at this moment was very much a star. And I was one lucky girl to have lassoed him.

23

Lost in Space

On Thursday I left my house before the sun even came up. Rex had arranged for breakfast on the set, then I would meet with the various department heads to go over the shots for the day. At that time I would make my final decisions for how each scene would be shot. By the time the cast and the rest of the crew arrived, we would have a plan set in motion.

As I drove, I had the most unusual sense that something big was about to happen. I'd had that feeling only a couple of times before in my life, and both times the "something" had turned out to be bad. Still, with my faith firmly intact, I kept a positive outlook. Why, in the last two weeks alone, I'd practically delivered a baby on my own and had a blind date stolen. Surely I could handle whatever life threw my way.

When I arrived at the studio, everything seemed in perfect order. Jason greeted me with a warm hug as I entered, and

Lenora seemed to be completely coherent and normal. Well, except for the Ben-Hur costume, but I'd come to expect that from her.

Yes, God was in his heaven, and all was right with the world, as Anne with an *e* would say. And despite my earlier concerns, this day would go down in history as one of our finest. How could it not with Brock Benson still on board, along with his new love interest?

Around nine thirty, the cast and crew arrived. I prepped them and then slipped back to my office for a couple minutes. For whatever reason, I felt the strongest urge to pray. Afterward I headed out to the soundstage, smiling as I saw the ushers seating our audience. I glanced at the crowd of people, stunned to see my father in the second row. What in the world?

I hurried his way, and he gave me a shy smile. "Hey, Tia-mia."

"Dad . . ." I wanted to add, "What are you doing here?" but decided that would come across as rude. "You've never been to one of our tapings before. Glad you could come."

"I figured it was about time. Besides, Beni asked me to. She's very proud of her work here." His eyes filled with tears. "She's proud of you too, Tia-mia. I heard all about it last night. She thinks you're the best director in town."

"Really?" Looked like our little sister-to-sister chat had paid off.

I'd just started to ask, "Where's Mama?" when she appeared at the end of the aisle, looking lovely in a colorful new blouse and black slacks.

"Tia-mia!" She began to rave in Spanish about how excited she was to be here at the *Stars Collide* set. I gave her a hug and headed off to make sure my cast was ready to roll.

By ten, our stage manager had the audience prepped and ready. I buzzed back and forth between the greenroom and the set, making sure everything was in place. Hopefully we could get this episode knocked out in a few hours.

As always, we started by introducing our cast to the crowd. An extra-loud roar went up as Brock entered the stage. He waved and smiled, which sent the women into a tizzy. Hopefully they would be just as enthused by his characterization.

With the snap of the scene board, we were off and running. Usually the first scene was the toughest, but not today. Even though Lenora had several lines to deliver, she did so without missing a beat. I could hardly believe it. No retakes at all. Well, unless we noticed something in the dailies. Could things get any better?

We were about halfway into the second scene when the floor underneath my feet began to tremble. For a moment, I thought I was imagining it. Sometimes when the larger cameras rolled across the floor, they created that same eerie vibration. But only a couple of seconds later, the shaking intensified.

Halfway into her line, Erin stopped cold and stood frozen. Over her head, the chandelier began to sway. Then the sofa slid a few inches to the right. Several audience members screamed. By now the whole room was quivering, and set pieces were tumbling around me.

I'd been through dozens of earthquake drills, of course. As a child, I had vivid memories of hiding under my desk during one. But this was different. I yelled, "Cut!"—probably not necessary under the circumstances—and Jason jumped from his spot behind the camera to rush my way.

I watched, completely in a mental whirl, as members began to scramble. I wanted to holler, "Stop! Stay where you are!" but couldn't. The words were stuck in my throat. Besides, what did one yell in the middle of an earthquake? All of my directorial skills went straight out the window.

I watched as Brock, who'd been sitting on the back of the

sofa, flipped off and disappeared behind it. Erin did a swan dive of sorts, also disappearing behind the couch.

Jason held me tight as the tremor now shook us both. I lost my footing and went sprawling. As I began to crawl, Jason called out, "Find a door, Tia. I'll be right back."

Somehow I made it to the doorway, only to realize it wasn't a real door. It was just a set piece. Still, I had to think I'd be safer here, so I settled into the doorjamb and didn't move.

Off in the distance, the cries of the *Stars Collide* children rang out. I could hear Candy's shrieks and Joey's wails. They pierced my heart. I wanted to run to them but couldn't make them out through the crowd. Oh yes, there they were, just beyond Scott and . . . Jason.

Yes, Jason had gone to be with the children. God bless him. I would have to remember to kiss him later. If we survived.

Stop it, Tia. Of course you're going to survive.

The shaking continued, and I held my breath. Surely this whole thing was a dream. I would wake up and laugh about how silly it had been.

No, this was no dream. As the shaking intensified, I thought of my parents, seated in the audience. I tried to find them but couldn't. I'd never prayed in such a frantic way before, but a thousand prayers went up at once, all of them involving my parents, siblings, nieces, and nephews.

Behind me, Lenora began to trill with glee. "Ooo, we're on a roller coaster! Look, there it goes again!"

The room swayed, and a camera toppled from its stand, nearly hitting Rex. Thank God he managed to get out of the way just in time. The roar of what sounded like a train coming through the building now took over. Most of our audience members added their voices to the fray, and the cacophony of sounds nearly deafened me.

The walls of the set began to tremble, and strangely, in that moment, I was reminded of the conversation I'd had with Jason about the walls I'd built up in my life. Who knew it would take something like this to bring them down?

Thank goodness the physical walls remained intact, though several things that had been attached to them—a picture frame, a shelf, and a faux window—came toppling down, nearly striking one of our tech guys who'd sought refuge nearby. He managed to scramble away just in time.

All of this I watched as if I were someone in a movie. It was real. No, it couldn't be. And yet it was.

Just as quickly as it had started, the shaking stopped. The sofa was somehow back in its original position, but not much else remained intact. Everything we'd worked so hard to put together—the set, the cameras, the lights—were all tipped, tilted, or broken.

Not that I cared. Not one whit. No, right now only one thing mattered to me—we had made it through.

Jason rushed my way, grabbed me, and whispered, "You okay?"

When I nodded, he offered up a "Praise God," then took me by the hand. We made the rounds together, checking on the children first, then Lenora, Scott, Brock, and Erin. Though badly shaken, no one appeared hurt.

"I've got to find my parents." Staring out into the audience, I finally caught a glimpse of my father rushing toward me with my mother just behind.

I'd seen my father emotional before, but never like this. He grabbed me and held me close. Mama joined our circle, and seconds later, Benita linked arms with us as well.

My father dove into a lengthy speech, all in Spanish, about how much he loved us, about how scared he was that he might've lost us. Everything we'd longed to hear him say for twenty-plus years came out in less than a minute.

My mother's tears broke my heart. I did my best to be a big girl. To nod and say everything was fine. But it wasn't. Inside, I quivered like Jell-O.

As my father cried out words of love over me, every bit of self-control I'd fought to maintain on the set of *Stars Collide* unraveled. I released my hold, my control, and just let 'er loose. The tears came—slowly at first, then in a river. All around, my cast and crew watched in what I could only guess was stunned silence. So much for the charade that I was tough as nails. Now they all knew the truth . . . I was anything but. And all it took was an earthquake to prove it.

My father continued to whisper words of love and comfort, and for the first time in years, I relinquished my anger toward him long enough to be comforted. As I rested in his arms, years of internal pain melted away like butter. Right now I was just my daddy's little girl. Not a famous director. Not someone in control. No, I was someone willing to let her guard down long enough to get real. To stop pretending. To be me, even if it meant looking vulnerable.

And it felt good. Very, very good.

It took a few minutes, but the Morales family finally managed to get things under control. I took a step back and tried to remember where I was and what I should be doing. Strange. We'd trained for all sorts of problems on the set, but never an earthquake. How did one go about putting a set back together after something catastrophic?

Hmm. Probably the same way one would go about putting a life back together—by handing it over to the only one capable of handling something so big.

Jason drew near, phone in hand. "Just checked the headlines. That was a 6.1."

"Are you serious?"

He nodded. "There's been a lot of damage around the

246

city. But from what I can tell, the Topanga Canyon area was hardest hit."

I shook my head, still unable to take it in. "We made it," I whispered.

"*A mas honor, mas dolor*," my father said.

"The more danger, the more honor," Jason echoed from behind me. "I agree. I think a lot of people deserve honor today."

"Yes." My father turned to him and gave him a respectful nod. "I watched you taking care of my daughter." He extended his hand. "Thank you."

Jason shook his hand, and they ended up in a bear hug.

Minutes later, the ushers opened the back doors to release the audience. Many stayed put—clearly shaken—but several went shooting out of the doors in record time. My parents headed out to check on the rest of the family, though we'd already received word that everyone was safe and sound.

Our remaining audience members were mostly on cell phones. Interesting, since they weren't supposed to have them inside. But who could fault them? All around the room I could see the concern etched on people's faces as they checked on loved ones.

I made the rounds from one crew member to another, grateful to see that our writers and wardrobe folks were fine. Athena seemed more shaken than the others, but Stephen never left her side.

After calling home to check on Kat, Scott took off in a hurry. I didn't blame him. Thank God Kat and the baby were both fine. Brock and Erin left next, in a rush to check on his after-school facility.

After they left, I walked the perimeter of the soundstage with Jason and Rex, taking inventory.

"Looks like much of the damage is cosmetic," Jason said.

"The cameras are intact, and the set pieces are all fixable. Nothing huge. In the grand scheme of things, I mean."

Thank you, God.

"How much time are we talking to pull things together?" I asked. "Days? Weeks?"

"Days." He took my hand. "But we should probably look at pushing production back a full week."

I looked at Rex, who nodded. "Our viewers will understand. Nothing—and I repeat, nothing—is more important than caring for our cast and crew. They come first, before the viewers."

"Amen," I whispered, feeling completely at peace about this decision.

We dismissed the rest of the cast, and the tech crew got busy right away, cleaning up as much as they could. I made my way back to my office, finding things topsy-turvy. Hardest hit? My Prada handbag. When the desk toppled, the bag was destroyed for the most part. Oh well. What were expensive things when my life had just been spared? I could always get another bag.

I returned to the soundstage and joined Rex and Lenora as they helped with cleanup. We were all still badly shaken—so much so that we scarcely spoke a word as we worked alongside one another. The whole thing just felt surreal. I wanted to go home and soak in my bathtub.

My house! Was my house still standing? Would all of the work we'd done on it be for nothing?

Deep breath, Tia. It's just a house.

I released a slow, steady breath, remembering my vow to take a calmer approach to life. Of course, when I'd made that promise, I hadn't exactly counted on an earthquake. But a promise was a promise. And if I'd ever been given an opportunity to prove that I wouldn't overreact, this was it.

"Tia Morales!"

I turned as I heard the gravelly voice and saw a fellow, maybe in his forties, with a sly smile on his face.

"James Stevens from *The Scoop*."

Now? In the middle of all of this?

He took one look at Lenora with her hair in shambles, makeup contorted, and feather boa strewn about, and pointed to his photographer, who started snapping photos.

"Oh no you don't. Not this time." Rex reached out, and I thought he might knock the camera to the ground. "No cameras allowed inside. You know that."

"Well, yeah, but under the circumstances, I assumed—"

"You assumed wrong." Rex gave him a warning look. "Now get out of here before I call for security."

James laughed. "I'm guessing they're a little busy right now."

Lenora fussed with her hair but only made it worse. She turned to James and offered a half smile. "Mr. Holliday, it's so great to see you."

"Holliday?" James snapped another photo, catching her as her hairpiece came loose.

Lenora sighed as she attempted to maneuver it back into place. "Years from now, when you talk about this—and you will—be kind."

Rex slapped himself in the head and chuckled. "Even under duress, she still amazes me."

"Deborah Kerr, *Tea and Sympathy*," Lenora said with a smile. "1956, I believe." She turned to face Rex. "Do you remember going out to dinner with Deborah back in the late fifties? She was always such a lady. I used to aspire to be just like her."

"You far surpass her, my dear." Rex took Lenora by the arm. After a couple more camera clicks, she disappeared with him down the hallway. I hoped that would be enough to send the reporter running, but it turned out he was not alone.

"Over here, Tia," an unfamiliar woman hollered. "Jenny Collins from *Tinsel Talk*. What was it like to face death and live to tell about it?"

"Face death?" Should I tell her that facing the paparazzi was scarier than any storm we could possibly face during an earthquake? Maybe not.

I offered a smile, gave some sort of halfhearted answer, then repeated Rex's warning that we would call security if they didn't leave the premises. A short time later they cleared out.

I took a seat in the audience, still badly shaken in every respect. I looked at our set in shambles and tried to think clearly about what to do, but I couldn't.

Jason sat in the chair next to me, reaching for my hand. "You okay?"

I shook my head. "That's a question for another day."

"Right." He leaned back in the seat and closed his eyes. "So, I'm thinking . . ."

"Oh? This is a good time for thinking?"

"Yeah. We should get the writers to do an earthquake episode. After today, I think we can do it justice."

"No way." I turned to face him, wondering if he'd lost his mind. Probably the trauma making him crazy.

Jason smiled. "I was just kidding, trust me. It's the last thing on earth I would do. Just trying to find the humor in all of this."

"Is there humor in it?" I asked. "If so, I'm having a hard time locating it in the midst of all the rubble."

"I've always believed that we can find humor in just about anything. If I didn't feel that way, I would've chosen a different show to work on."

"You had offers from other shows?" I'd never heard this before.

"I did. Three, in fact. But I chose this one because *Stars Collide* is funny. It lifts spirits and makes people smile. It's always been about finding the humor in life's tragedies. Like having a baby in an elevator, for instance. Or losing the kids at NASA in a space shuttle. It's contrived, sure, but it's hysterical."

I thought back over the many episodes I'd directed. Sure enough, every single one had been a "laughter in the midst of tragedy" tale. How had I missed the message?

I sighed. "Maybe that's where I've gone wrong."

"What do you mean?"

"I've always been so serious. Here I am, working on the funniest show in television, and I don't know how to laugh."

All of a sudden the image of Lenora with her hairpiece falling off flashed through my mind, and I got the giggles. I thought back on the sight of poor Brock flipping over the back of the sofa and almost couldn't contain myself. I remembered trying to brace myself inside a fake doorjamb for protection and realized how funny that must've looked from the audience's point of view.

My laughter poured out, energizing me as never before. On and on I went, giggling my way through the pain. By the time I'd worked my way through the laughter, the tears took over. Cleansing, honest, refreshing tears gripped me, and I rocked back and forth, a river of emotions. Through it all, Jason held tight to my hand, tenderness pouring from his eyes. And when I looked at him with a woeful sigh, he dried my tears, told me a funny joke . . . and got me laughing all over again.

24

Clean House

On the Saturday after the earthquake, I stared at my partially renovated house with new eyes. All around the Los Angeles area, people had lost their homes. Mine looked as if it had been hard-hit by the earthquake—on the inside, anyway—but nothing had really changed from two days before.

No longer would I complain, however. At least I had a home. I had a roof over my head and plenty of time—Lord willing—to get the work done. In the meantime, I would stop stressing over it and just take things as they came. Well, just as soon as I started those allergy shots. In the meantime, antihistamines were my best friend.

I shared my allergy tale with Carlos, who took it more seriously than I'd expected. He paced my living room as I told him about my conundrum.

"I'm not sure what to do." I sat on my plastic-covered sofa, shoulders slumped forward. "If this renovation lasts much longer, I might have to find another place to stay because of the dust and mold. I can't go to Mama's because of the dog. So I'm stuck."

"We'll just have to get through it quicker than we'd planned, that's all." He looked confident for a change. "We'll work double-time if we have to. I won't let you down this time. I promise."

"Yeah." I looked around at the mess he and Humberto had made. "I'm grateful for your hard work. I really am. But we're probably talking at least another month's work, right?"

"Yeah, at least." He shrugged. "Look, I'm not a professional. We both know that. But I can work harder. I really can." He hung his head, then gave me a sheepish look. "Tia, I'm really grateful for the work. I didn't want to tell you this, but Maria and I were two months behind on our mortgage when you asked me to help out. Having the extra income has saved my neck."

I suddenly felt about two inches tall. While I'd been fussing and fuming over sneezing, my brother and his wife and kids were facing very real problems. Sure, he'd probably caused some of them with his drinking, but maybe he was ready for a change. I hoped so, anyway.

He sat on the sofa next to me. "This earthquake shook me up, and not just in the way you think. I'm going to be a better husband. And a better worker. You'll see."

I reached to take his hand. Giving it a squeeze, I whispered, "I know you will." I gave him a huge hug.

He stood and took inventory of the kitchen, the next room to be remodeled. "I think I can get these old cabinets out of here today once Humberto gets here to help."

"Sounds great."

"I know how you are, Tia. You're going to want to hang

out here and help. But I'm not going to let you. Not with this allergy problem. Do you have someplace you can go?"

"I've already got a plan. Jason is coming by to pick me up. We're supposed to go to lunch and then maybe see a movie this afternoon."

"A movie?" My brother looked stunned at this news. "Really?"

"Yeah, I know. I'm taking a break from my work and doing something normal for a change."

"High five, Tia." He put up his hand. "If anyone deserves a break, you do."

I sprinted up the stairs to my room, where I changed into a pair of jeans and a cute but super-casual green shirt. As I applied my makeup, I tried to remember the little tricks Benita had taught me. The results weren't half bad. And I did a pretty good job with my hair too.

At 11:00, Humberto arrived, ready to work. At 11:45, I opened the front door and ushered Jason inside my home for the first time. He took one look at me and grinned. "Tia, you look awesome."

I glanced down at my jeans and T-shirt and shrugged. "It's the more natural version of me. The post-earthquake version."

"If this is the 'all shook up' version, then more power to you. You look amazing."

"Thanks." Suddenly I felt pretty amazing.

I pulled him further into the house, wondering what he would think about the chaos inside.

Jason took his time looking over the work my brothers had done. "I like the banister on the stairway. Is that new?"

"Yes. Carlos picked it out."

"And that crown molding? Your brothers did that?"

"They did." I winked. "With my help." A sneeze followed.

"Mm-hmm. Sounds like I need to get you out of here."

"Maybe. I've been"—another sneeze followed—"sneezing all morning."

I said goodbye to my brothers and we hit the road. After all of the drama and trauma of this past week, I could hardly wait for some downtime. If anyone deserved it, Jason and I did.

As he rounded the turn off of Mulholland, Jason glanced my way, his expression serious. "Tia, I want to talk to you about something."

"Oh?"

"I'm worried about your health."

"Oh, that." I waved my hand. "It's going to be fine. I'll start allergy shots this coming week, and my stress level is already going down. I can feel it." I smoothed my jeans with my palms. "Besides, I've already figured out how this house thing is going to end."

"You have?" He looked perplexed.

"Yep. Ty Pennington is going to show up at my door one morning and holler, 'Good morning, Morales family!' Then I won't have to finish this house by myself."

"I'm pretty sure *Extreme Makeover: Home Edition* doesn't come to Bel Air." He chuckled.

"Hey, you never know. They might consider it. My allergies are serious business, mister."

"Mm-hmm." He focused on the road. "Well, speaking of which, I've come up with an idea that just might work for both of us."

"What idea?"

Jason gave me a quick glance before crossing over the 405. "I think we should switch houses."

"Switch houses?"

"Yes. You can stay at my place and I'll stay at yours. That way you'll be in a safe environment and I'll be able to supervise your brothers. And I could help them. I enjoy home improvement stuff. I've always been pretty good at it."

"You . . . you would do that for me?"

He grinned. "Tia, I'd do a thousand times more. I need you to be healthy."

I was so floored by his offer that I didn't know what to do. In my thirty years of living, I'd never had anyone offer to look after me in such a caring way.

I'd just started to gush over him when my phone rang. I saw Mama's number and wondered why she'd picked this morning to call when she knew I had a date. Her first words totally threw me.

"Tia, I need you."

"Mama, I'm right in the middle of a date with Jason, remember? We're going to lunch and then a movie."

She choked back a sob. "Tia, I had to call 911. Your father's on his way to the emergency room."

"W-what? What happened?"

Jason, probably alarmed at the sound of my voice, slowed the vehicle and pulled off the road.

"I don't know, honey." She switched to Spanish, her words flying by so fast I could hardly make them out. "I was in the kitchen getting things ready for tomorrow. He was working on that hole in the Sheetrock in Gabe's room when all of a sudden he started having chest pains. I thought it was indigestion—you know how much he loves my chorizo and eggs—but it didn't go away. Then . . . " She began to cry. "Then he clutched his chest and told me to call 911."

"Oh, Mama."

"When the paramedics got here, your daddy's heart rate was way too high, and they hooked him up to an IV. He's on his way to the ER, and I'm in my car, following the ambulance."

"Where?"

"CHW."

"CHW? Jason and I are on our way."

I ended the call and looked Jason's way, feeling almost as shaky as I had after the earthquake.

"Your dad?" he asked.

"Mama had to call an ambulance. I think he's had a . . ." The lump in my throat wouldn't let me finish. I planned to say "heart attack" but hated to voice the words.

"I heard you say CHW. Is that where he is?"

I nodded, and Jason put on his turn signal, heading south. "Good thing it's Saturday. Won't be a lot of traffic." He pointed the car in the direction of the hospital, and we arrived twenty-five minutes later.

Mama met me in the waiting room, and we went into my father's room together. Seeing him hooked up to all of those tubes almost sent me into a panic, but I managed to keep things under control.

The heart monitor kept a fast and chaotic beat. The doctor couldn't find evidence of a heart attack but was extremely concerned by my father's high blood pressure and erratic heartbeat. Dad was immediately put on IV fluids and given several medications. After a few minutes, he fell asleep.

My brothers and sister arrived in short order, and we all remained at our father's side throughout the afternoon. Around four o'clock, I managed to talk the others into going to the cafeteria for some food. My mother resisted, but I knew she needed to get out of the room for a while, so I suggested Jason go with her. He readily agreed. My mother, on the other hand, did not. I found it interesting that, after all the times my father had left her, she now refused to leave him.

"Mama, let me sit with him for a while," I said. "You go get something to eat."

257

After a couple minutes of arguing, she finally agreed. She and Jason walked toward the cafeteria with the others, and I remained in the room.

A few minutes later, my father awoke. He looked my way and stretched out his hand, muttering something I couldn't quite make out. I stood and grabbed his outstretched hand.

"Tia, what are they saying?"

I tried to keep my voice on an even keel. "The doctor said it wasn't a heart attack. But they're going to run tests. And you've got to take it easy."

"I can't take it easy." He tried to sit up but struggled to do so. "I have so much work to do around the house. I owe it to your mama. She's put up with that beat-up old house too long."

"She'll understand, Daddy."

He shook his head and a tear rolled down one cheek. After a moment of silence, he gestured for me to come closer. "Tia, I have to tell you something." His voice cracked. "And I need you to listen."

"I'm listening."

I'd seen him cry before. He'd turned it into an art form. But I'd never witnessed anything as gut-wrenching as the tears that now flowed. After a couple minutes, he managed to get himself under control. Good thing, because his heart monitor went off. The nurse came in the room, fixed the machine, and adjusted the drip level on his IV. She took one look at his tearful state and insisted he remain calm and quiet. He nodded in response.

After the nurse left the room, he looked up at me, teary-eyed. "I love your mama, Tia." Tears now ran like a river down his cheeks. "I can't explain why I've hurt the one and only person who's ever truly loved me for me—in spite of myself." He paused and dabbed at his eyes. "If it takes the rest of my life, I'm going to make it up to her. She's going to have the husband she always wanted."

I wanted to respond, but the lump in my throat got in the way. Looking into my father's tear-filled eyes, I couldn't help but believe him. He'd laid bare his soul, and this time it was legitimate. Perhaps the decision to turn his life around had happened in the trenches—the ER—and I had the strongest sense he would not go back on this promise.

"Daddy, you're going to get well, but it's going to take resting and doing what the doctor says. You're not a kid anymore."

"You're telling me." He smiled. "Okay, I'll do what they say. I have to get well. I want to dance at my daughter's wedding."

"Beni's getting married?" If so, I'd certainly missed the memo. Sure, she'd talked about marrying Bob, but . . . to actually do it?

"Not Beni." My father shook his head. "You, of course. I want to do the father-daughter dance with you after walking you down the aisle. I can't do any of that from a hospital bed."

My mind reeled. Did he really think I was getting married?

"Tia, don't look so surprised. I've been around awhile. I know the real deal when I see it." Apparently the medicine had kicked in, because his words now sounded a little slurred.

"O-oh?"

He nodded, his eyes fluttering closed. "You and Jason are going to get married, and you're going to have a houseful of babies."

"Whoa. Stop right there." I put my hand up. "Married, maybe. A houseful of babies? We'll have to talk about that."

My imagination began to run wild. How could I raise a houseful of babies and direct a show at the same time?

"Deep breath, Tia." My dad spoke from a near-slumber state.

"Oh, I don't get worked up. Not anymore. That's the old Tia. The new and improved version is calm, cool, and collected, no matter what comes her way."

"I see."

Only, he didn't. Because he was now snoring.

I watched my father resting, completely overwhelmed by what he'd said. For the first time in years, I had complete peace that my parents' marriage was on the right track. No doubt about it. And I also knew my father had enough fight left in him to get well and actually become the better man he'd promised to be.

And then there was that part about him dancing with me at my wedding. I'd have to give that a little more thought. Someday. When things calmed down.

Right now, I just needed to relax . . . and trust that God had all of this under control.

25

The Amazing Race

The following morning, Daddy returned home from the hospital in time to celebrate Sunday dinner with the family. We all gathered at my parents' place. Well, all of us but Angel, who'd been banished to her crate in my parents' room. Thanks to my medication, I barely sneezed at all.

Mama outdid herself with the meal, but the person who really impressed us was Benita. She made all of the desserts. Who knew the girl could bake? Bob beamed with delight as he told us all about it. Cooking really was more fun with two people involved, I had to admit. With Jason's help, I'd provided a potato casserole. It was a little lumpy but oh so tasty.

Spending the day with my family turned out to be a huge blessing, and by late afternoon Jason and I decided to stop by his parents' place in Newport Beach for round two. Their luxurious home near the beach totally blew me away, but so did the relaxed ambience. I fell hard and fast for Jason's mother, who seemed to love everything about me. The feeling was definitely mutual. In fact, I felt as if I'd somehow stumbled into a whole new world of family members I'd never known existed.

The following Saturday, Jason and I switched houses. I'd never lived in an apartment before, but I loved his place right away. And he'd no sooner moved into my place than he started helping Carlos with the construction. Turned out the boy was amazing with a hammer and nails. And talk about fast! He helped my brothers stay on task but also kept everyone sane and cheerful.

By late May we were both settled in, relaxed, and happy. Instead of me driving myself to work, Jason now stopped by to pick me up each morning. Interesting idea, riding to work with someone else, particularly someone you happened to be crazy about. Sure, it meant a missed call from Mama, but she understood. In fact, I had it on good authority that she and my father enjoyed watching the news together each morning.

As Jason drove, I took the time to look out the window, to observe my surroundings. In the countless times I'd made the drive to the studio, I couldn't remember actually seeing what was going on around me.

"When did they finish that hotel?" I pointed to my right, mesmerized by the luxurious new hotel. "And what's up with that dry cleaner? Has it always been there?"

"For as long as I can remember." Jason chuckled. "You're like a kid in a candy shop today. Haven't you ever actually looked at Hollywood before?"

I shook my head. "Obviously not. I mean, I've seen it thousands of times, but never from the passenger seat." For some reason, that statement gave me the giggles. My whole life had changed since I'd climbed into the passenger seat.

I started humming, and before long, I was singing at the top of my lungs. "Oh, you can't get to heaven on roller skates."

Jason echoed, "Oh, you can't get to heaven on roller skates."

We sang together: "Oh, you can't get to heaven on roller skates. You'll roll right by those pearly gates. All my sins are washed away, I've been redeemed."

He harmonized with a rich bass on the last line, which got me tickled, so I started laughing again. "Hey, we sound pretty good together."

"Yes, we do."

"Maybe if this television gig doesn't work out, we should think about hitting the road with that act."

"Never in a million years. I only sing in the car." He paused. "And the shower."

"Same here." I glanced out the window, noticing a sign ahead. "Ooo, can we stop for ice cream?"

"Ice cream?" Jason looked at me like I'd gone crazy. "This early in the day?"

I nodded. "Yeah. Just sounds good for some reason."

"Okay, ice cream it is. If you think we have time."

"Time?" I shrugged and pointed to the ice cream shop in the distance. "It'll wait for us. Rocky Road sounds good, don't you think?"

"I think bacon and eggs sounds better, but that's just me." He laughed and pulled the car into the parking lot.

Unfortunately, the ice cream shop wasn't open yet, but I didn't let that stress me out. Instead, I settled for a Frappuccino from Starbucks just a few blocks away. As we pulled away, I leaned back in my seat, took a swig of the ice-cold coffee, and sighed.

"I feel like Dorothy about to leave Oz."

"Oh?" Jason grinned. "Should I put on my Tin Man costume?"

"Nah." I took another swig. "I've come such a long way over the past few weeks. I feel like someone should ask me, 'What did you learn while you were here, Dorothy?'"

"Okay, I'll bite." Jason waggled his brows, then said, "What did you learn, Dorothy?" in a voice that sounded like the Tin Man's.

I put on my best Dorothy voice. "Well, I think I've learned that a family isn't something to be tolerated. I need to see each person as an individual, loved by God. Flawed, sure, but still loved by God."

"Anything else?" Jason took a sip of his coffee.

"You can't run away from where you've come from. Even if you change your wardrobe, your makeup, the way you speak—you're still you. Embrace the fact that God is writing the script. Let him take the reins."

He chuckled as he put his coffee down. "Wow, this does sound like the script from *The Wizard of Oz*. But you left out one part."

"I did?"

"Yep. There's no place like home. There's no place like home. There's no place like home."

"Which home?" I asked. "The one I'm living in now, the one you're renovating, or my parents' place?"

"All of the above." He gave me a wink that sent my heart into a tailspin. I decided right then and there that home would be wherever he was.

"Okay then." I repeated the words "There's no place like home," suddenly believing it. Though my family drove me nuts at times, I had to admit there was no place like home. Home was where I went when the world was crumbling around me. A few laughs with my family members, along with some of Mama's tamales, could make everything better.

"Hey, you're even wearing ruby slippers." Jason pointed down at my feet and I gasped.

"No way." I'd put on my new pumps this morning. Perfect! I wiggled my feet and laughed. "I remember why now. The end-of-season party. I wanted to look festive."

"You look festive, all right. That blue blouse is . . ."

"Reminiscent of Kat's Easter Bunny suit?" I offered.

He chuckled. "No. I was going to say *beautiful*, but it didn't seem like the right word." He reached for my free hand and gave it a squeeze. "It's a good thing you're ready to go back to Kansas, Dorothy. I hear Oz is highly overrated. Besides, the party today just wouldn't be the same without you." He paused, his expression growing more serious. "In fact, nothing would be the same without you."

I managed an "Aw," then turned my face to the window, hoping he wouldn't see the shimmer of tears in my eyes. What had I done to deserve this amazing guy? I turned back to face him, tears and all. When he saw them, he squeezed my hand again. Unspoken words traveled between us.

Well, unspoken for a while. After a couple minutes we dove back into the conversation, covering everything from my house to the upcoming end-of-season party.

We arrived at the studio in short order. With yesterday's filming behind us, we were free to take care of the one thing on the agenda today—the party. And what a party it was going to be! We'd spent all week planning. With Erin's and Athena's help, I got the soundstage prepped and ready.

Kat arrived with the baby just as the festivities got under way. The children went crazy when they saw little Katherine for the first time. Lenora—God bless her—was completely discombobulated, though she did look rather dashing in her Tinkerbell costume.

"Oh, is this the baby from the elevator?" she asked as Kat passed the baby into her outstretched arms. "He's so cute!"

Tears rose in Kat's eyes, but she quickly brushed them away. "Yes, I have to admit, I have the cutest baby in town."

Lenora nodded and began to make silly faces. Before long, the kids were circled around them, doing the same. Rex looked on, a bittersweet look on his face. I could only imagine what must be going through his mind.

As the children oohed and aahed over the baby, I watched them, my heart swelling with pride. For the first time, a new sensation arose. Genuine caring for a child. Motherly instincts. Weird. Who knew I had those?

Candy took a few steps in my direction. "We have a special present for you, Miss Tia."

"You do?" She passed the gift my way and I smiled. "Do you want me to open it now?"

"Yes, please, but let me get the other kids." She hollered for the younger cast members to join us, and then I opened my gift. I gasped aloud when my eyes fell on the Prada handbag, identical to the one that had been destroyed.

"We're sorry about what happened to your purse, Tia," she said. "I hope you like this one."

"Like it?" I stared at the expensive bag, completely overwhelmed. This had to have cost the kids a fortune.

"Mama said you were worth every penny." Candy offered the sweetest smile.

What? The ultimate stage mother thought the director actually had value? If I hadn't heard it from Candy's lips, I wouldn't have believed it. I turned to Bianca with tears in my eyes and mouthed, "Thank you." She nodded and smiled.

I turned my attention back to the children and clapped my hands. "I want to say something to all of you."

The kids looked up at me, likely curious about the ease in my voice as I spoke to them. They usually saw me only in director mode.

"I just want you to know how proud I am of you. You're all very talented." My gaze lingered on Candy. Though she'd been a challenge at times, her talent was undeniable. "This show wouldn't be the same without you, and I want you to know that. I'm grateful for all of you."

Just then the boys began to argue. I tried to speak above them but found it difficult.

Joey punched Ethan in the arm. "Stop talking, stupid," he hollered. "Tia's trying to say something to us."

Ethan settled down, and I resisted the urge to say, "We don't say 'stupid.'" Instead, I settled on my rehearsed speech. "We wanted to make the end of this season very special for you, so we've got a little surprise."

I gestured down the hallway. Brock and Erin emerged, arms loaded down with gifts.

Jason appeared at my side and gave me a little nudge. "Great call on your part. The kids won't ever forget this end-of-season party. It's like Christmas all over again."

"I won't forget it either." A contented sigh followed.

Jason slipped his arm around my waist and planted a kiss in my hair. "Just one more reason why I love you. You've got the jolly gene."

For some reason, that got me tickled. I started laughing and couldn't stop.

In the middle of my giggle fest, Erin approached with a broad smile on her face. She grabbed my hand, her ruby-red lips curling upward. "Tia, I couldn't wait to tell you."

"Tell me what?"

"I got the best gift ever."

"You finished out your semester at film school? Passed your exams?"

"That too."

Brock approached with a boyish grin.

"Brock is coming back to Texas with me for a few weeks," she said.

"Oh?" I looked his way.

"I'm going to meet her family," he explained. "We're spending the month of June together."

Wow. Things had clearly progressed.

He slipped his arm around her waist and drew her close, and she released a sigh.

"You once told me that you saw more for me than I saw for myself," Erin said. "And you were right. I've learned a lot from being on the set, but most of all I've learned that the script of my life had more pages than I ever dared dream. The story I'd created in my head—about being a director someday, about working with famous directors like you—wasn't big enough. I had no idea my real story would include falling in love with someone like Brock." She looked over at him with an expression so sweet, I couldn't help but be awed.

I threw my arms around her neck, whispered half a dozen well wishes, and turned my attention to Brock. "Don't steal her away from us."

"I wouldn't dare. She's fallen in love with everyone here." He shrugged. "I have too, to be honest."

"The feeling is mutual. And we hope you stick around a long, long time."

"I'd like that. Might have to work out that whole *Dancing with the Stars* thing, though. You okay with that?"

"Very. We're family now, and family members always accommodate one another."

"We are family, aren't we?" Erin shook her head. "I still can't believe I've only been here a couple of months. It feels like forever. I can't even remember what my life was like before *Stars Collide*."

"Funny you should say that," Jason chimed in. "I can't either."

"I guess that's what it's like when you're with family. You lose all track of time." Erin giggled, then gazed up at Brock, her eyes dancing with delight.

They went back to the children, now singing silly songs and acting like kids. Oh, but she was right! We were family—every cast member, every tech person . . . all of us. One big, happy family.

Thinking of family got me thinking about Benita. I noticed her standing off in the distance, gabbing with Bob. I walked toward her, seeing something in her eyes that I never had before. Peace. Tranquility. And as she gazed at Bob, I also saw something else. Innocent love. The kind that most people experienced when they were young.

Her face lit with joy as she took several steps in my direction. "Tia, can you believe it?"

"Believe what?"

"I'm dating Bob."

"Bob . . . and only Bob?" I really couldn't think of a better way to phrase the question.

"Mm-hmm." She nodded. "He actually wants me to be his steady girlfriend. Isn't that awesome?"

Now here was a strange turn of events. What could I say to her? "Why wouldn't he? You're an amazing woman."

She wrinkled her nose. "But he usually dates the smart girls. The ones who've been to college and have a degree."

"You have a degree."

"Oh yeah." She giggled. "I guess I do. But cosmetology's not exactly brain surgery."

"Doesn't matter. You're still brilliant at what you do. But even if you weren't, he would still care for you."

"You think?"

"I *know*. I see the way he looks at you."

She sighed. "I'm a lucky girl."

"Luck doesn't have anything to do with it. I'm convinced that God brought you here—at least in part—so you could meet Bob."

"Funny." She giggled again. "That's exactly what I was going to say about you and Jason."

I couldn't argue with that. The Lord had indeed brought the two of us together. And there was no turning back.

"So, just out of curiosity, what do you suppose ever happened to Julio?" I asked.

"Oh, him." Benita shrugged. "If I had to guess, I'd say he's gazing at his own reflection and talking about how beautiful he is." She released a breath. "He *is* beautiful, there's no denying it. On the outside, anyway. But there's only so much a person can take of hearing someone go on and on about how gorgeous they think they are." She rolled her eyes.

"My guess is he's talking to some poor, unsuspecting soul about her car insurance as we speak. She's won over by his good looks, so she's spending a lot more on her coverage than she would ordinarily."

"Blinded by his shocking good looks." Benita sighed. "I was that woman once. But no more. Now I've given my heart to a man who's beautiful all the way to the core." She smiled. "And he thinks I'm pretty special too."

"You *are* special, Beni. More than you know."

She gave me a long hug, then sashayed over to Bob once again. Minutes later, they were hand in hand.

The rest of the day was sheer bliss. Though Rex and I managed to sneak in a few minutes of work time with the writers, most of our day was filled with that bittersweet feeling that always accompanied end-of-season events. And when we dismissed the cast and crew, I realized just how much I would miss them over the summer months. They had truly become like family.

I happened upon Bob just as he prepared to leave. He reached to grab my hand—an unusual gesture for him—and gazed at me with such a serious expression that I thought perhaps something had happened.

"Everything all right?" I asked.

He nodded. "More than all right." He paused, looking a bit nervous. "Tia, I'm a writer," he said at last.

"A great one," I added.

"Thanks." Another pause followed. "I know how plotlines work. Boy gets girl, boy loses girl, boy gets girl." He gave me a penetrating look. "What's important is that the boy gets the girl in the end."

"Amen," I whispered.

"Some things are worth waiting for."

"Yes, they are."

"I just wanted you to know . . . that's why I hung around your parents' house that night after she took off with Julio. I saw something in her—in us—that was worth waiting for. And it was a great opportunity to get to know your parents." He shrugged. "I really like your dad, by the way. Seems like a great guy."

"He . . . he is." I wanted to throw my arms around Bob's neck and thank him, but decided against it. Instead, I squeezed his hand and whispered, "Beni is a lucky girl. I'm so happy for both of you."

And I was. In spite of my sister's formerly crazy ways, I wanted the best for her. And from everything I could tell, Bob truly was the best for her.

Around four o'clock, Jason met up with me in the conference room. "You almost ready to go?" he asked. "I was hoping to stop off at Pink's for a hot dog on the way home."

"Sounds good. I just need to make a call before we leave, if you don't mind."

"Not a bit. Just let me know when you're ready." He disappeared into the hallway.

I reached for my cell phone and called Mama. She answered right away, sounding as cheerful as ever.

"Tia! How are you?" She spoke in Spanish, which put me at ease.

"Great. We just wrapped up our end-of-season party, and I'm in a festive mood."

"Glad to hear it." She laughed. "Your father—God bless him—insisted on mowing the lawn today."

"He's supposed to be taking it easy," I said.

"I know, I know. Still, he insisted. He just finished up the front yard and is in the back now. Isn't that sweet?"

"Very." I marveled at how sweet, in fact.

Still, I hadn't called to talk about yard mowing. I had something entirely different on my mind.

"Mama, what's the one thing you've always wanted but never got?"

"Honey, I have it all. I have a wonderful husband. I've got five great kids who love me and come to visit regularly. No one has landed in jail. Recently. That's pretty good, considering the neighborhood. Everyone is healthy. Yes, I'm good."

"What do you and Dad talk about more than almost anything else?" I asked.

She paused. "How we wish they'd put in a Walmart close by so we didn't have to drive so far to go shopping?"

"No, think bigger than that."

"Hmm." She paused. "How we both wish we could go back and redo some things in our marriage?"

"Well, that too. But what do you say when you're dreaming the big dreams?"

"Oh, that's easy." She giggled. "We want to go on a cruise together."

"What kind of cruise?" I asked.

"Alaskan, of course. We want to go north to see the glaciers and pan for gold." An exaggerated sigh followed.

"Well, pack your bags. You leave next Sunday for ten days."

"W-what?" She began to ramble in Spanish about how she must have misunderstood me.

"I bought your tickets yesterday."

"But . . ."

"It's your anniversary gift."

"But our anniversary isn't for two weeks," Mama argued.

"Doesn't matter. You're celebrating now with a cruise. So pack your bags. You're off to see the snow-capped mountains, glaciers . . . everything you've ever wanted and more. I booked a ton of one-day excursions, so prepare for cold weather."

"Oh, Tia, this is the best gift ever." Mama began to cry. "Your father and I never had a honeymoon. We got married on a Saturday afternoon, and he was back at work on Monday."

"I know. And that's exactly why I think you need this now. Get away. Relax. Have a blast. Forget about the past."

I found myself flooded with hope for the future. I couldn't control what had happened with my father, but I could hope for the best. For a change. And I could speak positive, faith-filled words over their situation.

"Hold on, Tia. I want to tell your father."

Mama disappeared for a few minutes. I could hear her squeals over the phone line. Then my dad came on the line, his words breathless.

"Tia, I don't know why you've done this for me after all I've—"

"Daddy, don't." I pondered my next words. "You just go

273

and show Mama the time of her life. I've got a gift card for her to do some serious shopping before you leave. Make sure she has everything she wants. And treat her like a princess. Promise?"

"Oh, I promise. She is one, so I won't have to work hard to treat her that way."

Jason stuck his head in the door just as I ended the call with my parents. "How did they take the news?" he asked.

"I've never heard them more excited about anything in my life."

He leaned against the doorjamb and smiled. "Well, it's the adventure of a lifetime."

"No." I walked his direction. "*This* is the adventure of a lifetime." Cuddling up against him, I felt his heart beat in sync with mine. Alaska could wait. I had all the presents I could ever need . . . right here.

26

King of the Hill

The summer months passed as none before—loaded with excitement and God-breathed joy. My parents had the time of their lives on the cruise. And when they arrived home, there were no lingering doubts in my mind. They had worked things out—permanently. Not that I could fix it if they hadn't. But I could trust in the one who could.

July brought several surprises, including the news that *Stars Collide* had garnered not one but four Emmy nominations, including one for yours truly for directing. Every time I thought about it, I felt giddy. Well, giddy and a little nauseous. After all, winning awards wasn't what this was about. Nope. I'd settled my heart and mind on the fact that relationships were the only things that mattered.

By the first week in August, the *Stars Collide* cast and crew prepared to jump back into gear for a brand-new season. I breathed a sigh of relief knowing my house would be complete by the end of the month. Then I could return to it and enjoy it in style. Thanks to Jason.

Jason. Every time I thought of him—of the sacrifices he'd made for me, of the way he made me feel—I felt hopelessly, blissfully in love. I knew he felt the same. We'd shared those words dozens of times. But watching his love in action as he worked on my house, seeing him play with my youngest brother, observing his kind heart as he engaged my father in conversation—all of these things won me over again.

Sure, life went on. We still had to work. And I still felt safe inside the walls of the studio. But something had changed. I no longer wished for my life script to be rewritten. Gone was the angst over all I'd suffered. Now I could see only happy days ahead—for me and Jason, and for our cast and crew.

I met with our *Stars Collide* family for our new season's first roundtable reading on the first Monday in August. Kat—who had trimmed off all evidence of a baby bump—showed up with little Katherine, ready to be added to this season's script. Having Kat back was the icing on the cake. And I could tell it made Scott's day too. He fussed over her and baby Katherine all day long.

So did Lenora, though she seemed a bit out of sorts. She couldn't seem to read her lines, at least not with the usual flare. And her costume of the day—*Is she supposed to be Pocahontas?*—seemed to be missing a few pieces. I did my best to shrug it off and offer support. That's what directors did, after all—offered support.

After we finished in the conference room, Rex asked me to meet him in his office. When I arrived, he was sitting in his chair, facing away from me. He swiveled my direction and I noticed the tears in his eyes. "Tia, I think it's time to talk about something. I . . . I've put this off a long time."

"What is it, Rex?"

"Lenora." He stood and began to pace. "It's getting harder and harder to deny the obvious. The Alzheimer's is getting worse."

"What are you thinking?" My heart began to pound.

"I don't want to take the show away from her. This set, these people—this is her home. It's pretty much all she knows. If I remove her from this building, these people, she'll be more lost than ever."

"Of course."

"Still, I can't deny that the time has come to rethink her role in the show. I hate to say it, but I guess it's time to ease Lenora out of the story."

"Ease her out?"

His eyes filled with tears. "I haven't really thought it through, but the writers will come up with something. Maybe she could show up occasionally for a line or two, but I honestly don't know for how long. By the end of this season . . ." He shook his head. "I just can't predict the future."

"None of us can."

And aren't you glad? If we could see what lies ahead for Lenora, chances are pretty good we wouldn't like it.

"The viewers love Lenora's character on the show," I continued. "So we'll have to handle this carefully."

As I pondered the situation with Lenora, I thought about all of the many times she'd come into the studio dressed in costumes from the golden era of Hollywood. It always struck me as fascinating that she could remember the names of the movies from her youth—even the actors and actresses who played the lead roles—when she couldn't even remember what had happened yesterday. Guess that's what Alzheimer's looked like, at least the Hollywood version. I suddenly felt very, very sad.

"Tia, last season was wonderful. You somehow managed

to keep things going to the very end, even without one of our lead players."

"Oh, you can thank the writers for that. I just play off the script they give me."

"No, you've been an integral part of the decision-making process from the get-go, and I can't tell you what a relief it's been." He paused. "Maybe when things reach an inevitable point, you'll be the one to take my place."

My heart quickened. "W-what?"

"Oh, don't get nervous. I don't plan to go anywhere anytime soon. I'm just saying someday." He gave me a knowing look. "Pray about it?"

"Of course." I stood in the doorway, unable to say anything else until I'd thought it through. Finally an idea came to me. "Rex, remember a while back we talked about the role Brock's character would play on the show? How I told you that it would be fun to have him try to steal away some of the *Stars Collide* actors?"

"Right. I remember."

"We talked about having him steal Candy's character, but what about Lenora's too? Maybe he somehow talks her into breaking her contract with Stars Collide and joining him at A&B Talent."

Rex looked intrigued by this idea. "And then what?"

"And then there could be a lot of conversation about her between the talent scouts. Over a period of weeks, I mean. It could turn into a tug-of-war. That way her character's name would still get mentioned a lot, but she wouldn't have to actually be in the scenes. At least, not many. We could use her in snatches, just a line or two per episode." I hesitated. "We'll have to balance this against Brock's time on *Dancing with the Stars*, but other than that, what do you think of the idea?"

"I think it's the only thing that makes sense, given the circumstances. It's the perfect solution."

"Okay. I'll get with Athena later this afternoon and tell her." I put my hand on Rex's shoulder. "And just so you know, we all think you're an amazing man and an even more amazing husband."

A lone tear rolled down his wrinkled cheek, nearly breaking my heart in the process.

"I waited for years to marry that blessed woman," he said. "It took an act of God to bring us back together after being apart for so long. I promised to be with her in sickness and in health—and I made that promise already knowing her condition. Don't ever feel sorry for me, Tia. I made this decision with a clear head because I love her so much. She's worth it. And every minute we have together is a gift."

"I love you, Rex." I walked over and planted a kiss on his head. "You're more than a producer to me. You're like family. You . . . well, you all are."

"Thank you, Tia. I feel the same about you." The tenderness in his expression made me feel warm all over.

"Speaking of family . . ." a familiar male voice rang out behind me. I turned to see Brock standing in the open doorway with Erin at his side. "We have something to tell you guys."

"Come on in." After they stepped inside, Rex closed the door behind them. "What's up?"

"We thought you two should be the first to know that we got married last weekend."

"W-what?" I stared at them, totally confused. "Where? How?"

He laughed. "I know. It's a miracle the tabloids didn't catch on. My pastor flew down to Texas and married us at a wedding facility in Galveston."

"Well, congratulations!" Rex wrapped him in a bear hug while I latched onto Erin, all giggles.

After the excitement died down, Brock slipped his arm around Erin's waist and drew her close. "I'm not sure how to explain it." He leaned over and planted a kiss in her hair, and Erin's cheeks turned the prettiest crimson color. "There's something about her heart that pulled me in right away. For one thing, she's so great with the kids. They love her."

"And vice versa," she whispered.

"You know I started that after-school community center a couple years back, and I go there at least once a week to hang out with the kids. I've always known that the woman I fell in love with . . ." His words trailed off as he gazed into Erin's eyes. "She had to love kids as much as I did. And it's a given that she had to understand the movie business. I'm pretty sure I'll be in Hollywood for years to come. In fact . . ." He looked at Rex. "I'd definitely like to stay on at *Stars Collide* for a while, if you'll have me. Turns out I prefer television to movies."

"Funny you should say that," Rex said. "We just had a conversation about how we plan to keep your character going and still give you time to appear on *Dancing with the Stars*."

"Perfect." Brock looked like he'd won the lottery. Go figure. The megastar was content to stay put on a sitcom.

I found it rather ironic that we'd given Brock a Pied Piper sort of character, one interested in luring folks away from Stars Collide. In real life, he'd become a Pied Piper of another sort—he'd won all of our hearts. No doubt about that. But he'd cast a spell on someone else too. Erin.

"What about you, Erin?" My heart pounded a little harder at the idea that she might leave. "Are you going to stick with us? We have great plans for your character and would like to have you sign a contract."

"Oh, I'm not going anywhere." She gave me the sweetest

smile. "Why would I? You guys are like family to me now. And it would kill me to leave the kids."

"Whew!" Relief washed over me. "Now that we've made you Brock's love interest on the show . . ." I paused, realizing what I'd said. We'd somehow done it again. Kat and Scott had started out as love interests on *Stars Collide*, then fallen for each other in real life. Now these two?

I got so tickled that I started laughing. In fact, the more I thought about it, the funnier it got. The Stars Collide name had always represented the merging of Jack's and Angie's talent agencies, but now I realized it meant even more. How many of my talented co-workers had come together over the past year? Kat and Scott. Athena and Stephen. Erin and Brock. Benita and Bob.

Tia and Jason.

A smile immediately followed. How wonderful it felt to find love—not the Hollywood version but the real deal.

We celebrated a bit longer, and then I went in search of Jason to tell him Brock and Erin's news.

Athena caught me just as I entered the soundstage. "Hey, you."

"Everything okay?" I asked. "Got those kinks worked out with next week's script?"

"Yes. All kinks are gone." She grinned.

"Well, I for one think it's perfect. You've outdone yourself this time."

"Yes, I have."

I gave her a curious look, and she began to giggle.

"What are you trying to tell me?" I asked.

"We, um, well . . ." She giggled again. "I know we haven't been married all that long, but for Pete's sake, we didn't want to wait."

"Wait." Suddenly it hit me. "You're pregnant?"

She nodded and laughed. "Can you believe it? A little Cosse, running around my parents' gyro shop and wreaking all kinds of havoc here at the studio." She paused. "I mean, I'm assuming I can keep working. You're okay with that, right?"

"Okay with it?" I laughed. "Oh, it's perfect! You'll know just what to write for Kat because you'll be a mommy as well."

"And one day you will be too!"

I was taken aback by that idea. "Well, maybe one day."

"Life can change a lot faster than you think, Tia. One day you're single, saying you'll never get married. The next day you're buying a house in the suburbs and remodeling."

"Hey, I've already done that."

"See? You're halfway there. Now all you need is the husband and baby."

"Slow down, slow down!" I chuckled. "I'll take them . . . in God's timing." A lingering sigh followed.

"Why the sigh?" she asked.

"It's just so ironic. I used to say that if I'd been handed the script of my real life in advance, I would have changed several things."

"Who wouldn't?" Athena laughed.

"Now I'm not so sure. I've been through a lot of things I wouldn't wish on anyone. But in some ways I thought I was content. I was one of those 'perfectly happy single' people."

"Puh-leeze." Athena rolled her eyes. "You were not."

"Well, I thought I was. Does that count?"

"I guess." She shrugged. "So what do you think now? Still happy single?"

"I can't even imagine not having Jason in my life. He's . . . he's . . ."

"Yep, he's all of that and more. And just for the record, you are too." She grinned. "So why are you standing here talking to me? Get over there and give that man a kiss. Tell him you're nuts about him."

"I've already done that."

"Do it again. Men are slow. They need to be reminded."

That got me tickled. In fact, I couldn't stop thinking about her words as I walked across the room to Jason, who had taken up residence in my director's chair.

"Oh, sorry." He rose when he saw me coming.

"No, don't be silly." I gestured for him to remain seated. He stood anyway. "Just thinking about something."

"Oh?"

"Thinking through this week's episode. It's going to be great." He leaned close and whispered, "And by the way, I have no doubt you'll take home the Emmy award for best director in a few weeks too."

I shrugged, realizing that it didn't mean as much to me as it once did. "Win or lose, I'll just be Tia."

"You'll never just be Tia." He kissed the tip of my nose. "You'll always be Tia-mia. My Tia."

I cradled into his arms, completely content.

Content. There was that word again—the one that had eluded me for so long. I hadn't found contentment in the director's chair. I hadn't discovered it in my Bel Air home. Funny, after all of my hard work trying to prove myself, I'd found it in the arms of a man who—just as Lenora predicted—rubbed away my rough edges and loved me simply for being me.

Then again, who else would I be? I'd tried pretending to be something I wasn't, and it hadn't gotten me very far. From now on I'd just relax and enjoy the process.

I looked around the room, a memory overtaking me.

"What are you thinking about, Tia?" Jason asked.

"About how I always said that I like to keep my drama on the set."

He looked my way, an "I know better" look on his face. "How's that working out for you?"

"It's impossible." I grinned. "I think I've finally figured out that life is filled with drama no matter where you go. Whether I'm eating tamales at my parents' place in South Central or flipping a house in Bel Air West or riding out an earthquake on the set, it's all unscripted. And there's nothing I can do about any of it."

"But that's the joy of it," Jason said. "Because you didn't plan for it—and you don't know what's coming next—you can see it as an adventure."

"I guess." I shook my head.

"What?"

"I just had the weirdest flashback. I saw Lenora in the middle of the earthquake, squealing with excitement because she thought it was a roller-coaster ride."

"It kind of felt like one."

"I was thinking how ironic it was that even in the midst of something catastrophic, she saw it as the ride of a lifetime." I paused to think about what I'd said. "So I guess you're right. Life really is an adventure."

"Mm-hmm." He grinned. "And if you think that was fun, wait until I get you out on the water on a surfboard. Summer's not over yet, you know. Just because we've gone back to work doesn't mean I won't get you to the beach."

I put my hands up in mock despair. "Oh no you don't!"

"Okay, okay. We won't talk about it now. But someday." He gave me a kiss on the cheek, then whispered, "I'm starved."

"Me too. Want to go out to eat?"

"Nah. I was thinking we'd cook."

I did my best not to groan.

"I know this great cook." He waggled his brows. "She makes a mean tamale."

"My mother's on a date with my dad tonight, so you're out of luck."

"Not your mom. You."

"Oh." Wow. Make tamales . . . by myself?

He laughed. "You're hysterical, Tia. You can bring a script to life, you can corral dozens of people, you can direct a scene like nobody's business . . . but you're afraid to conquer a tamale."

"Hey now." Those were fighting words.

Nah. On second thought, looking into those beautiful green eyes, I had to conclude, what would be the point of fighting? No, my fighting days were behind me once and for all. With Jason at my side, there were only happy days ahead.

He wrapped me in a loving embrace and kissed me soundly. "That's a thank-you in advance."

"For the tamales?"

"No, for giving me the courage to say what I've been dying to say all day long."

I gave him a curious look. He wasn't making much sense. "What did you want to say?"

"Just this." He squared his shoulders and looked me in the eye. "When you realize you want to spend the rest of your life with somebody, you want the rest of your life to start as soon as possible."

I knew the reference. *When Harry Met Sally*. Billy Crystal. 1989. But was he teasing me, or . . .

As Jason dropped to one knee, the soundstage filled with all of the people I loved—my family members, the cast, and the crew. Most were cheering or laughing. My thoughts began to whirl.

I caught a glimpse of my parents off in the distance, arm in arm, tears streaming. My brothers cheered from the sidelines as well. And Benita? Well, this certainly explained why she had encouraged me to wear my new teal blouse.

Looked like the director had been duped. Yep, duped. But as I gazed into the eyes of the man holding open the ring box—*Wowza! Check out that solitaire!*—I could conclude only one thing: no movie, no television show, no previously recorded love scene could even come close to what I was witnessing right here, right now. And if I tried for the rest of my life, I could never come up with a lovelier script.

SPECIAL FEATURE

"LET FREEDOM RING!"

DIRECTED BY
Brock and Erin Benson

STARRING
Tia Morales and Jason Harris

A CALIFORNIA BEACH at sunrise. Tight shot on TIA, standing along the shore dressed in a bright pink bathing suit. "CALIFORNIA GIRLS" plays overhead.

Tight shot on two surfboards, which appear to be standing of their own accord in the sand.

JASON steps out from behind the surfboards wearing red swim trunks, hair slicked back.

> JASON
> (flashing confident smile)
> You ready?
> (picks up surfboard)

Tight shot on TIA'S face. She looks as if she might be ill but manages a nod.

> TIA
> (biting her lip)
> As ready as I'll ever be.

Wide shot on ocean. Waves are rough. JASON shows TIA how to paddle out to their starting point.

Tight shot on TIA as she tries to stand on the surfboard.

She falls. She gets back on it and tries again, wobbly but hanging on.

Wide shot on JASON and TIA standing alongside each other. A wall of water

rises in front of them, and TIA looks
terrified at first. Then, just as quickly,
she smiles.

                    TIA
            (raising her arms
                triumphantly)
        Woo-hoo! Here we go!

Wide shot on ocean. TIA and JASON disappear into the wall of water and emerge
seconds later, floating in the water.
They swim toward each other, all smiles.

Tight shot on TIA. She waves at JASON,
who grabs his surfboard. He pushes it
toward her, and she climbs aboard. He
joins her.

Tight shot on the couple wrapped in each
other's arms, drifting on the waves.
They begin to kiss.

FADE TO CIRCLE. TIA PEEKS THROUGH AND
SNAPS A SCENE BOARD. FADE TO BLACK.

Author's Note

Dear Reader,

I've had such a wonderful time writing the three books in the Backstage Pass series. I've always wanted to write a story set in Hollywood. Perhaps this desire came from my earlier years when I actually lived in Bel Air West and belonged to the Screenwriters Guild. Oh, what wonderful, sunny memories I have of those carefree California days!

When I think about the many believers who live and work in Hollywood, I'm floored! Several years ago I took a team of Christian drama students to L.A. to meet with the folks from Act One, a training and mentorship organization that focuses on the next generation of Christian artists and professionals. Oh, how our eyes were opened to all that God is doing in Hollywood! Soon after that, I joined the Hollywood prayer network so that I could be apprised of prayer needs among industry pros.

Speaking of industry pros, it's hard to say goodbye to Kat, Lenora, Athena, and Tia. In my mind, they—and the show—live on. I see Kat and Scott happily married with at least two more children. Kat is offered a major movie deal, which she refuses. She'd rather spend her days on the *Stars Collide* set with the people she loves.

Lenora's struggle with Alzheimer's continues, sadly, but she still shows up on the set each day dressed as a movie star from the golden years of Hollywood. Though her memory is fading, she has Rex with her through it all.

I see Athena and Stephen raising a whole houseful of Greek babies, hanging out in her parents' gyro shop, and bringing all of the kids—and the dog—to the studio with them when they work. They continue to produce funny scripts for *Stars Collide* and even go on to win major awards. In between visits to Greece, of course.

And what about Tia? Well, she lives happily ever after. She learns the ultimate lesson that the true happily ever after isn't really about earthly relationships anyway. It's about giving her life, her problems—and yes, even the reins—to the one who created her. (Not an easy lesson for a control freak.) I see her running rehearsals with a baby on one knee and a script on the other. And I see Jason, once focused only on the action through the camera, now wholly given over to his family. Oh, and they're both nominated for Emmys for the "Angie Gives Birth in an Elevator" scene. Tia's acceptance speech is shaky but heartfelt.

And Brock and Erin? Brock wins *Dancing with the Stars*, and he and Erin become Hollywood's power couple. They're offered major motion-picture deals, which they accept but carefully balance against their time on *Stars Collide*. In the end, they start their own production company so they can raise money for Brock's after-school facility. They also take a trip to Texas to visit with Bella and D.J. from the Weddings by Bella series. Speaking of which, if you're a fan of Weddings by

Bella, stay tuned for more news about the characters you've grown to love in an upcoming series from Revell.

So there you have it! I hope you've enjoyed your trip backstage with the *Stars Collide* cast and crew. They've been happy to have you. And remember, if you're ever in L.A., stop off at the studio and take a tour. Maybe—just maybe—you'll get to see one of our stars pass by. For now, I wish you a blessed and happy journey as you continue to act out the role you've been given. May your life's script be filled with blessings every step of the way.

Janice Thompson

Acknowledgments

Because I've worked as a director at a local Christian theater, I connect with Tia on so many levels. There's such a fine line between being a control freak and giving good, solid direction.

I would like to thank my good friend Brenda White, who serves as my co-director on all of our Curtain Call Café productions. Thank you for linking arms with me and working alongside me. Together, we are Tia-riffic!

Many thanks to sweet Janetta, who read every word of this manuscript, sticking with me till the very end. Girl, I couldn't have done it without you.

To my editor, Jennifer Leep. Bless you for allowing me the privilege of writing this series for Revell. What a distinct honor to write about something so near and dear to my heart. You've blessed me beyond belief.

Many thanks to my copy editor, Jessica English. Girl, I sing your praises from shore to shore. You are truly the best copy editor I've ever worked with, providing the perfect balance of polish and encouragement. Thanks for your kindness and your expertise.

To my marketing gurus, Michele, Donna, and the others who spend so much time marketing and promoting my books. Bless you! Oh, what fun to work alongside you.

To Chip MacGregor, my faithful agent. We are quite the team, aren't we? You will never know how grateful I am for your presence in my life. If not for you, these stories wouldn't exist.

JANICE THOMPSON is a Christian freelance author and a native Texan. She has four grown daughters, four sons-in-law, four beautiful granddaughters, and two grandsons. She resides in the greater Houston area, where the heat and humidity tend to reign.

Janice started penning books at a young age and was blessed to have a screenplay produced in the early eighties, after living in the Los Angeles area for a time. From there she went on to write several large-scale musical comedies for a Houston school of the arts. She continues to direct at a Christian theater and enjoys her time in the director's chair.

Currently, she has published nearly eighty novels and nonfiction books for the Christian market, most of them lighthearted.

Working with quirky characters and story ideas suits this fun-loving author. She particularly enjoys contemporary, first-person romantic comedies. Janice loves sharing her faith with readers and hopes they will catch a glimpse of the real happily ever after in the pages of her books.

Come meet
JANICE THOMPSON
at www.JaniceAThompson.com

Read her blog, more interesting facts
about her books, and other fun trivia.

Follow Janice on Twitter
booksbyJanice

"I hope you enjoy this romantic getaway as much as I did."

—Kristin Billerbeck, author of *Perfectly Dateless* and *What a Girl Wants*

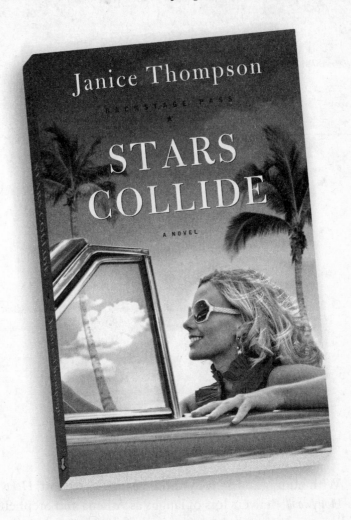

Catch the start of Janice Thompson's hilarious new series, Backstage Pass.

When it comes to *love*, one thing's for sure—it doesn't follow a script!

With humor and a Hollywood-insider viewpoint, *Hello, Hollywood!* delivers lots of laughs as Athena and Stephen discover that not being in control of the plot of their lives might just be the best thing that ever happened to them.

A Romantic Comedy That Will Have You Laughing All Day

Don't miss book I in the Weddings by Bella series!

When *Hollywood's* most eligible
bachelor sweeps into town,
will he cause trouble for *Bella*?

Don't miss book 2 in the Weddings by Bella series!

*Get ready for a double dose
of wedding frenzy!*

Don't miss book 3 in the Weddings by Bella series!